THE COLLEAGUES

DANIEL HURST

www.danielhurstbooks.com

›ok

If you would like to receive a FREE copy of my psychological thriller 'Just One Second', then you can find the link to the book at my website *www.danielhurstbooks.com*

PROLOGUE

Unsurprisingly, the meeting room was full as everybody in the office crammed inside it to hear about their dead former boss and their ex-colleagues who allegedly killed him.

While it was barely 9 a.m. and the caffeine inside all the cups had not yet entered the bloodstreams of the workers in the room, everyone was alert and awake, far more than they ever had been at this time on a Monday morning before. The simple reason for that was because this was no normal day in the office. Instead of trudging through the door, slumping down at their desks and logging on to their computers to sift through a pile of emails, every employee of Van Dekker Logistics was waiting for their anxious colleague to start speaking. The colleague in question was Amy, and she was the one who was first put forward to talk about the crazy rumours circulating around this office in her role as Personal Assistant to the manager.

Well aware that it was unrealistic and most likely impossible for the employees of this company to concentrate on work after what had been reported in the news over the weekend, a decision had been made. The reports were going to be addressed before everybody could get on with their jobs, and that was what was about to happen now.

'Thanks for getting here on time,' Amy began nervously, her seven years of experience not having prepared her for the kind of speech she was having to make today. 'I know you're all very busy, and we have a lot of work to do, so I'll be brief. I'm sure you have all seen and heard the reports in the media over the past forty-eight hours.'

If Amy wanted confirmation of that, she got it in the form of all thirty-two employees in the room instantly firing back questions at her as to whether or not what they had seen in the news was true.

'Did they do it?'

'Did they kill him?'

'Is it safe for us to work here?'

'What is going on?'

The questions came fast, but Amy was out of her depth and slow to respond to them, which meant this tense situation quickly got out of control.

'Please, let me speak,' she tried. 'I need to make it clear to you that you are all contractually obliged not to speak to any members of the media about this or any other matter relating to this company in the news. If you are approached by any journalists, you will simply say 'no comment' and then come to me, okay? I cannot stress this enough. Failure to follow this procedure could result in the termination of your employment here.'

If that was supposed to calm everyone down then it didn't work because the volume in the room only increased, rendering anything Amy said after that indecipherable. What this situation called for now was for a calm head to come in and de-escalate matters, and much to the overwhelmed PA's relief, that is exactly what happened.

Everybody in the room went quiet the second they saw the door to the meeting room open, and in walked their manager. His name was Phillip, and he looked resplendent in his navy blue suit as he approached Amy and politely told her that he would take it from here.

As Amy gratefully moved to the side of the room to join some of her colleagues who were standing on the periphery of the room, Phillip cleared his throat before he began.

'I'm not going to waste anybody's time here. I respect you all, so you deserve the truth,' he said, and as he paused, the room was silent, nobody daring to speak now in case they missed what was said next. It turned out it was worth the wait.

'Edwin, my loving father and the man who led this company before me, was a flawed man but a good man,' Phillip said, taking a few liberties with the word flawed but carrying on before anybody could question him on it. 'While he might have made some mistakes in his time, he most definitely did not deserve to pay for those mistakes with his life. However, we all know that my father has been missing for quite some time now, and after this weekend, you may all know why that is.'

Still silence. It felt like the truth was coming. When it came, it was as if all the air was sucked out of the room.

'The news reports are correct. An ex-employee here was involved in the death of my father,' Phillip said with a grim expression on his face.

The bombshell hit before everybody had more questions again, questions like why they had done it, how they had done it and, almost just as importantly, how they had almost gotten away with it for so long. But Phillip simply raised his hand and didn't lower it until everybody in the room had fallen quiet again. Then he spoke with a calm authority, one that suggested he was very much in control of this crazy situation.

'Rest assured, I am just as shocked as you are about all of this,' Phillip said, his eyes moving from one of his aghast employees to the next. 'But also rest assured that the guilty party will pay for what they have done. The police will see to that. They are currently in custody, and once convicted of their crime, they will be facing a lengthy punishment. Until all that is resolved, I don't want to hear their name spoken around this office. Do you understand?'

With that, Phillip nodded and straightened out his tie before striding out of the room before anybody could ask him anything else. But if he really thought his little speech would do the trick then he was sadly mistaken. That's because no sooner had he left then everyone in the room immediately began asking each other more questions.

They also broke the golden rule he had just given them.

They talked about the guilty party. They talked about the mastermind behind the whole grisly plot that the police and the media were currently trying to unravel, and there was no way they wouldn't because it was simply too juicy a story to not gossip about.

They were all talking about their ex-colleague, the one who had seemed so nice when they knew her but was now accused of carrying out a truly awful crime.

The Colleagues

They were all talking about Liz.

ONE WEEK EARLIER

1

'Liz? Hello? Is there anybody there?'

I'm snapped out of my daydream by the female voice to my left, and when I swivel around in my chair, I see one of my colleagues frowning at me, her fake eyebrows furrowed and her false eyelashes fluttering as she blinks while staring at my older face. She's barely twenty; I'm nearly forty, and as well as begrudging her for being half my age, I begrudge her because she has apparently just dropped a load of work on my desk and is only speaking to me to make sure I understand that it all needs to be finished by the end of the week.

'No problem,' I mutter before she turns and saunters away from me back to her own desk, all high heels, a short skirt, and a badly fitting blouse that only makes me shake my head but makes every male in this office like putty in her hands.

How did someone her age end up giving orders to someone my age when I have way more work experience?

Two words.

Sex appeal.

Annoyed at her, my lustful male boss, and the pile of extra work I now have, I grit my teeth and think about my life. When I do, I am certain of one thing.

I really hate my new job.

No, hate isn't a strong enough word.

I *loathe* my new job.

It's not hard for me to express why that is. The work is tedious, the pay is pitiful, and the commute to get here is soul-destroying. But the worst part of it all is undoubtedly the sense of loneliness it fosters inside of me. Whereas, in my old job, I was surrounded by many colleagues of a similar age to me, things are very different here. I might only be thirty-eight, but I'm the oldest person in this office by at least a decade, and in comparison, I feel as though I might as well have a walking stick, a plastic hip, and a bus pass that allows me to travel for free as a senior citizen. That might seem a little overdramatic, but how else am I supposed to feel when those who sit around me in this office all day talk about things I have no clue about?

TV shows, music, fashion choices – I can't relate to them over any of those things because their tastes are so different in comparison to mine, and it's not difficult to see why. The average age at this company must be about twenty-five, and that's with me bringing that average up a few notches when my years on this earth are taken into account. Even the CEO is in his twenties, and that is particularly galling.

I'm working at one of those start-up companies that was founded on the internet, on a laptop in somebody's messy bedroom before becoming big enough for its creator to require several employees to complete admin tasks in an office. It must be amazing to be so young and literally create your own job. I've only ever known life as an employee, and here I am again, working hard for my living.

All I do here is the accounts, and that is literally all I do because, as far as conversations go, most people gave up talking to me once they realised I had little in common with them beyond us sharing the same place of work. Still, I shouldn't complain too much because after what happened in my last job, I'm just grateful to have found gainful employment, and I know how lucky I was to be given a role here.

As I sit back in my chair and momentarily look around this office full of people with better clothes, tighter bodies, and far fewer wrinkles on their faces than I have, I let out a weary sigh, which is not something that a young person does but is a thing that becomes quite high up on the to-do list of someone approaching forty. Once I've done that, I once again wonder if there was some sort of a mistake in me being hired here. There had to be because I really don't fit in here with my other colleagues at all. Then again, I am good with a spreadsheet full of numbers and also believe I came across very well in my interview, so maybe that's why the young CEO here offered me a place amongst his very young team. Oh, who am I kidding? I was hired here because I was most likely the only person who was willing to accept a demanding position on a meagre wage.

What's that famous saying? *Beggars can't be choosers*. That certainly applied to me because, with my 'unique' employment history, it's almost a miracle I do not have to spend the rest of my life claiming unemployment benefits. Then again, I wouldn't be any financially worse off if I was getting a handout from the government, not when I receive my pay packet from here at the end of the month and wallow in how pathetic it is for a woman of my age and experience.

Not for the first time, I curse the extreme bad luck that saw me end up in my current position. It wasn't my fault I ended up working for a truly awful man in my last job, though it was at least my fault what ended up happening to him. The fact that I still haven't had to face justice for that means my luck is not all bad, and as long as I stay a free woman then, overall, I have to consider myself to be winning.

Still, it doesn't feel like it on a slow Monday like this one, and as I check my phone, I'm in desperate need of something to boost my mood. Fortunately, I find it in the form of a message from my friend, Bev.

Can't wait to see you both later. Lots to catch up on and even more to drink!

I smile at the message that was sent to both me and our friend, Natasha. The three of us in this particular WhatsApp group are all ex-colleagues, a trio of women who ended up working for the same evil boss. Thankfully, we all escaped his clutches, though it wasn't easy or particularly legal in the end, though we don't tend to dwell too much on that. What we do is stay in touch so that even though we no longer see each other every day at work, we make an effort to meet up every couple of weeks or so for a few drinks and a good chat.

Chatting was precisely what the three of us used to spend most of the day doing when we were sitting at neighbouring desks, and I really miss having dear friends in the workplace. But at least I have them outside of it, and as I type out a reply to the group, I am just as excited for this evening as Bev clearly is.

I'm so looking forward to it! I'm bored out of my brain right now!

I wonder if either of my friends will reply quickly because I know they will both be at work too, but it doesn't take Bev long to respond.

Oh no, trouble at the nursery? Have you tried changing their nappies and burping them?

I smile at my friend's joke, and it's the same one she has made before. After I told her about my new job and the fact I'm now working with people much younger than me, Bev has taken to referring to my workplace as a nursery and my colleagues as babies. It's just a bit of fun, and it makes me smile, which is something Bev was always good at. Natasha too, for that matter, but she is being uncharacteristically quiet today because there are no messages from her. I guess that, unlike her two friends, she is actually doing some work right now, so I don't think too much of it as I send a couple of laughing face emojis back to the group before putting my phone down and refocusing on the task at hand, namely this spreadsheet on my computer screen showing all the figures for the last sales quarter. It's not exactly riveting stuff, but I never became an accountant for the excitement.

However, despite my seemingly mundane job title, I've ended up with more than my fair share of drama in my career.

I shouldn't dwell on something so dark when I'm not at home in private, but for a few minutes, I am unable to help myself, and before I know it, my thoughts are on my past and, in particular, the one thing I have done in my life that could see me get in serious trouble with the police. I always imagined I'd go my whole life being a law-abiding citizen. As a child, I never stole so much as a penny sweet from the local shop, and once I was an adult, I was far too aware of that place called prison to ever contemplate doing something that might see me end up there. *Or so I thought*. But I was wrong because despite thinking I didn't have a criminal bone in my body, I proved that theory incorrect six months ago, and since then, I have been looking over my shoulder, afraid that the police might come calling for me at any moment.

So far, they have not, and hopefully, they never will because I was careful, just like my co-conspirators were. But you never know, do you? Maybe I will get caught for what I did, and maybe I'll have to go to prison one day to serve the sentence I should have already started serving by now.

If it does happen, it will undoubtedly be a very long sentence. What's the going rate for pre-meditated murder these days? Ten years? Twenty? Life? I dread to think about it, mainly because I am confident that I wouldn't be able to last more than two minutes inside a prison with a load of dangerous criminals for neighbours.

Let's hope it never comes to that.

Let's hope the police never figure out that I am the one who killed my old boss, Edwin.

Well, me and my two friends.

They are just as guilty as me.

Natasha and Bev. The three colleagues. The three amigos. *The three killers.*

We'll all be together again tonight. When we are, we'll be sure to raise a toast to our dearly departed boss.

If I was being polite, I would say rest in peace, Edwin. But if I was like Bev, I would say something more honest and the same thing she says every time we refer to that man who we got rid of half a year ago.

I'd say rot in hell, you evil piece of work.

2

It's not difficult to spot Bev as I enter the busy wine bar and survey the scene. She's the one sitting at the table right in the centre of this crowded room, flirting with the handsome young man who is currently opening a bottle for her.

As I get nearer to her table, I see her fluttering her eyelashes at the employee before hearing her laugh loudly at something he just said, something that most likely wasn't very funny, but Bev isn't going to let that stop her. By the time I reach her, she is already touching the guy, lightly putting one of her hands on his arm as he leans over and pours a measure of white wine into one of the three sparkling glasses set out on the table. There's surely no need for her to touch him; it's unlikely his arm is unsteady and needs the extra support, but Bev is initiating contact anyway, and I'm pretty sure that if I wasn't just about to interrupt proceedings then she'd be asking for his phone number any second now.

'Sorry I'm a couple of minutes late. Work was busy,' I say as I announce my arrival at the table, and the waiter quickly gets to work on pouring me a glass too.

'This is Pablo. He's from Argentina,' Bev tells me, smiling at me as if I needed to know that crucial piece of information.

'Shall I pour the third glass?' Pablo asks in a heavy South American accent, but Bev asks him if he can wait for the last member of our party to arrive, before explaining why.

'That way, you have to come back here in a minute, and we get to talk to you again,' she says, her lipstick-covered lips curled up into a devilish smile.

Pablo laughs nervously before placing the bottle down in a cooler and walking away to go and serve another thirsty and flirty female patron.

'He's cute,' I say as Bev and I hug.

'He'll look even cuter when he's lying in my bed,' Bev replies without skipping a beat, and I laugh before I take my seat and Bev retakes hers.

'Relax, it's a Monday,' I jest. 'Give the poor menfolk of this town a day off from your clutches.'

'There is no time for days off at my age,' Bev says as she fixes her eyes on the back of Pablo's trousers as he leans over another table and pours wine for another happy customer.

I laugh at Bev's comment, though I can't help but be reminded that while it was made as a joke, it comes with an undertone of truth, and it's a truth tinged with some sadness and more than a little tension. The sadness comes from the fact that, just like me, Bev is in her late thirties and, as of yet, has not found a man to put a ring on her finger or help her have a baby or two to fill her home. The tension, on the other hand, comes from the fact that our biological clocks are ticking louder by the day, but so far, there are no signs we are going to be able to beat them before they run out of time.

Neither of us dwell too much on the fact that we'd love nothing more than to settle down with someone special and start a family, opting instead to just accept life as it comes and trying to make the best of things. At least that's the way we are when we have company anyway. However, I do wonder if Bev is like me when she is alone, and by me, I mean shedding the occasional tear whilst lying in an empty bed and wondering if this is all life really has to offer for us.

To prove my point about Bev never dwelling too much on what we lack, she picks up her glass of wine and raises it in front of me.

'It's good to see you, mate,' she says, using the 'm' word as her affectionate way of addressing me, which is something she has always done since we became friends a year ago.

'You too,' I say as I pick up my own drink, and as we clink glasses together, I'm more than ready for a sip of wine. But something makes me pause for a second.

'Do you think we should wait for Natasha?' I ask, noting that we are still one person short at our table for three.

'She's always late, and she won't mind,' Bev says with a shrug that is not an uncaring gesture but simply one that reminds me just how common it is for Natasha to struggle to keep to a set time between us. It's not that Natasha is rude and turns up late because she doesn't care. She has just always struggled a little when it comes to being on time, and having seen how late she would be for work when we shared the same office together, it's not surprising she isn't right on time for our little catch-up tonight. Then again, there could be another reason for her not being here yet, and it might be one much worse than just poor timekeeping skills.

'Do you think she's okay?' I ask Bev after we've both taken a refreshing sip and set our glasses back down on the table beside the expansive wine menu that makes this place our favourite watering hole in town.

'Natasha? Yeah, I'm sure she's fine.'

'She didn't reply to any of our messages today.'

'She didn't?'

Bev doesn't seem to have noticed, but as she checks her phone, she sees that I am right.

'Must have been a busy day at the office,' she adds. 'I'll tell her we're here now.'

Bev types out a text before taking a photo of our two glasses full of wine alongside the empty one that is waiting for our friend, before sending the image to her.

'Do you think it could be more than that?' I ask as Pablo rushes past our table on his way back to the bar.

'Huh?'

'Might it be more than just a busy day at the office? Natasha was quiet the last time we came out, wasn't she?'

I'm reminding Bev of the last time the three of us got together. It was a fortnight ago, and we came here, sticking to our routine, although that was where the familiarity ended because while Bev and I were gossiping away like always, Natasha had been uncharacteristically withdrawn, simply sipping on her wine and listening rather than actively joining in with all the chatter. What made it even more unusual, or so I thought at the time, was that while she didn't say much, she drank at least twice what Bev and I consumed, even though it was a work night, and we all had an early start the next morning.

'I'm sure she's fine,' Bev says with another shrug. 'Speaking of fine, I can't wait for that waiter to come back over here. I'm definitely getting his number before we leave.'

'You're too old for him,' I tease, but Bev is having none of it.

'I could teach him a thing or two,' Bev insists, and I'm sure she is right, but best not to dwell on that, and after being reminded of such a thing as a sizeable age gap between people, my thoughts return to my workplace and how unhappy I am with my current situation there.

'Speaking of being too old, I think I'm going to have to try and find another job,' I say. 'It's just not working. I've got no friends there, and I suppose it would be okay if the work was rewarding, but it's far from that. I hate it.'

'I'm sorry to hear that,' Bev says, putting aside her lust for the waiter to be a good friend for a moment. 'But do you not think you should try and stick it out a little longer? I mean, it took you a while to get that job, right?'

I nod my head without saying anything more because Bev already knows just how difficult it was for me to find employment. She knows because she's had the same trouble as Natasha. All three of us have suffered when it comes to our careers, through no fault of our own, but we have suffered all the same, and I know what Bev is getting at, even if she won't say it outright.

She thinks I'm lucky to just have a job, even if it is as bad as I say it is.

'It just feels like we're still being punished for what he did to us, even though he's gone,' I say, moaning about our old boss and how, even in death, he is still negatively affecting our lives. 'Don't you think so too?'

Bev nods her head in agreement but says nothing, inviting me to go on.

'I know I shouldn't complain. I mean, Natasha had it way worse than we did, and she is carrying on, so I should be able to manage it myself,' I say, but Bev cuts me off there.

'Hey, don't be so hard on yourself. We all suffered at his hands, and we're still trying to move on from it now. It's only been six months. We just have to give it more time. What did I say to you both after we left his house that night? We'll be feeling so much better about all of this in a year's time. So just try and give it time.'

I do remember Bev saying that, and it was quite a wise thing to say, but it was also difficult to really appreciate the astuteness of it when she first said it, what with all the blood on my clothes and the guilt over what I had just done already taking hold of my tired body. But I've made it through these first six months, and I'm sure in another six, things will be looking a little better.

I change the subject then, preferring not to dwell on the past and opting to look to the future instead, which is why I ask Bev if there has been any progress in her love life recently, beyond trying to pick up hot waiters in wine bars on a Monday night. It turns out that there is a little news for her to pass on, nothing too spectacular but a little titbit of gossip about one of her new neighbours who might be potential boyfriend material one day. It's enough to make the two of us lose ourselves in conversation for the next twenty minutes or so, but by the time she has finished telling me about him and how she definitely knows he is single, we realise Natasha really is late now.

'She hasn't replied to my message,' Bev says after checking her phone again, and that's when I decide to try and call her. But there is no answer, and now I'm starting to worry because it's not like Natasha to be entirely unreachable all day, especially when we are due to see her. Even Bev shares my concern now, and that is proven when she quickly dismisses Pablo when he returns to check on us, putting her friend's wellbeing above her need for a night of passion with the Argentinian man. But it's not just Natasha who she is worried about. Bev is also concerned for herself and me.

'She wouldn't do something stupid, would she?' Bev asks me. 'Like tell someone what we did?'

'What? No, of course not!' I cry, perishing the thought.

'She's not as strong as us.'

'She's been through much worse than we have.'

'I know. So what if she's cracked? What if she's confessed to someone? What if she's at the police station right now, and that's why she's not answering us?'

‘Calm down. Natasha wouldn’t go to the police.’

I’m trying to be confident of that, but my actions deceive me because I’m no longer interested in drinking my wine, seeking out more gossip, or even just admiring Pablo as he continues to wander around nearby. Now, all I am thinking about is that we need to check on Natasha as soon as possible, and if she isn’t going to come to us, we need to go to her.

‘Let’s go to her place,’ I say, and Bev is quickly in agreement.

‘I was just going to suggest the same thing myself,’ she says before she tosses a £20 note onto the table to cover our drinks and a tip. Then she grabs her coat and follows me out of the bar and onto the street, where we hail a taxi and tell the driver to get us to our destination as quickly as he can.

But the rest of the journey is made in silence because, unlike back at the wine bar, Bev and I are far too nervous to talk anymore.

3

The taxi driver did as we asked and got us to where we wanted to be in a quick fashion, and as he parks his vehicle outside Natasha's house, Bev and I are already looking for clues as to whether or not our friend is home. The fact that Natasha's car is parked on her driveway is a good sign, though the fact all the curtains are closed despite the sun not quite having set yet is not so good.

'Here you go, thank you,' I say as I hand the driver his fare before following Bev out onto the pavement. Then, as the taxi moves on, the pair of us make our way to our friend's front door.

'She might be ill,' Bev says, not having failed to notice the closed curtains too and already coming up with a plausible reason why Natasha might be seeking some darkness and privacy inside. 'That would explain why she didn't text us back. She's too sick. Maybe it's the flu or something.'

'Maybe,' I say, but I'm not entirely convinced because even if she was ill, surely she would have been able to muster up the energy to send us at least a text message to let us know she wasn't going to make it tonight.

Bev reaches the door first, so she is the one who knocks while I keep my eyes on the curtains to see if any of them move, which would be a good sign that Natasha really is in there somewhere. But Bev is forced to knock for a second time after her first one goes unanswered, and while the door hasn't moved yet, neither have the curtains. All is quiet and still, and the longer this goes on, the more I don't like it.

'I'll text her and tell her we're outside,' I say. 'She might be in bed.'

'Go for it,' Bev replies, and I send Natasha a quick message to let her know we are the ones at her door, before adding that we are here to make sure she is okay. I sign off by writing that we are just worried but will go once we know she is fine.

Waiting for a reply that I'm not sure is going to come, I am starting to grow more concerned by the second, and that concern only strengthens when Natasha's next-door neighbour comes out of their house, presumably having seen or heard us knocking nearby. It's not the neighbour's appearance that troubles me but what they have to say.

'I'm not sure she is in there,' the female neighbour tells us. 'I've been home all day, and I haven't seen her go out or go in. I didn't see her at the weekend either.'

'Her car is here,' Bev says, pointing out the obvious, but that doesn't seem to make much difference to the neighbour.

'I'm guessing she went away on holiday or something,' she adds.

'Why do you say that?' I ask the nosy neighbour, although at least her nosiness is giving us some information to work with.

'The curtains have been shut for days,' she replies. 'If she was in there, she'd open them, wouldn't she?'

With that, the neighbour drops a couple of bottles into her recycling bin and goes back inside, leaving Bev and I to figure out the rest of this mystery by ourselves.

'Did she mention a holiday to you?' Bev asks me, but I'm already shaking my head as I make my way towards the side of the house.

'No, she didn't,' I reply, and as Bev follows me, she must be aware of the same thing I am. Our friend would not go away on holiday and not tell us, particularly if we were due to meet up during that time.

There is a horrible sinking feeling in the pit of my stomach as I reach Natasha's back garden and check the windows at the rear of the property. When I do, I'm pleased to see that the window to the kitchen is unobscured, so I lean in to the glass to try and get a good look inside. No sooner have I done that then I note the poor condition of the scene inside.

There are two empty wine bottles on the kitchen table, as well as a further two more on the countertop beside the microwave. Alongside those are several small measures of vodka, those tiny bottles that can be purchased from supermarkets or off-licences, though quite why Natasha has so many of them in her home is strange because she's never been a vodka drinker as far as I know. As for the rest of the kitchen, it's safe to say the place is a mess, with dirty plates in the sink and two pizza boxes stacked on the floor in the corner beside an overflowing bin.

Either Natasha had a party last night or she has been living like this for a while.

'What can you see?' Bev asks me, and I turn back from the window before telling her that the place looks like it needs tidying up.

'Natasha? The clean freak?' Bev says, and that's a good point because, as far as we always knew, Natasha kept everything in an orderly fashion. Her desk at work was always uncluttered, so much so that we would tease her that she had no work to do because our desks were overflowing with paperwork, but really, she was just more organised with her things than we were. But seeing the state of her kitchen now makes me worry as to what could have made her lose that sense of pride in her environment.

Of course, I know she has some good reasons to care less about tidying up these days, given what she has been through in her past, but this mess, alongside the drawn curtains and the neighbour who hasn't seen her for days, is now making me think something bad has happened to our friend.

'We need to get inside now,' I say, and Bev is already on the same wavelength as me because she gets to the back door before I do and tries the handle. There's no reason why it wouldn't be locked, just like the front door is, but it is not, and as the door opens, I shoot Bev a troubled look.

'People don't go on holiday and leave their doors unlocked,' I say before Bev steps inside, and I follow her in.

Now I'm standing in the kitchen, I get an even greater sense of what a poor state the room is in, and if it looked bad from the outside, the smell is even worse on the inside.

'That bin stinks,' Bev says before putting her fingers to her nose and pinching shut her nostrils.

She's right about that, and the leftovers in the pizza boxes or on some of the dirty plates aren't helping matters either, and all I can wonder is how long our friend has been letting standards slip around here. It worries me that it could be quite a while because we usually meet in public places rather than at each other's homes, so it may have been a long time, and we still wouldn't be any the wiser if we hadn't come here tonight. But we're here now, so we can do something about it, but first, we have to locate the owner of the house.

'Natasha! Are you here?' I call out before Bev has a go too, shouting for our friend as we leave the pungent aromas behind in the kitchen and move into the dark hallway. Things aren't much brighter in the lounge as we enter, but I pull open the curtains to get some light into the room. Once I have done that, we see this room is just as messy as the last one we were in. A few more dirty plates and cups litter the coffee table, as well as there being even more evidence of alcohol consumption in the form of another two empty wine bottles. There's another bottle lying on its side on the sofa, though this one appears only half drunk. But it's what I see lying next to the cushion on the other side of the sofa that worries me the most.

Rushing towards it, I pick up the empty bottle of pills and study the label to see what used to be inside the container.

'Sleeping pills,' I say to Bev before I check the date on the prescription sticker on the bottle and see these were prescribed on Friday. If that's the case, and I have no reason to think it isn't, then there is one big problem. There's no way all these should have been consumed in such a short space of time and beyond that, no way they should have been consumed with alcohol at all.

'Where the hell is she?' I say to Bev before we rush out of the room and head for the stairs.

Taking them two at a time, we quickly make it to the first floor, and as Bev pushes various doors open, I keep calling to Natasha. She's not in the first bedroom, nor is she in the bathroom. But then we find her in a second bedroom, and when we do, I almost wish we hadn't.

She's lying in a bed, and her eyes are closed, and for a moment, she simply looks asleep and peaceful. But I start to doubt she is asleep when she fails to wake up to Bev shouting her name and slapping her face, and as Natasha fails to stir, I tell my friend to check for a pulse.

She does just that, but while it's easy to put her fingers on Natasha's throat, it proves harder for her to find any signs of life, and as tears fill Bev's eyes and she begins to panic, I realise what has happened here.

We're too late.

If the lifeless body in the room wasn't enough to make it obvious what has gone on here, there are plenty of other pieces of evidence all pointing to the same sorry conclusion too.

More empty wine bottles, another empty bottle of pills - and a handwritten letter on her bedside table that I pick up and begin to read before quickly dropping it to the floor once I realise what it really is.

It's not a simple letter.

It's confirmation that we are too late to help our dear friend.

It's Natasha's suicide note.

But as awful as that is, there's something that makes all this even worse.

As part of her final thoughts, she has expressed who is to blame for her taking her own life.

She blames us.

4

I've just gone through the same motions Bev did a moment ago in checking our friend for signs of life. I've called her name, I've slapped her face, and I've felt for a pulse, but none of it has changed the facts.

Natasha is still and cold, and no matter how much we wish for her to still be with us now, it's obvious that she has gone.

'I'm calling for an ambulance,' Bev tells me when it's clear this situation is beyond desperate, and she turns her attention to her phone. While that is usually what a person should do when they realise someone else is in grave health, I quickly realise this is no ordinary situation.

That's why I tell Bev to pause before sending for help.

'What? They might be able to save her!' Bev cries, no doubt stunned that I would even consider delaying getting the paramedics on the scene. But that's only because she hasn't read what I've just read, and it's time to change that before her call connects.

'Look at this!' I say as I hold out the letter towards Bev, and she stares at the piece of paper in my hand.

'What is it?'

'It's Natasha's suicide note.'

'Oh my God!'

I feel as sick as Bev does that Natasha has gone to such extreme lengths without making a cry for help that we or somebody else could have responded to because if that had happened then she wouldn't be in this position now. But Natasha never told us exactly how low she was feeling.

We knew it was bad, so we made sure to be good friends and offer support when we could.

But we didn't know it was this bad.

'You need to read it,' I say, continuing to hold the letter out towards Bev until she takes it.

'I need to call for help!' she replies, still not listening to me, so it's time to make myself clear.

'We can't call anybody yet because if the emergency services come and read this, we'll be spending the rest of tonight in a prison cell!'

That gets Bev's attention, and she lowers her phone.

'What are you talking about?'

'Just read it!'

I throw the piece of paper at Bev then, and while it misses her and floats down to the carpet, she soon picks it back up and starts reading. When she does that, she finally understands why I don't want any third parties here just yet.

'She blames us?' Bev gasps, looking up from the letter and staring at me, only the bed with our deceased friend lying on it between us.

'It sounds that way. But whether that's really how she felt or whether it's just the last thoughts from an intoxicated, overdosed mind, that's not the biggest issue here. The biggest issue is what would happen if the police were to read that letter.'

'So what do we do?' Bev asks, and I'm surprised she is going to make me spell it out for her.

'I don't see how we have a choice. We have to destroy that letter.'

'We can't do that!'

'We have to! Unless you want to explain to a police officer why your name is mentioned in connection with a missing person who we killed and buried?'

Bev might be shocked and upset but she isn't stupid, and she knows I'm right. This letter cannot be seen by anybody else because it clearly spells out the crime we committed together, and we should just be thanking our lucky stars that we're the first people to have read it.

If I get my way, we'll be the only ones who read it.

'But what about Natasha's family?' Bev asks me.

I don't want to be cruel because I know they are going to be devastated when they learn she has passed away, but I don't know how else to ask my next question.

'What about them?' I say for lack of better words.

'They're going to want answers. They'll want to know why she killed herself. If we destroy this letter then they'll never know!'

'But they can never know. No one can!'

Bev must understand this, and I'm sure she does, but she isn't making it easy, so I walk around the bed, closing the gap between us before I take hold of her arm.

'I know this is a horrible situation. I'm devastated that Natasha did this, and I'm heartbroken for her family, but you know as well as I do that we cannot let anybody know what happened to her and what we did about it.'

Maybe it was me holding onto her arm that did it, or perhaps it was the urgency in my voice, but either way, Bev finally comes to her senses and hands me the letter. Once she has, I don't waste any more time.

Tearing the paper into pieces, I keep going until not even the most skilled jigsaw professional could put it back together again in the right order, but that's still not enough. Not wanting to take even the slightest chance and have somebody aware that the letter even existed at all, I leave the bedroom and go downstairs in search of the final thing I need.

Fire.

I find that in the kitchen, and once I have turned on one of the gas cookers, I drop all the pieces of the letter on top of the circular blue and orange flame, and no sooner have I done that then the pieces disappear before my eyes.

Some might consider that overkill, but I'll do whatever it takes to guarantee I don't go to prison, and once that is done, I turn off the cooker and think about what my next move should be. We do need to call the emergency services; there is absolutely no way around that, but before that happens, Bev and I need to get our stories straight.

Returning to the bedroom, I find one friend crying over the body of another, and as Bev mourns

Natasha, I wish I had the luxury of doing a little grieving myself. But I'll have to process the pain of what I have lost here later because right now, time is of the essence, and even though the letter is gone, we could still get in trouble if we don't discuss exactly what we will say to whoever is going to come here when we call them.

'We'll have to explain to the police why we were here,' I say. 'We tell them the truth. She's our friend, and she was due to meet us tonight, but she failed to show up. We were worried about her because it was out of character, so we came here and looked around for her. The neighbour will confirm that. Then we tell them we found the back door open, came inside and discovered the body. That's it.'

Bev says nothing, and for a moment, I think she might not have heard a single thing I just said, which would be annoying because with time of the essence, I could do without having to repeat myself. But then she turns to me and nods her head, and with that cleared up, I am finally ready for her to make that phone call to the emergency services.

But before she does that, Bev has something she wants to say.

'Natasha was right. This is our fault. We are to blame for her death.'

'What?'

'She killed herself because she felt guilty over what we made her do.'

'We didn't make her do anything. It was a joint plan, and all three of us agreed on it.'

'Maybe we pressured her into it.'

'We did no such thing. We were just trying to help her!

'Were we? Or were we trying to help ourselves? We hated that man too. It wasn't just her that he hurt. He screwed our lives up too. What if we forced her into doing something we wanted to do more than she did?'

'Shut up! You're talking nonsense!' I cry, but the fact I feel so shaken as I speak tells me I have the same fears as my friend does. But I can't express them here because that would mean both of us are having a crisis of confidence, and one of us has to hold it together long enough for us to make it out of this situation with our freedom intact.

Bev is stunned by my outburst and falls silent, and it's long enough for me to take the phone from her and attempt to use it myself.

'I'll make the call,' I say. 'We just need to get this over with, then we can talk about it somewhere calmer.'

The sooner we are out of this bedroom and away from the dead body lying beside us, the sooner we'll find it easier to think clearer, and Bev doesn't argue with me anymore as I dial 999 and wait for it to connect. It barely takes a second before I'm through to an operator, and after they have asked me what I require, I tell them I need an ambulance as soon as possible.

'It's my friend! I think she's taken an overdose! She's not breathing!'

None of those things are lies, and it sure does feel good to voice some truths, for the time being. That's because it won't be long now until I'm going to have to be telling lots of lies. Bev is in the same boat. We're going to have to lie our way out of this, but that's okay because we're both good at it.

We've done it before.

Of course we have.

How else could we have gotten away with murder?

Accomplishing such a thing takes skill, courage and strength, and Bev and I have those in spades. I thought Natasha did too. Sadly, for all of us, it seems she became broken along the way.

I hate that this has happened. I hate that our friend felt she had to do such a drastic thing. Most of all, I hate the man we killed because he started this whole sorry chain of events.

He might be dead but it stings that he has now taken Natasha with him.

This has to be where it ends, doesn't it? There can't be any more loss of life, can there?

Bev and I have to survive this.

Whatever it takes, we can do it.

Right?

5

I appreciate how hurried the two young paramedics are as they exit their ambulance and rush towards the front door of Natasha's home with their medical bags in hand. I know that the man and woman are here to do their job and try their best to save a life, and I also know they are more than qualified to be able to do such a thing, so long as there is still a life to be saved. Unfortunately for them, and their professional enthusiasm, that is not the case because Bev and I both know Natasha's heart has stopped beating, and it seems the time for helping her has long since passed.

I'm not going to get in the way of the paramedics trying, however, and I'm hoping the pair of them can work miracles as they quickly get to work at the side of the bed, talking to each other as well as Natasha, not that she offers much by way of a response.

As I stand in the bedroom helplessly and watch the paramedics trying to revive Natasha with all sorts of scary-looking equipment, I'm struck by a strange and not particularly helpful thought. It's a thought that says the writers who work on hospital television dramas are clearly doing their research because what I have seen on screen over the years very closely mirrors what I am seeing right in front of me now. Of course, it was far less frightening when it was on screen because I knew that, ultimately, it was just a work of fiction being carried out by a bunch of actors following a script. But this is far more real.

This is life and death. These paramedics are real people with a serious job to do. And that is my friend they are working on so urgently.

But all their efforts are for nothing because despite trying to resuscitate Natasha for the best part of twenty minutes, it's obvious they are fighting a battle that has already been lost, and there is nothing they can do.

Unlike the TV shows, there is to be no happy ending here.

Bev must have still been holding onto a sliver of hope because she lets out a pained cry when the paramedics stop their work, and it becomes official that Natasha has gone. But I just stay quiet, probably because I already knew it was a lost cause by the time the ambulance arrived here.

Of course there is no miracle.

Miracles don't happen to people like us.

We just get left with all the usual stuff like pain, regret, and paranoia.

'The police will be here shortly to ask you a few questions,' the female paramedic tells me as I'm trying to console Bev, and I tell her that I understand, before I suggest to my heartbroken friend that it might be best if we go and wait for them in a different room. I'm sure it will be better for our mental health if we aren't staring at Natasha's body for the next half an hour, and a change of scene will do us good. But I'm also aware that going into another room will give us both the chance to have one more talk in private before we do what we have to do.

As I thought she might be, Bev is a little reluctant to leave Natasha, thinking that our friend still needs us, even though, sadly, that is not the case. But I manage to carefully lead her out of the bedroom and down the stairs as another ambulance arrives, and two more paramedics come in to either help their two colleagues already upstairs or simply confirm what has already been decided as far as the patient goes.

Taking a seat on the sofa beside Bev, I hold onto her hand and tell her that we are going to get through this together, before noting that Natasha must have been in more pain than we even knew about and that at least this means she is at peace now. Of course, I'd rather still have my friend here with us and would give anything for this night to have gone to plan and the three of us to be in that wine bar now, gossiping about our lives and gawking at Pablo as he poured us another glass of wine. But that is not to be, and no amount of crying or wishing is going to change that for any of us.

I know I get this from my mother – this ability to process grief in a slightly cold and calculating way. She possessed that ability too, and I guess it was passed down to me in the genes I inherited. I never saw Mum cry. Not when I cried in front of her as a child after hurting myself playing in the garden. Not when I went with her to Grandma's funeral and stood in front of that coffin with her as lots of people in black suits and dresses walked around us. And not even when Dad died, when the doctor in the hospital told us that after years of heart problems, his ticker had finally given up and was no longer beating.

I was twenty-six when Dad passed, and even though it was devastating, what I remember most about that day is how practical Mum was. I knew she was upset but only because she had a tell, and it was in the form of her touching her face. She always touched her face when she was processing something sad. But she never shed a tear, nor did she let out a cry of pain, like Bev just did upstairs. I was the same. I didn't cry for the loss of Dad either, though I missed him terribly and still do to this day. Nor did I wail. I just sat next to Mum and held her hand while her other one kept going up to her face, scratching her cheek or her nose, telling me she was bereft, but to anybody else, she would have looked surprisingly calm.

Even all these years later, I still haven't decided if it is a good or a bad thing to be the way we are. Sometimes, it feels like a blessing to be able to process grief in such a stoic way because, let's face it, the alternative way of sobbing and screaming doesn't look particularly pleasant. On the other hand, it feels less human somehow, like I'm not in touch with my emotions as much as someone like Bev is beside me now, for example.

Does she think I'm callous for not crying over Natasha's death like she is? Possibly, though, at the moment, I'm not sure she is thinking about me or herself. She's in mourning. But it's my job to remind her that the mourning can't really begin until we are both safely back in our homes and the police are satisfied with the answers we have given them.

Aware that the officers in uniform will be here any minute, I do my best to comfort Bev while also gently telling her once again that we are not to mention the note Natasha left before her death. But despite trying my best to get Bev to give me clear confirmation that she understands, the police arrive before she has done much of anything other than wiping her tears and saying what a waste this all is. That's why, as the first police officer introduces himself as PC Marsden, I'm afraid this might not go exactly the way I want it to.

What if Bev blabs and mentions the letter? What if she tells these police officers what we did to our old boss? What if I'm going to be in handcuffs in a minute and my life as a free woman is about to be over?

As PC Marsden takes a seat on the sofa opposite us, I notice his colleague, PC Paul, observing the wine bottles on the table between us, and in that moment, I decide it's best if I just start talking because that way, I can not only pre-empt any questions but also fill the silence so Bev can't go and fill it herself.

I explain to the officers who we are and why we were here tonight, and that's the easy part because it only requires honesty. The next part isn't so bad either, the part where I talk about Natasha and how she has had a troubled time recently, what with being unemployed and developing a bit of a drinking habit. I'm not saying anything that Bev can disagree with there, which might be why my friend is keeping quiet beside me. But as I move on to discuss what we found when we arrived here at this house tonight, I'm aware Bev might interject at any moment and tell the officers about the incriminating letter I have already destroyed. That's why I speak more quickly then, explaining that we found Natasha upstairs and figured she had suffered an overdose, but I leave it at that before putting my head in my hands and doing my best to look utterly devastated. I am devastated, but I also want these police officers to take pity on me and leave it here, allowing us to go home without any more questions. Thankfully, it seems to do the job because PC Marsden thanks me before asking if we would be able to come to the station and give a formal statement at a more suitable time.

I confirm that I will be happy to do that, as does Bev, though she needs a little prompting from me, but as the two officers go to leave us, I am just grateful my friend did not mention the letter. But just before the officers depart, one of them pauses before turning back and asking a frightening question.

'I know you're upset, but have you seen anything in the house that might indicate why Natasha chose to take her own life?' PC Paul asks me, and instantly, my mind is filled with the image of those pieces of paper that I set fire to a short time ago.

I look at Bev then and see that she has gone incredibly pale, but at least she still has her mouth shut, and I better make sure it stays that way, so I answer for the pair of us.

'No, I haven't seen anything,' I say before PC Paul turns his attention to Bev, and I guess he wants her to speak for herself here too.

But what is she going to say?

'I haven't seen anything either,' Bev says quietly, and that's enough for the officers, who leave the room and go upstairs to check on the work of the paramedics.

It's also enough for me because I don't waste any more time, taking Bev's hand and getting up from the sofa.

'Let's go home,' I tell my friend seconds before my other friend is carried down the stairs inside a body bag.

6

It's late by the time I get home, but I only know that because I have enough awareness of my surroundings to see that it's dark, all the curtains in my neighbours' windows are closed, and there is not a single soul on the street as my taxi delivers me onto it. But I'm far too tired and upset to do something as simple as check the actual time on my watch, and it takes all my effort just to concentrate for ten seconds so I can pay the driver and exit his vehicle. Once I'm out of it, it takes me a while to get to my front door and unlock it, such is the heavy feeling in both my arms and my legs.

Natasha's death is still very fresh but is already haunting me, so much so that I already know sleep is going to be impossible to achieve shortly. That's why, once I'm in my house, I forgo heading upstairs to the bedroom and enter the kitchen instead, with my only intention being to retrieve the bottle of wine from the fridge that I opened yesterday.

Back when I first savoured the delicious contents of this bottle, it was a sunny Sunday afternoon, and I had a glass while sitting out in my garden and mentally gearing myself up for another week at work. I stopped at just the one glass, though, because I knew I was meeting the girls tonight and that always involved one drink too many. But tonight did not go to plan - far from it – so now I am more than grateful for the fact that this bottle in my hand is over half full.

Unscrewing the lid and pouring myself a glass, I chug down half of it before I come up for air, before topping it back up and then slumping down into one of the chairs at my kitchen table. While the wine is good, it's doing little to take the edge off so far, but I'll sit here and drink until I've achieved the desired outcome.

Seeing Natasha zipped up inside that bag as it was carried out of her house is an image that is most likely going to stick with me forever, and I'm sure Bev will be just as tortured over it too. Worrying about my friend, I send her a quick text to ask her if she is okay and got home safe, although I'm also aware a big part of me just wants to check up and make sure she hasn't done something stupid like going to a police station instead of going to bed.

Thankfully, the message I receive back tells me Bev is home, and while it sounds like she is as tormented as I am, I'd rather her be like that in the safety of her house than out there in the wild, spilling her secrets to anybody who might listen to them. As it is, she is spilling her secrets to me.

I bet Natasha wished she'd never met us.

That's the second message I receive from Bev, right after her first told me she was sipping on a strong drink, just like I'm doing the same thing here.

We were her friends, I type back, but even though that was true once, I'm not sure how much of a friend we were to her in her final hours. If we'd really been her friend, she wouldn't have apportioned some of the blame for her death onto us, would she?

I wonder if her family knows yet, Bev writes back, and it's clear she is up for a night of wallowing, though such a thing can't be healthy for either of us.

Try and get some sleep, I suggest, but that is ignored.

How are we going to get through her funeral? Bev asks me then, and while I wish she hadn't brought the subject up, it's a good question. The thought of standing at Natasha's graveside along with her devastated family and friends is a grim one, made all the worse by the knowledge we will possess that she might still be alive today if only I hadn't suggested what I did, six months ago.

It will be hard, but we'll manage it, I type back, hoping I'm right, before thinking of an alternative response. ***Maybe I could just go. You don't have to be there as I know how difficult it will be.***

My suggestion that Bev skips Natasha's funeral entirely is hardly likely to garner a positive response from my friend, but it's worth making. If Bev can stay away from that funeral, then not only would it make the whole day easier for her but it would make it easier for me too because then I wouldn't be worried about her having too much to drink at the wake and saying something we'd both regret. Unfortunately, Bev does not see it the same way, and I find that out when she calls me instead of texting me to reply.

'What are you talking about? I'm not missing her funeral,' Bev cries down the phone, and I'm almost regretting answering, such is the level of disagreement I'm hearing. 'I'm her friend. Of course I'll be at her funeral!'

'Okay, I'm sorry, it was just a suggestion. I was just trying to make things easier for you.'

'For me or for you?'

'Both of us.'

'Whatever.'

Bev surprises me by hanging up then, and even though I try and call her back, there is no answer. Worrying that she might do something stupid after our disagreement, I send her a message telling her that I'm sorry and that we just need to get some rest before we can talk about this in the morning. I almost tell her that things will look a little better once the sun has risen on a new day but decide against it at the last second because that might only serve to infuriate her further, and I dare not risk that.

Worryingly, Bev takes a while to respond but she finally does and it is to tell me that she is going to bed. That is a relief, and I wish her goodnight before deciding that I should probably look to do the same thing as her, so I finish my glass of wine and leave the rest of the bottle on the kitchen table, unfussed about refrigerating it because warm wine is the least of my worries for tomorrow.

Trudging up the stairs, I try my best to put my mind on my pre-bed routine rather than thinking about what those police officers I spoke to earlier might be thinking and doing now. It's obviously way more comforting to think about removing my make-up and brushing my teeth than it is to think that those officers might be analysing what I told them and wondering if it was the truth. However, despite trying my best there, it's impossible to rid myself of the anxiety I feel over not just tonight but everything that has happened, and as I get into bed, I feel even worse than I did earlier.

With the lights out and my bedroom dark, there is nothing for me to concentrate on, other than my even darker thoughts, and there is nothing anxiety feeds on more than a guilty mind with little else to occupy it. It's all well and good telling Bev what to do and suggesting things will get better, but it's much harder to put into practice, and if I'm lying in my bed, riddled with worry, I am damn sure she is too.

Turning my pillow over and rolling onto my left side instead of my right, I am hoping the change of position will improve my odds of sleep, but it's futile, and I soon give up, turning on my bedside lamp to at least allow me to see again. The light is somewhat soothing, though not nearly enough to relax me fully, but rather than try and do something else that might help, I foolishly pick up my phone and find myself looking at Natasha's social media accounts. It's a stupid thing to be doing, but I've gone down the rabbit hole now, and as I scroll further and further back, I see plenty of photos of Natasha in happier times. Unlike recently, when she practically withdrew from social media entirely, her online past is full of things that prove what a happy woman she once was. Photos of her smiling on holiday or on nights out. Status updates about some brilliant new TV show she has discovered or how she had the best meal ever at that Greek restaurant in town. Captions about her eating healthier, or joining the gym, or looking forward to her next chapter of life after a relationship breakup or change of job.

All very normal, average stuff, and there's nothing here that would suggest Natasha was any different to any other women using these websites to update their followers. But it's not what is here that is so telling as much as what isn't. As everybody knows, social media is not representative of real life, and while it appears that Natasha had a normal existence, as far as her online footprint goes, I know there is so much that didn't make it onto these pages.

The crying. The shame. The disgust.

The nights and decisions that changed her life.

The incident and, subsequently, t*he murder.*

None of that is on here, but unlike all of Natasha's followers, I know it all happened, and I know that is why, very soon, all those followers will hear the news of her death and flood her accounts with messages full of sorrow and respect. For example:

I can't believe what I have just heard. Say it isn't so!

I'm so sorry you were struggling, Natasha. I'll miss you so much xx

RIP my friend. Have a drink up there on me.

Everyone knows the kinds of things people post on social media when someone they once knew passes away, and while they won't win any awards for originality, it's more the sentiment that counts. Natasha's family may take comfort in knowing just how many lives their loved one touched and enhanced before her time here on Earth was up, and if so, there is no harm in all the messages that are soon to be flooding the deceased's accounts. I may even leave a message of my own, something short and sweet, stating my sympathies and wishing my dear friend is in a better place now.

What I won't do is write the truth.

I won't answer everybody when they all ask how a seemingly healthy, happy young woman like Natasha could choose to take her own life.

I won't get into the details because there are only four people who knew about those, and now, two of them are dead.

Bev and I are the last ones standing.

Natasha went before us.

But at least she lived longer than Edwin.

7

SIX MONTHS AGO

It's a chilly evening, and the last of the day's light is glinting off the office windows across the street from me as the sun sets on this particular Wednesday. That middle day of the week, 'hump day' as it is often called, can be seen as a milestone, one that once passed means the weekend is fast approaching and easier days are ahead, for a little while at least. But as I stand here and stare at the office, I don't have to wait for the weekend to come around with any great sense of anticipation. Not in my current situation.

Being unemployed means at the moment, every damn day feels like the weekend.

Unfortunately for me, while I might have a lot of free time on my hands, it's not as if I can enjoy it. Having no income means I have to be disciplined and guard what little money I have left in my bank account for fear of running out of funds before I find myself a new place of work. As of yet, I have no idea when I will be gainfully employed again and because of that, I can hardly spend my days drinking in bars, dining in restaurants, and catching a film or a show at the theatre. I can't even go into town and treat myself to something new to wear. I'm penny-pinching, living on a very strict budget, but even so, I still might not be able to stay financially afloat for much longer.

Bizarrely, though, potentially ending up homeless on the streets with nothing to my name is not my biggest concern. There's actually a more pressing matter to attend to than finding a job, and it's that matter that has brought me here tonight.

Staring at the dull, non-descript exterior of Van Dekker Logistics, there is a comfort in the familiarity of this place. Being an ex-employee here, I know my way around this place well. I parked in that car park, I walked in and out of that front door, I walked up and down the stairs, and I spent countless hours sitting at a desk on the second floor staring out at the street I now stand on. I wouldn't say I loved working here, and I certainly can't say my time here ended satisfactorily, but the history I have with this little section of the map means I feel quite comfortable to be back in these surroundings.

That is helpful because I need all the comfort I can get with what I'm planning to do tonight.

Checking my watch, I see that it has just turned 6 p.m., and with that, I start to make my way across the street, heading for the front gates of the office car park. As I get closer, I make sure to check on the camera that sits atop a metallic pole at the side of the left gate because I want to make absolutely sure that it is still in exactly the same position it should be in. The last thing I need is for it to have been moved because my presence here at the end of this working day needs to be kept a secret from everybody but the person I'm here to see. That includes Barry, the security officer who either sits in his office or patrols these premises, monitoring all the ins and outs and ensuring the place remains secure from thieves and other types of trespassers. Having had a brief fling with Barry, the cheeky and pudgy man whose bed I ended up in one night after I bumped into him in a bar in town and he offered to buy me a drink, it might not seem like a disaster if he was to see me here. But it would be because ever since that night, I told him it was a mistake and that I didn't want it to happen again, and while he tried to change my mind about that several times, I stuck firm, leaving him disappointed and frustrated.

So best to avoid Barry if I can help it.

That's why I'm pleased to see that the camera is exactly where it should be, and now I am confident that surveillance footage is only capturing what goes on in the car park and not just outside it, I stop at the gates. Then I make another quick check to ensure there are no new cameras that have been installed anywhere around here, a nasty surprise that could catch me out, and make my fairly miserable existence at the moment even worse. But again, I don't see anything I'm not expecting to see, and once I'm totally assured that I'm not in the line of sight of anything that could later be looked at by Barry or a police officer, I check my watch again.

It's now two minutes past six, and I'm right on schedule.

All I can hope is that the person I'm here to see is too.

Well aware that the owner of the company I'm currently standing outside of is a creature of habit, I fully expect to see him emerge from the front doors of this office any second now. I know he always leaves the workplace between 6:00 and 6:05 p.m., and he is always the last one to leave. Of course he is, no one else here is willing to work longer hours than the boss. I came close during my time here, but even then, I was always logging off and leaving my desk by half-past five. Everyone else was out as soon as the clock struck five, but I know the manager preferred to stay until six.

"The captain is always the last one off his ship," I overheard him saying once when somebody asked him how much later he worked compared to everybody else. The thing is, this isn't a ship, and he isn't a captain, but I guess he liked to make the whole thing seem a little more dramatic than it really was. At the end of the day, it's surely more exciting to use his description than to state the reality, which was that he was a middle-aged man coming and going from work with the same goal as everybody else in the working world – get paid, save for retirement, and hope to not drop dead before then.

My heart starts to beat a little faster at the thought of somebody dropping dead because if all goes to plan tonight, that's exactly what will be happening, but I'm not there yet.

It's three minutes past six in the evening now.

Where is he?

I know he's in there because his car is parked right beside the front door in its own designated parking spot. It's the only car left in the car park, all other vehicles having been driven out of here an hour ago and now parked up outside various houses around town, and it's as it should be. Any other car in here would worry me because it would mean somebody else was in the office too, somebody who could see me or distract from what needs to happen. But only the boss is inside, or to give him the title he prefers, the captain.

I'm a little surprised, given his penchant for referring to himself as a seafaring custodian, that he hasn't put that particular word on the personalised licence plate that is fixed to his BMW. Instead, he went for something a little different.

EVD 001

The first part of the personalised reg are his initials, Edwin van Dekker, while the numbers that follow it are just his way of letting everyone else know exactly where he puts himself in the pecking order of priorities. He is his first concern in life, the most important thing, the number one. That rather selfish outlook is distasteful in the best of situations, but considering he has a son, it's even worse. What kind of person puts themselves ahead of their offspring?

The kind of person walking out of that front door right now.

My chest tightens, and I nervously nibble on my lower lip as I lay eyes on the man I have been waiting for. He's a man I never wanted to see again and a man I never thought I would actually see again, but things have changed since we last crossed paths. Things have got worse, and for me to be here, they had to because I really, really wanted to stay away from this place and this man forever.

Seeing him sauntering out towards his car, the key in one hand and his phone in the other, I hate everything about him, from his fitted suit to his smug strut, to the way his hair is annoyingly trimmed and perfect. No matter what this man does in his day, and he has done some pretty terrible things, he always finds the time to make sure that there is not a single silver hair on the top of his head out of place.

This is my old boss.

This is the captain.

This is Edwin van Dekker.

And this is the man I want to murder tonight.

'Edwin! Over here!'

I call out to him before he can get into his car, and when he looks up and sees me loitering by the gate, it's not surprising that he looks confused. The last time he saw me, I told him I hated his guts, so I'm sure the last thing he expected was me coming to see him at his workplace. But here I am, and I'm not going anywhere until he acknowledges me.

'Liz?'

'Come here. I need to talk to you.'

Edwin looks around as if expecting to see a camera crew ready to jump out and surprise him by letting him know he's on some kind of reality show where ex-girlfriends and employees play pranks on their former partners and bosses. But there is no camera crew, just me and him, although he is currently in the line of sight of the camera on the gate, which is why I need to get him to come to me rather than the other way around.

'What?'

'Come here, I need to tell you something.'

Edwin looks unsure, as perhaps any man would be under the circumstances. But he's curious enough to want to know what I came here to say because he starts walking towards me, although as he reaches the gate, he stops and maintains enough distance, just to be sure. For all he knows, I'm here to slap him or throw something at him or start hurling abuse, all things that a woman in my position would be more than justified doing to a man like him after what he put me through. But like I told him, I'm only here to tell him something.

'You look nice,' Edwin says, unable to resist laying on his usual charm even though he must know the time for us two to ever be close has long since passed.

'It's Natasha,' I say, ignoring his comment and getting straight to the point.

'Natasha? What about her?'

'She's going to go to the police and tell them what you did to her.'

Now I really have Edwin's attention, and he takes a few steps closer to me to prove it before lowering his voice when he speaks again.

'What did you just say?'

'She's going to the police. I just heard about it from Bev. Apparently, she's in a bad way and can't carry on. She's going to tell them everything, Edwin. *Everything.*'

As he should, the man standing in front of me now looks very worried.

'But the money I gave her? The contract I made her sign? She'd be breaking the terms of our agreement.'

'She doesn't give a damn about any of that,' I tell him. 'She just wants to see you pay.'

Edwin is sweating now, and suddenly, that sharp suit of his doesn't look quite so comfortable. But unless he wants to swap it for a prison uniform, he better take what I am saying to him very seriously.

‘Why are you telling me this?’ he asks me then, and it’s a very good question because he would surely imagine I’d prefer to see him in handcuffs than get away with something else.

‘I don’t want it all becoming public knowledge,’ I say to him honestly. ‘I don’t want everybody in this town knowing the kinds of things that went on here. And I certainly don’t want the police knowing either.’

‘You’re worried you’ll get arrested too?’ Edwin asks, and I nod my head.

‘Of course I am. I don’t give a damn about you, but I need to make sure I don’t get dragged into this. If the police start poking around, I don’t want them coming to my door too, nor do I want them going to Bev’s. We don’t deserve to have people prying into our lives.’

‘So what are you saying?’ Edwin asks me as he looks up the street behind me, possibly to make sure the police aren’t already on their way.

‘I’m saying that Natasha needs to be silenced,’ I reply as calmly as I can. ‘And I’m saying we need to do it tonight, before it’s too late.’

8

PRESENT DAY

As would be expected for a woman who only yesterday saw the dead body of her former friend, I have not gone to work today, citing the stressful situation that I was recently a part of as the main reason for that.

My boss, the man in his twenties who is probably too young to know what it's like to lose a close friend, was at least sympathetic enough to allow me to stay home today, although he did say he would appreciate it if I was still contactable by email for as long as I'm away from the office. Whatever, I'd rather lie here on my sofa and check my inbox on my work phone intermittently than be sat in that office having to listen to all the people in there chunnering away about pointless things.

With my new boss dealt with for the time being, my thoughts turn to my old one and with Natasha now joining him in the afterlife, I'm dealing with all sorts of emotions based on my part in all of this. None of them are good, but seeing as it's far too early to start drinking again, I have no choice but to try and deal with them with nothing more than a strong cup of coffee for company. At least that's what I think until I hear the knock on my front door, and as I stay still on my sofa and wonder who it could be, I am afraid the police have come to ask me a few more questions. If they have, can I get away with delaying answering them, using the trauma of yesterday as an excuse not to be ready for it yet? Possibly, but first, I'd have to tell them that so they might leave me alone, and that means going to open the door to them.

Wearily dragging my sleep-deprived self off the sofa, I pull my dressing gown closed around me before making it to the door, but when I open it, I do not see any police officers. Instead, I see a woman I recognise, although in her current state, only just. She looks very different to the last time I saw her, which was at a party to celebrate her daughter's birthday. That night, the woman on my doorstep was a ray of light in the room, chatting with all the guests, drinking lots of champagne, and dancing the night away with women at least twenty years her junior. I even remember remarking to Bev that I wished my mum was like her; that's how impressive this woman was the last time I was around her. But now, she is a shadow of her former self.

Now, she is simply grieving the loss of her beloved daughter, Natasha.

'Can I come in?' Ruth says, her eyes tear-stained and her face pale and make-up-free.

'Of course,' I say, and as Ruth steps into my home, I do the only thing that feels right in a situation as horrible as this one.

I wrap my arms around the devastated woman and give her a hug.

As soon as I do, Ruth's tears start flowing, and it's a good few minutes before she calms down enough for me to suggest she takes a seat on my sofa while I make her a drink. The time it takes for my kettle to boil is painstaking but only because I know there is a woman in tears waiting for me to return to her. By the time I do that, handing over a hot cup of tea for her to hopefully take a little comfort from, I'm ready for what is surely going to be just as difficult a conversation as if the police were here instead.

'I believe you were the one who found Natasha,' Ruth says, after I have placed a box of tissues next to her.

'Yes. Well, me and Bev. We went to Natasha's house together.'

Ruth nods but doesn't touch her drink or the tissues.

'Why?'

'Did the police not tell you all this?'

'I'd like to hear it from you. The police were just…' Ruth trails off from her sentence for a second before completing it. 'Impersonal.'

I nod to show that I understand and that she's here to hear about her daughter's death from somebody who actually had an affinity with the deceased rather than somebody just doing their job.

'We were supposed to meet Natasha last night for a drink,' I say. 'Me and Bev.'

Ruth surprises me by smiling a little then.

'She loved having you two as her friends,' she tells me, although that only makes me feel even guiltier about what our friendship ended up costing her, not that I say that. 'I remember her telling me about you both when she first started working with you and how she felt you would get along well. It was so nice to see that was the case.'

'We loved her too. I'm glad I knew her. She was so lovely.'

'Yes, she was.'

Ruth's smile has disappeared almost as quickly as it came, so I go on.

'When Natasha failed to show up at the bar, we tried to contact her, but there was no answer, so we went to her house. A neighbour told us she hadn't seen her, but her car was there. All the curtains were drawn though, which seemed strange as the sun was still up. That's why I went looking around the back.'

'I should have gone to her house a few days ago,' Ruth says then. 'If I had, I could have seen how much she was struggling, and she'd still be here now.'

'Don't blame yourself for this. It's nobody's fault,' I say, but I know that is not true, and I hate having to lie to this devastated woman. I really wish I could tell her whose fault it actually is. I'd love to say Edwin's name. But even then, I'd still be lying because I wouldn't be giving Ruth the full picture, the one in which Bev and I are almost just as much to blame as that man was.

'But it is my fault. I should have known she'd be struggling, what with her leaving her job and being by herself at an age when most women are already married with kids,' Ruth goes on before she realises she has just described me too.

'I didn't mean…' she starts, clearly looking to apologise if she has offended me, but I dismiss it quickly.

'It's nobody's fault,' I repeat. 'Please don't blame yourself. Unfortunately, people can be good at hiding how they are really feeling, and often, it's their loved ones who are the last to know.'

Another lie. I was one of Natasha's loved ones, one of her best friends, and I knew. The problem is, while I was aware of how unhappy she was in her last few weeks, I had no idea she would ever have done something this drastic.

'I just find it hard to believe she wouldn't leave something behind,' Ruth says, after finally putting some of the tissues I gave her to good use. 'A note or something so we could at least try and understand what she was thinking in her final hour.'

'She loved you. You know that. A goodbye note doesn't change anything.'

'Doesn't it? At least if I had that, I'd have some kind of clue. Now I'm left with nothing. All I know is my daughter killed herself, and I don't really know why.'

I stare at Ruth while visualising the letter Natasha left going up in flames right in front of me, and just like Bev said, I shouldn't have done it because it wasn't fair on the family, who all need answers. But I had to do it. At least this way, Ruth can just think her daughter was struggling with being unemployed and a little lonely. At least this way, she doesn't know the full extent of the suffering Natasha really went through.

'I'm so sorry,' I say, relieved to get the chance to say something honest, and I move over to Ruth and put a comforting arm around her as she cries once more.

Her tears are such that she finds it impossible to carry on our conversation, and after leaving the drink I made for her untouched, she tells me she has to get going because she has funeral arrangements to think about.

I tell her to call me if she needs help with anything, and she assures me she will, before she leaves my house, as broken and lost as she was when she first arrived here.

As I close my door, I can't help but think I provided no comfort to that poor woman then. She most likely came here looking for more answers but left with none, which hurts because I actually hold all the answers; I just can't give them to her.

As I tidy up the tea and the tissues, I wish there was something more I could do.

But I've already done more than enough in this life.

I saw to that the night I lured Edwin away from his office and straight into a dangerous situation from which he would never recover.

9

SIX MONTHS AGO

I have persuaded Edwin to leave his car at the office and join me in my vehicle for our journey to Natasha's house. My car is parked across the street from the office and again, well out of view of any cameras, so I am confident that nobody will know I was here tonight or that Edwin was in my company. With him sitting beside me in the passenger seat, I start the engine and begin the drive, though my nerves are jangling as I do because I can't relax whilst in such close proximity to a man as dangerous as the one riding with me currently. Fortunately, we have plenty to talk about on the way, so there is a little less time to think about just how much I hate being around this man.

'You really think it will work?' Edwin asks me as I turn a corner. 'The overdose thing?'

'It will work,' I say without skipping a beat. 'Natasha drinks a lot these days, and I know she's on prescription meds, so there are plenty of pills in her house. All we need to do is make it look like she has taken her own life. I can get us inside because she'll answer the door to me, and once it's open, we can both get in.'

'But she's going to fight, isn't she? There'll be a struggle, and that means there'll be evidence. How is it going to look like she killed herself if she is fighting for her life? There'll be cuts and bruises, not to mention our DNA under her fingernails.'

'Open the glove compartment,' I say then as I turn another corner, and when Edwin does as I say, he sees the plastic bottle in there alongside a black handkerchief.

'What's that?' he asks me.

'Chloroform.'

'What?'

'We use that to knock her out. Then we stuff the pills and booze down her throat and get out of there. I've got a bottle of wine in the back of the car.'

My eyes might be on the road ahead, but I can tell that Edwin is staring at me, and when I turn to look at him, I see that he looks horrified at the plot I have planned and prepared for. Funnily enough, me suggesting that we silence Natasha tonight didn't bother him too much, but seeing that I have chloroform in my car seems to have been the thing that makes him see me as crazy.

'Have you got a better idea?' I ask him.

'No, it's just that…'

'What?'

'Well, I thought she was your friend.'

'She was. But she stopped being my friend the second she started talking about going to the police and telling them about her experience working at Dekker. If she talks about everything, including the accounts and what you were trying to have me do, it's bad news. At best, for my future career and at worst, I could go to prison. I'm not risking that, no way, and if that's the chance I have to take with her around, she is no longer my friend.'

Edwin seems satisfied with that answer, and I turn the next corner in silence. But he's soon back with more questions.

'So what do we do when this is all over?'

'I'll drive you back here, and you go home. That's it.'

'That's it? We just act as if nothing happened?'

'I'm sure you can manage it, Edwin. You've had plenty of practice at that in your life. You're the master of hurting people and moving on.'

Edwin knows I'm right there, although, despite his many sins, murder is a step up, even for him.

'You really think we can get away with this? How do you know Natasha hasn't already started talking to the police? If she has and she turns up dead, they will be very suspicious.'

'She hasn't.'

'How can you be so sure?'

'Because she still thinks I'm her friend, so she tells me everything, and I know for a fact that she has not gone to the police yet. I know it because I was with her last night and listened to her talking for over two hours about what she was thinking about doing.'

'Didn't you try and discourage her?' Edwin asks me then. 'Couldn't you just talk her out of it?'

'Don't you think I tried? But it's hard when she's been through what she has for me to just sit there and tell her not to try and seek retribution. I couldn't make it obvious that I wanted her to stay away from the police, or she would have just pushed me away, and then we'd never be able to get near to her, would we?'

I'm giving Edwin plausible answers for all of the questions he has, and as we enter the final stretch of our journey, his concerns turn away from what has gone before and more on to what is going to happen next.

'So let's say we do this, and it all goes well. What happens with us?'

'Us?'

'Yeah, I mean, we're bonded by this for life, aren't we? We can't just go back to how things were. We'll need to talk. Discuss how it's going. Keep each other updated and make sure the police aren't on our scent at any point.'

'No, we do this, and then we never see each other again,' I say firmly. 'I still hate you and what you did, and I am only doing this for me. Once it's done, we just get on with our lives as if it never happened.'

Edwin looks like he is unsure that it will be as easy as that, but the time for talking is over, and I bring my car to a stop by the side of the road.

'What are you doing? Natasha's house is on the next street from here,' he says as he looks around at the row of houses on the other side of the windows.

'I know that, but I'm hardly going to go and park right outside her property so her neighbours can see my car on the day she died and pass my licence plate number on to the police, am I?'

After turning off the engine, I lean over and remove the bottle and handkerchief from the glove compartment before unscrewing the lid and pouring some of the contents onto the handkerchief. Edwin watches me work until I'm satisfied there is enough chloroform on this rag to subdue Natasha, and then I tell him what will happen next.

'I'm going to go to her place and knock on the door. You walk several yards behind me so nobody who sees us tonight would think we're together. When I get to her house, I'll knock, and when she answers, I'll show her the bottle of wine and tell her I've come to cheer her up. She won't see the handkerchief because it will be in the shopping bag with the wine, but once I'm in, I'll use it. When she is unconscious, I'll then open the door to let you in.'

I'm just about to open my door and get out of the car when Edwin grabs my arm, and feeling his hand on me is enough to turn my whole body instantly cold.

'Wait a minute,' he says to me, and if I didn't have enough to worry about before this, now I've got the fact that I know this man is dangerous enough to turn on me at any second and make it so it's actually my life in danger here instead.

'What?'

'I was just wondering,' Edwin says, his fingers still curled around my slender forearm. 'If you can get inside the house and render Natasha unconscious, what do you need me here for? It sounds like you could do all of this yourself.'

He has a good point, and I did wonder beforehand whether he would pick up on that fact but because of that, I already prepared an answer for such a question.

'Let's remember that I'm not the only one who could get in trouble if Natasha does go to the police and has them start digging around into your affairs,' I say, fixing Edwin with a steely glare. 'You have way more to lose here than I do, so the question should be, why wouldn't you help me? I could do with the extra pair of hands in there, and considering what you have put me through in the past, I'd say the least you can do is help me now.'

I stare at Edwin and hope he accepts that answer, but I guess I'll know for sure if he removes his hand from my arm or keeps it there. It's a tense few seconds before Edwin chooses to release me from his grip and once he has, I ask him if he is going to help me or not.

'Let's go,' he says, and with that, the plan is back in motion, and we finally exit my vehicle.

After picking up the shopping bag from the back seat, the one with the bottle of white wine in it, I stuff the soaked handkerchief into the bag and then get on my way. As per my orders, Edwin lingers back before following me, so by the time we walk onto Natasha's street, there is a sizeable gap between us as we pass under the street lights and move in and out of the shadows.

The street is quiet, all residents already inside their properties after work and preparing their evening meals, or still out and continuing their commute home, and we don't see anybody on our way, which is perfect. I only slow down when I reach Natasha's house, and after glancing back and seeing Edwin move himself out of view behind an overgrown garden bush two houses down, I approach the front door.

Knocking twice, I stand back and wait until I hear the sound of the door being unlocked. When it is pulled open, I lift the bottle of wine out of the shopping bag and flash it to the homeowner.

'Hey! Only me! I thought we could have a drink tonight. What do you say?'

Natasha smiles at me before inviting me in, and as I step inside, I take one more glance to my left, spotting the top of Edwin's head peeping out from behind the bush and seeing that he is watching me going in, thus knowing the plan is still in play.

As the door closes behind me, Natasha stops smiling and just stares at me, but she doesn't have to say a word for me to know what she is thinking. All I do in return is nod my head, and that's enough to tell her that Edwin is here and that the real plan, the one he doesn't know about, is actually the only thing still in play.

'I'll open the door in twenty seconds,' I say to Natasha but also to Bev, who is right in position where she should be, standing behind the front door in the corner where she wouldn't be spotted by anybody who walked in.

Bev and Natasha are fully on board, and as the seconds count down, I know there's no going back now.

'Let's do this,' I say before going back to the door and as I do, Natasha lies down on the floor and closes her eyes while Bev pushes her back to the wall and stays well hidden.

Opening the front door, I find Edwin waiting on the doorstep, and he rushes inside while asking me if I have done it. But he gets his answer when he sees

Natasha lying on the floor looking totally unconscious, and I make sure to confirm that everything went as it should have.

'Okay, so we get the wine and the pills now?' Edwin asks me, looking to move quickly on this.

'No, first we move her,' I say. 'We need to put her on the sofa. Come on. I'll take her arms, and you grab her legs.'

I move around to the other side of Natasha while Edwin bends down and takes hold of her feet but as he does that, his back is turned to the front door, and that means he cannot see who is behind him in the corner, nor what she is about to do.

That's why he's utterly powerless to stop Bev bringing down the rolling pin hard on his head, and only when he is lying on the floor with blood pouring from his skull does the person he is lying next to get back to her feet.

As Natasha stands up beside me and Bev, the three of us stare down at our former boss and know that the first part of our plan has been a success.

Now it's just about completing the second part.

The part where we make sure he dies.

10

PRESENT DAY

After Ruth's emotional visit, I need to get out of the house, so I've put my coat on and am going for a walk. I left the house ten minutes ago, and in that time, I've managed to navigate my way down to the canal that runs all the way through the centre of town. It's nice to walk beside water, even if the water in this case has a slightly green layer of algae floating on top of it and is definitely not the kind a person should think about going swimming in. But it's nice to be out of the house, and as a small barge slowly sails past me and the owner of it waves to me and the other pedestrians on the embankment, I can't help but feel my mood improve ever so slightly.

Still, it's going to take a lot more than receiving a smile from a stranger and working on getting my 10,000 steps daily goal to make me feel truly better, and I know it's going to be a long time until I'm anywhere near happy again.

Even now, as I walk along enjoying the freedom that comes with being off work today and having nothing more strenuous to do than decide when and where to turn back and walk home again, I can't help but feel guilty. Does a woman like me, with what I have done and the secrets I harbour, deserve to have freedom like this? There must be people serving time in prison for crimes lesser in severity than mine. Then again, the type of freedom I am experiencing only exists in the outside.

Sure, I'm free to wander where I like today, but on the inside, mentally, I'm trapped in a prison of my own making.

I always knew the night I lured Edwin to his doom was going to live with me forever. Making a deadly plot and then executing it is not the kind of thing one forgets about after a couple of days, though I wish it was. Was I surprised that it worked? I was, simply because Edwin was a clever man and could have potentially figured out that I was laying a trap for him at any point while we were in my car driving to Natasha's place. He could have run from the car while I was stopped at a traffic light, and if he had, my chance at revenge would have left with him. Or worse, he could have realised I had deadly intentions and hurt me first, murdering me and burying my body, rather than the other way around. At least I'm the one who is here and not him, though I'm hardly revelling in the spoils of my victory at present.

As I cross over a small footbridge about fifteen feet above the canal, I look down at the murky depths, and as I have done every time I have come to this place in the last six months, I wonder if Edwin's body is still rooted to the same spot I dumped it in or if it has moved by now. Is it lying on the bottom of this canal exactly where I dropped it, or has the current taken it away forever? I hope it's still where I left it because that means the bricks I tied to his corpse are keeping it well hidden on the canal bed, and rather that than his body floating up and bumping into the bottom of somebody's barge while they're out for a Sunday sail. But the most important thing is that it remains undiscovered, and I just pray that is the case until I die.

The police are free to discover it one day.

Just as long as it's not in my lifetime.

Pausing on the bridge, I put my hands on the edge of the railing and look down at the canal stretching away from me in a southerly direction. If my eyes were to follow the path of the water all the way as far as I could see, then I would end up looking at some of the taller buildings in this town in the distance. But I'm not looking that far because my eyes are fixed on the bench about one hundred yards ahead of me on the left of the embankment. That bench is currently occupied by an elderly man who looks like he has just taken a moment to sit down and enjoy the little bit of sunshine that is peeking out from between the clouds. If only he knew what happened here six months ago in this scenic, tranquil spot.

I'm staring at this particular part of the canal because it's here, just to the right of that bench where two friends and I dumped Edwin's body into the water. I hadn't noticed the bench at the time because it was dark, and I had more pressing matters on my mind, like trying to make sure I wasn't caught with a corpse, but once Edwin's lifeless face had disappeared under the water, I saw the bench and actually sat on it for a moment to get my breath back. Bev sat down with me, and the pair of us took a moment to discuss what we had just done and what would happen next. The only person who didn't sit on that bench or join in on that discussion was Natasha. That's because she chose to stay standing on the edge of the embankment, staring down into the water without saying a word.

To watch her, it almost looked like she was making sure Edwin didn't rise back up from the depths to torment us all again, but that was a silly notion because that man was most definitely dead when he entered the water, and nothing could resurrect him after what we had done to him. Still, Natasha had stood there for what felt like ages, monitoring, making sure, getting confirmation Edwin really was gone for good. Or at least that's what I thought she was doing at the time. But now, as I stand here and look down upon the scene of the crime, I can't help but wonder if what Natasha was doing that night was not revelling in the end of Edwin but rather, commiserating the true end of her innocence.

Before that night, she was just a victim, like Bev and me but after it, she was guilty in her own right, as we all were then. That quiet moment she had by this canal that night may have been the moment her spirit became broken beyond repair, and while it might have taken six months for the true extent of that devastation to manifest itself, the damage was already done. Did she know she was going to end up taking her own life half a year later, as she stared at the water on that chilly, moonless night? Or did she only decide to kill herself yesterday when things had finally worn her down to the point where she couldn't go on any longer?

The only thing that can help answer that is the letter she left, and based on the references she made to what we did to Edwin, I have a feeling that Natasha already knew she was doomed by the time we left this canal and went back to our homes to try and act like we had done nothing wrong.

I could stand here and stare at this canal all day, but that's not going to put me in a better place mentally, so I decide to seek out a better place physically, walking down the steps of the bridge and moving on, though I do choose to pass right by the spot where Edwin's body was last seen. As I do, the old man on the bench briefly looks up at me before smiling, and as I return the expression, I think about how he would not be smiling if he knew the true depths of my character. Just like this canal, there is far more beneath the surface, and while he might go home soon and remember the friendly woman he smiled at by the water, he'll never know that same woman is a cold-blooded killer who hid a body right by his favourite spot to sit and enjoy the sunshine.

The old man's eyes are no longer on me once I have passed him, but the same can't be said of the man I see on the other side of the canal. I noticed him earlier, a little further back from here, and we made eye contact as we passed then. He's in his thirties and walks with a very upright posture, as if his mum told him to stand up straight when he was younger, and he's been trying to obey her order ever since. Now here he is again, and just like the first time, our eyes have met. But once they have, he looks down at his feet before carrying on his way, although the action of him hanging his head down goes against his usual erect body shape, and I wonder why a man as tall and purposeful as him suddenly shelled up a little bit when I looked in his direction.

As he goes, I keep watch, unsure why I sense something off about him but just checking to see what else he does. That's when I see him turn back and look over his shoulder, and when he does, our eyes meet for a third time today.

No sooner has he seen me catch him looking then he turns back around and walks away, hurrying his pace somewhat until he rounds the curve of the canal and disappears out of sight. But even though I can no longer see him now, I don't feel as if I can forget about him quickly. Am I just being super paranoid, or was that man paying me a strange amount of attention? If so, why here, in this place of all places? Does he know why I'm here? Does he know what I did at this exact part of the canal? Is he following me or keeping tabs on me to see what I do next?

'This was a bad idea,' I say to myself out loud, referring to my decision to come here, and when I say it, the man on the bench must have heard me because he speaks then.

'Excuse me?' he says, checking if I was saying something to him.

But I just ignore him and start walking, not wishing to engage in chit-chat. I also don't wish to go in the same direction as that other man who seemed to be looking at me, so I go the other way, putting more distance between us, and by the time I leave the canal, I'm expecting that I'll never see him again.

Or maybe I'm just hoping it.

Come on now, Liz, my mind says to itself. *He can't possibly know what you did.*

It's annoying, but I don't feel better for telling myself that.

All I do feel is that, as I suspected at the time, what I did that night with my two friends would not end there.

It would always come back to haunt me.

After all, you can't kill a man without there being serious repercussions one day.

11

SIX MONTHS AGO

'Come on, we need to move him before he wakes up,' I say, and I grab Edwin's arms, noticing they are limp but already aware that he still has a heartbeat, so while he might look and feel lifeless, he is not quite there yet. But despite my simple statement, my two accomplices don't spring into action alongside me, and instead of helping me move the man we just tricked and trapped, they stand by uselessly and just watch.

'What are you doing? Come on! Help me!' I urge them, and only then does Bev snap out of it and put her hands around Edwin's ankles. But Natasha still does nothing to help us, although she's going to have no choice but to once Bev and I realise we cannot move him by ourselves.

'Natasha. Grab a hold of him!' I say, but Natasha does no such thing, and it's pretty clear I need to change tact if I am to get her back on board with what we planned to do tonight.

Letting go of Edwin's arms for a moment, I take a step towards her and put a hand on one of her thin, bony shoulders.

'If you want to tell him what you have to say to him and if you want to hear him apologise then we need to get him into position before he wakes up,' I say as calmly and clearly as I can, and only then does Natasha seem to remember what this is all about tonight.

She nods her head, and as she makes a move to help, I grab Edwin's arms again, and once the three of us have hold of him, I make the count.

'One. Two. Three. Lift!' I cry, and on three, Edwin's body moves upwards, though it's not easy, even with six hands doing the heavy lifting.

'Wait, this isn't working,' I say when I realise the only thing that's likely to happen in the next few seconds is one of us putting our back out and being left unable to stand up straight, due to the physical exertion of trying to lift a weight that's far too heavy for us.

'We'll have to drag him,' I say, feeling slightly annoyed that I've had to slip into the role of leader here tonight, but what choice have I had but to when both my friends have so far proven to be pretty passive. Okay, so Bev and Natasha did what they were supposed to do when Edwin entered this house, but since then, they've seemingly been happy enough to let me figure out what happens next. But we're all in this together, and I'd do well to remind them of that now.

'We've come this far, and there's no going back now,' I say, after both Bev and Natasha have once again been slow on the uptake. 'Let's finish what we started and get this over with.'

'Why can't we just do it here?' Bev asks me.

'What?'

'Why do we have to move him? He's too heavy. Let's just do it here.'

'We can't do it here.'

'Why not?'

'Because that wasn't the plan,' I remind her, but she doesn't seem too bothered about that.

'It doesn't matter where we kill him,' Bev says, but I disagree.

'If you want us all to get away with this then we do it as we planned,' I say, and it must be the reminder of what is at stake here that gets her to stop delaying this process and join me at Edwin's head so she can grab one of his arms while I take the other one.

'Grab the collar of his shirt,' I say to Natasha, and while she's reluctant to, she slowly does as I say, and with her getting purchase on his shirt, all three of us start pulling Edwin towards the living room door.

It's tough work, but we slowly but surely drag the body out of the hallway, and we only stop dragging once Edwin is in the position I want him in.

Lying right in the middle of the plastic sheeting Natasha laid out before we all got here, Edwin is in the best spot for what is to come, or rather, he is in the best spot if we are to get away with what we are going to do to him.

Glancing at the knife that sits on the coffee table, I'm tempted to just pick it up and get this over with. But I know I'd regret it because before this man can die, he is going to hear what all three of us have to say to him. That's why, instead of reaching for the knife, I reach for the pair of handcuffs that sit on the table beside the blade, and once I have them, I quickly loop one of the cuffs around Edwin's right wrist before wrapping the second cuff around the leg of the heavy sofa that lies just behind Edwin's head.

When he wakes, the first thing he will try and do is break free of his restraints, but there's no way he'll be able to free himself from the sofa and once he realises that, he'll also realise that he is then powerless to stop what will happen next.

Checking the cuffs and ensuring they are secure, I can finally relax, but only a little bit. Just because Edwin won't be able to get up and run out of here when he wakes up, it doesn't mean it's plain sailing from here on out. This situation still has its challenges, but best to work through them one at a time.

First challenge now – waking Edwin up so he can hear what we have to tell him.

Aware that Bev struck him hard over the head, it's to be expected that Edwin is dazed and confused but that we could work with. But at the moment, he's simply unconscious, so that's why I begin slapping him on the face and calling out his name to try and stir him.

'I hit him good,' Bev says as I try and rouse Edwin, and I'm not sure if she is saying that to clarify why Edwin is so out of it or because she wants me to know just how well she executed her stealthy attack. Either way, it's not really helping me, but I keep working on Edwin, shouting and slapping him until I hear a groan escape his lips.

It's another sign of life, albeit not much of one, and his eyes still haven't opened yet. But I keep trying him until they do, and as he tries to focus and figure out his surroundings, he looks very confused. Another groan is followed by him putting his free hand to his head to tenderly touch the area where he was struck by Bev. As his hand makes contact with the wound on the top of his skull, I see blood on his fingers, and Edwin sees it too. But that's not the thing that causes him to start to panic. That happens when he tries to use his other hand, only to realise that it is handcuffed to the sofa behind him.

Trying to sit up is not easy for him, but it's made even harder by the plastic sheeting he lies upon, and after slipping for several seconds, Edwin gives up when he realises he's not getting anywhere fast. That's when his eyes land on me, and presumably, after remembering that I was the one who convinced him to come here tonight, he will now want to know what happened after that.

'What's going on?' he asks me, his groans now replaced by an uncharacteristically meek voice.

'I'll tell you what's going on,' I say, pleased that the real show is about to begin. 'My plan worked. Or should I say, our plan.'

I turn and gesture to the two women standing over us, and as Edwin looks past me and up at them, he only grows more anxious to get out of this situation. But it's no good because those handcuffs mean he's not going anywhere.

'Now, you are going to listen to what each of us has to say to you,' I tell him, and while he protests and wastes half a minute telling us that we're crazy and that we have to let him go, I wait for him to shut up before I carry on.

'You screwed me over,' I tell him, not saying anything he doesn't already know. 'You ruined everything I've worked for. You messed up my career and my life. Do you think you can just do what you did to me and get away with it? Did you think there wouldn't be any consequences for the threats you made and the damage you left behind?'

I wonder if this might finally be the moment when Edwin offers an apology and tries to put right all his wrongs, but when I see his reaction, I feel foolish for even contemplating the thought of him doing such a thing as saying sorry. Of course he doesn't. A man like him has no remorse, and I get confirmation of that as I look down at Edwin laughing at me.

'You stupid bitch,' he says in between chuckles. 'What the hell did you think you could achieve with this? Have you any idea the trouble you'll be in when I get out of here and go to the police?'

While it's galling not to have Edwin grovelling and begging me for forgiveness, I can at least take comfort in the fact that he is way off the mark if he thinks he is going to get the chance to go to the police and tell them about this little chat of ours.

'Fine. You won't listen to me. Bev, how about you have a go.'

I move away from Edwin then, allowing Bev to lean in closer to him, and when she does, she looks the stricken man up and down before shaking her head.

'You're despicable,' she tells him, and she's not wrong there, though obviously, Edwin disagrees.

'What is this? Therapy? Get these damn handcuffs off me now, or you'll regret it!'

I note that Edwin is starting to get a little bit flustered now, and perhaps the severity of the situation he finds himself in is slowly dawning on him. But it's not nearly quick enough, and as Bev gives him a few more disparaging labels before telling him that what he did to her will not define her for the rest of her life, I wonder how long it will take for her to be done.

When she is, she moves away from Edwin too, and that just leaves Natasha to say her piece. Out of the three of us, it's most important that she gets to have her say because as far as our suffering at the hands of this man goes, she's by far and away had it the worst, which surely makes what she has to say the most scathing. But while Natasha does lean in over Edwin, she doesn't say a word as she looks him up and down. All she does is one simple action.

She spits at him, and with that, she has made her feelings clear.

'What the hell! I'll kill you!' Edwin cries as he writhes around on the sheeting and tries to free himself whilst dealing with what Natasha just did to him, a gross act and normally one I would abhor, but in this case, I can make an exception.

'You've got it mixed up,' I say, looking down on Edwin with a smirk on my face. 'You won't kill us. That's because we're going to be the ones to kill you.'

Edwin stops wriggling then and goes very still and quiet, and once I have his full attention, I pick up the knife and hold it aloft so he can clearly see the instrument that will soon take his life. But while I'd love nothing more than to plunge this knife into him myself, Bev and I made a decision to let Natasha do it.

She needs it. *She deserves it.*

Handing the knife to her, I watch as Natasha regards the weapon in her hands. But the longer she takes to do anything with it, the more Edwin starts to call our bluff.

'Okay, fine. You've got me. I made mistakes, and you have a right to be angry at me. But stop messing around and pretending you're going to hurt me because we all know that none of you have got it in you. So put the knife down, take off these handcuffs, and then we can talk about this like adults, okay?'

Edwin must be expecting Natasha to do as he says, and while I'm not, she is taking a worryingly long amount of time to put the knife to use. The delay only allows Edwin to grow in confidence, and the longer he is still alive, the more he begins to taunt the three of us and tell us that we are as stupid and useless as he always knew we were.

'Do it,' Bev says to Natasha, but she doesn't move.

'This is what you wanted,' I remind her, but still she doesn't act.

'You stupid women,' Edwin says, chuckling again now. 'You stupid, stupid women. What have you done?'

Edwin seems to be enjoying himself, so much so that the moment suddenly becomes too much for me to bear, and that's why I grab the knife from Natasha's hand and do what she should have done two minutes ago.

I drive the knife down into the centre of Edwin's stomach as hard as I can, and with the full force of my bodyweight pushing down upon the blade that is now wedged in between his rib cage, it doesn't take long for the gravely wounded man to begin coughing up blood. But I don't move a muscle, keeping the knife in place whilst Edwin squirms desperately beneath me.

I keep it there until he stops moving, and then, using my blood-soaked left hand, I touch his neck to check for a pulse. Only when I find that there is none do I let go of the handle of the knife.

But the blade itself stays buried in the body of its victim. It can stay there for a moment because I'm in no rush to take it out. It won't make a difference when I do because it's done the job.

Edwin is dead, and that means one thing.

Bev, Natasha and I have just got our revenge.

Now all we need to do is get away with it.

12

PRESENT DAY

After my walk along the canal yesterday, something I quickly regretted after becoming paranoid that I was being watched, I went home and spent a torrid afternoon and evening trying to take my mind off Natasha, Edwin, and the events that link those two people with me forever. But it was impossible, and after realising that taking the day off work had actually been a hindrance to my mental health rather than a help, I have made the decision to go back in today.

I'm dreading being in the office with so much playing on my mind, but it's either that or be by myself all day, and I think being surrounded by irritating colleagues is better than being alone with my thoughts, or at least I'm hoping it is. I'll find out soon enough because as I smooth out the front of my blouse across my stomach and check my appearance in my bedroom mirror, I see that I look presentable enough to make a return to the workplace.

Grabbing a breakfast bar to chew on during my commute, I leave the house and start walking in the direction of the centre of town. There is a bus stop five minutes from here that will get me to the office quicker, but I was up early after a restless night, so I have the time to walk, and with the sun out as well, I might as well make the most of it.

However, the fresh air, blue sky, and moderate physical exertion is not doing much to lift my mood and neither is my breakfast after I have chomped down the granola bar. I think I'll have to give in and get a coffee on my way and hope that does the trick of perking me up enough in time for my busy day. If not, I'm out of ideas as to how to make myself feel a little bit better.

Wondering how Bev is doing today, I send her a quick message as I walk, asking her if she is okay before telling her I've decided to go in to work. But she doesn't reply, and while she could be asleep or busy making her own commute, my paranoia is such that I immediately start imagining her sitting in a police station telling everybody there that she knows why Natasha killed herself.

'No, you're not doing this to yourself all day,' I say under my breath as a reminder that I need to try and stay positive and not always come up with the worst possible outcome, and my very short pep talk helps snap me out of it.

The rest of my walk is peaceful enough, and by the time I enter the coffee shop just around the corner from my office, I'm feeling better than I was half an hour ago. As the aroma of the coffee beans lifts my spirits a little more and I see there is only a small queue to join before I can place my order, I'm thinking this day might not end up being as difficult as I'd thought it could be. But it's while I'm standing in the queue that all that changes. That's because as I watch the barista behind the counter working, I catch a glimpse of my reflection in the mirror behind him and when I do, I also see who is standing across the street outside this shop and looking in my direction.

It's the man I saw by the canal.

Turning around quickly, I look through the large windows at the front of this shop, and sure enough, I see him standing out there on the pavement, but no sooner have I done that then he is on the move, walking away and disappearing quickly amidst a steady wave of pedestrians making their own commutes. But it's too late for him to try and pretend because I've caught him looking, and I quickly give up my place in the queue to go after him because no matter how good that coffee might have been, finding out why this man seems to be following me would be much better.

Rushing out onto the street, I look to my left and just about make out the top of his head before he disappears around a corner. But I'm quickly in pursuit, and after running across the road during a break in the traffic, I round the same corner he just did and see him up ahead of me, about eighty yards away or so. He's not running like I am, but he's walking quickly, and that tells me he is keen to get out of here after I saw him, but I'm determined not to let him just walk away from me this time like he did by the canal. I knew there was something off about him then, and I should have tried to get to the bottom of it at the time, but at least now I have a second chance.

'Hey! Wait!' I call out to him, but he doesn't turn around or slow down, so I call out again. 'Who are you? Why are you following me?'

Still no answer from him, but as I see him turn down a side street, I know I'm making up ground on him, and I fully expect to be close enough to reach out and grab him any second now.

Running into the side street, I anticipate seeing him running away, but if that's his plan, he's surely gone down the wrong street for it because I'm pretty sure this one ends in a dead end. But I'm wrong because he is not running. Instead, he is very calmly standing and seemingly waiting for me.

'Hello, Liz,' he says calmly after I have stopped in my tracks, completely caught off guard by my pursuit being over so suddenly.

'How do you know my name?' I ask him, getting the final bit of confirmation, if I needed it, that this man is taking a very keen interest in me.

'Oh, that's not all I know, Liz,' he replies with a smug grin. 'I know a lot about you. Your past. Your career. Your friends. *Your enemies*.'

The emphasis he puts on that last part of his statement sends a chill down my spine, but as he must be referring to Edwin, I maintain enough composure not to overreact to it and give myself away entirely.

'Who are you?' I say, trying to turn this conversation onto him for a minute.

'I'm somebody who has been asked to look into you and report back with what I find,' he says, and that response is almost as frightening as what he just said about me and my enemies.

What the hell is he talking about? Look into me and report back?

Report back to who?

'Excuse me?'

'You might think you've done well to catch up with me, Liz, but it really doesn't matter,' he says. 'In fact, I think it is better that you do know about me and what I'm doing. That way, I think you're even more likely to make a mistake that will lead me to the truth I am looking to uncover.'

The man steps towards me then, but I'm far too stunned to say or do anything in response, and as he leans in towards me, he lowers his voice, not that any of the pedestrians rushing past this side street could probably hear our conversation anyway.

'I'm on to you, Liz. You and your friend. You both must think you're so clever, but we'll see about that. Now, until next time, have a good day.'

With that, the man walks away, but I don't turn around and watch him go or try and do anything to make him stay. I'm simply in too much shock to function properly, and it's a good minute before I can pull myself together enough to try and process what just happened.

As tears run down my cheeks and I think about how I wish I hadn't chased this man down this side street, because at least I could still have some blissful ignorance about all this before I did, all I can think now is the awful truth.

This man knows what I did to Edwin, and with his reference to my friend too, he knows that Bev was involved as well.

Finally coming to my senses after the initial shock has worn off, I run back out of the side street and try to find the man again, but he's already vanished. Grabbing my phone out of my handbag, I try Bev, but she doesn't answer my call, so all I can do is leave her an urgent voice message instructing her to call me back as quickly as possible. Then I see the time on my phone's screen and realise I'm due at work in five minutes, so I better get a move on. But can I even go into work after what's just happened? Or should I try and find this man again? Or maybe it's too late for that, and the best thing for me to do now would be to go home and start packing, hoping I can make it to the airport to catch a flight out of the country before the police swoop in on me to make their arrest.

No, calm down, Liz. Relax. There are no police here. If they knew what I'd done, I'd be locked up already.

Trying to calm myself, I think about one of the things the man said to me before he left.

"I think it is better that you do know about me and what I'm doing. That way, I think you're even more likely to make a mistake that will lead to me to the truth I'm looking to uncover."

Those words tell me that he wants me to make a mistake. He wants me to panic and run or do something else out of character for me. He wants to draw a mistake out of me.

He said he's looking for me to lead him to the truth.

That means he doesn't quite know what it is yet.

Sucking in a very big gulp of air, I feel the vice-like tension in my chest lessen slightly as I contemplate the fact that this might not be as big a disaster as I had first feared. Then, as I start walking to my office, I tell myself that I just need to do the opposite of what that man wants. I need to stick to my routine. Try and carry on as normal. Not slip up. Not give him anything, whoever he is.

By the time I walk through the doors of my office and pass through the reception area on the way to the elevators, I'm telling myself that man is just a weirdo who probably has some obsession with the mystery of Edwin's disappearance, just like everybody else in this town is interested in it. After all, it's not every day a rich, successful businessman goes missing, and after six months, all sorts of theories have been put out there about where he might have gone and what happened to him. Some say he simply boarded a private flight and left the country. Others say he met a grislier fate. All I care about is that none of them know for sure, and as far as I could tell then, that man did not know for sure either. That's why he was following me. He's hoping I might lead him to something. But so what if he suspects me of being involved in Edwin's disappearance? He can think what he wants as long as he gathers no evidence to back up his beliefs, and I'm more than determined to not give it to him.

Pushing the button for the elevator, I stand back and wait impatiently for it, and as I do, I notice the young woman sitting on the sofa in the reception area. She's dressed smartly, her hair and make-up is immaculate, and she is nibbling her bottom lip.

She's waiting for an appointment. She's made an effort with her appearance. She's nervous.

She must be here for a job interview.

That's all it takes for me to remember the job interview I sat through, not to get my job here but to get my previous one.

It was the job interview where I met Edwin for the very first time.

13

ONE YEAR AGO

I hate job interviews. Then again, is there anybody out there who enjoys them?

The waiting. The stressing. The desperation. There are plenty of 'experts' online who make out as if they have this whole process decoded, and it's as simple as smiling, asking questions and projecting confidence, but we all know it's not really as simple as that. Interviews can be as easy or as difficult as the person hosting them, and as I wait to meet the man who will decide whether or not to hire me, I am wondering what I am going to get.

All I know about the man so far is his name, what he looks like, and a short career history gleaned from the bio on this company's website. But while it has been helpful to be able to put a face to the name by way of his professional headshot, as well as find out about his background in this industry, there is so much I cannot get from the internet. I can't get whether this man has a relaxed or serious personality. I don't know whether he will appreciate a few jokes in the interview or whether I'd be better off keeping things simple. Basically, I don't know how he is going to respond to me when he meets me any moment now, and as such, I'm not entirely sure how to respond myself.

The tips online say it's all about trying to create a rapport with your interviewer. Do that, and apparently, the job is as good as yours. It sounds basic enough, but that's what worries me. I'd almost rather this whole process be simply about the strength of my resume and my experiences in previous jobs that I believe make me qualified to apply for this one. That would be okay because then my experience almost speaks for itself. With over a decade as a financial assistant in a couple of different accounts teams, I have gathered relevant work experience and am here as I seek to carry on my climb up the career ladder. But apparently, that's only a very small part of it, and what will matter just as much is whether or not the person asking me the questions feels like I am someone he will enjoy making a part of his team.

He needs to spot qualities in me that a piece of paper can't give him. Basically, he'll know within the first five minutes whether he likes me or not, and nothing I have done before this meeting can help me there.

Swallowing hard before picking up the plastic cup of water from the glass table in front of me, I am grateful the kind receptionist here offered me a drink while I wait. The water is refreshing as I sip it and is helping to hydrate my dry throat, and it'll need all the lubrication it can get if I am to spend the next hour or so 'selling myself' to the man who calls the shots around here.

So far, there is no sign of him, but I know that is only because my interview is not due to begin yet, and I'm sure he is very busy with lots of other things before he gets to me. But I also expect he will be on time for our appointment because even though it's not as critical for him as it is for me, he'll still want to make a good impression too. First impressions last, which is why I remind myself to sit up a little straighter, relax my face a little, and, of course, make a conscious effort to stop my left foot from tapping loudly on the marble floor of this impressive reception area.

Tapping my foot has been a nervous habit of mine since I was a little girl, and it's followed me all the way from the exam halls at school to the offices I frequent in adulthood. But because it's clearly going to give away the fact I am nervous, I force myself to stop fidgeting, and it's just in time because as the clock above the receptionist's head strikes ten in the morning, the door to her left opens and out walks the man I am here to see.

My interviewer is ready.

It's time to meet Edwin van Dekker in the flesh.

As I try and focus on making a good first impression, it's impossible not to be dazzled by the impression this man is already making as he strides confidently towards me with a big smile on his face. I detect muscle beneath his perfectly fitted suit, and there is not a hair out of place on his head. For a busy man, he looks incredibly relaxed, and I wish I possessed one-tenth of the composure he seems to have as I quickly get to my feet and force an awkward smile onto my face.

'Liz? I'm Edwin, lovely to meet you.'

His handshake is firm, and his eye contact is strong as I try not to mumble or stutter the first words out of my mouth in his presence.

'Hi, Edwin. I mean, Mr Dekker. I mean, I'm sorry. I'm Liz.'

Well, that was a disaster. Not only have I fumbled over his name, I've also given him mine when he clearly already knows it. Edwin laughs then, but it's not a nasty laugh or the laugh of someone who already thinks I'm a complete waste of time. It's a charming one to show me that it doesn't matter if I'm nervous because he's going to help guide me through this process as gently as he can.

'Follow me, Liz, and let's get started. It's right this way.'

Edwin leads me back to the door he just emerged from, and as the heels from my shoes echo on the marble flooring, I smile at the receptionist and thank her again for the water as I pass. Then I'm suddenly in a carpeted corridor, and then it's an elevator, and as we make the short ascension to the fourth floor, Edwin asks me how my journey to the office was today.

It's a simple question and could be construed as just making conversation, but I'm also aware he could be gauging whether or not I enjoyed the commute here to this office because if not, that could mean problems if he was to hire me. As it was, I had no trouble finding my way here and after telling him that, we step out of the elevator and onto the second floor, where several of my potential future colleagues are based.

The office is a hive of activity - men in suits taking phone calls or dashing to pick up a piece of paper from the printer, while women in blouses and skirts type on keyboards or flip through folders full of documents.

Everyone is busy.

Everyone is paid to be here.

Everyone but me.

I notice that I draw the gaze of a few curious employees as I follow Edwin through the office, and I wonder if they are already sizing me up as a teammate or potential rival for a future promotion somewhere down the line. But it's far too early for any of that because I haven't even got the job yet, and as Edwin shows me into a room with *Meeting Room Three* inscribed on the door, I just need to take this one minute at a time.

'We're in here,' Edwin says, before he looks past me for a second and calls out to one of his employees.

'Hey, Bev? Will you do me a favour and call Amy for me and tell her to move my ten-thirty appointment to tomorrow. I'm going to need an hour here.'

I look back to see who he is talking to, and when I do, I see a brunette woman of a similar age to me.

'Sure thing,' she says, before she notices me looking at her and shows me a polite smile.

I watch her hurrying away to complete the order her boss just gave her, and I wonder if I will soon be doing the same thing, as I enter the meeting room and Edwin invites me to take a seat.

I'm expecting him to take the seat opposite me at this large table, but he doesn't do that, opting instead to sit down in the seat directly beside me, so there is no obstacle in between us.

'Look, I know these interviews are no fun for anybody, but I try my best to make them as relaxed as I can because I think that's best for both parties,' Edwin says to me as he straightens out his tie and sits back. 'So this won't be anything too formal. Let's keep it simple. Tell me about yourself.'

'Oh, erm, well, I've been working in accounts for the last ten years,' I start with. 'I originally studied geography at university but felt a little foolish after graduating because I always knew my real strength was with numbers, so I went to night college and got my accountancy degree in my mid-twenties. That's why I was a little later than usual in starting my career.'

Edwin brushes a hand through the air.

'Don't worry, I know all about your career history. Your resume tells me that,' he says, tapping the piece of paper on the table beside him. 'Tell me about yourself, unless you are one of those people who allows your job to define you.'

I'm not sure if that is supposed to be a statement designed to trip me up. Does he want me to tell him that I'm most certainly not somebody who just lives to work and then launch into some spiel about all my hobbies, passions, and pursuits beyond the workplace? Or is he testing me to see if I'm actually a super-focused, dedicated worker bee who has no life beyond the office because that's the kind of person he is looking to hire?

I'm not sure, and if I'm not sure, how can I say the things he wants to hear so he'll give me this job?

Edwin picks up on my hesitancy but breaks the ice by laughing, and it does help put me at ease a little.

Then he gives me a clearer indication of the type of man he is.

'Look, we all know you wouldn't be here if you didn't have to be. Hell, I wouldn't be here if I didn't have to be. But we all have to earn a living, right? So let's remove the elephant in the room. You don't have to spend the next hour pretending to be fascinated with me or my company or anything we do here. The truth is, everyone here just does their jobs until the clock hits five and then they go home, and that's absolutely fine with me. I stay until six every day myself, but that's only because I'm disorganised and procrastinate half my time away while everyone else gets on with actual work.'

I laugh at the self-deprecating joke before Edwin goes on.

'I know you can do this job because your references have already told me you can, so this interview isn't about me trying to figure out if I can trust you to do the work given to you. What it is about is me trying to ascertain whether or not I think you'll be a good fit here. Will you get on with me and my team? Trust me, I'd take a friendly accountant who is half-good at their job over a brilliant accountant who everybody hates.'

I get what Edwin wants now and because I do, it's much easier to give it to him.

'Thanks for letting me know. I was just about to waste an hour of your time boring you to tears with my adventures in the world of accounting, but you've saved us both the torture of that.'

Edwin responds well to my humour, so I carry on.

'Well, when I'm not number-crunching or pushing paperwork around my desk, I guess you could say I'm a simple woman. I like films, I love to go on holiday, and basically, when it gets to the end of the week, I love nothing more than opening a big bottle of wine and enjoying the contents.'

Edwin flashes me a big smile, and I guess I'm on the right track, so I carry on, riding the wave of optimism I feel now about how this interview might end up turning out for me.

'My father always used to say how you do something is how you do everything. It's some quote he read in a book, or online, I think, but because he always said it, it's stuck with me, and I guess you could say I live by it now. That means I do everything the same. I work hard, and that means I play hard. You give me a task to do, and I will focus on it until it is done. But likewise, you give me and the rest of the team here access to a free bar at the Christmas party in December, and I will focus on those beverages until your expense account is exhausted.'

Edwin laughs hard at that, and now I feel like I can't mess this up. I can't believe it's been as easy as this, but I'll take it. I'm eager for a new job because there was no room for growth in my last one, both promotion-wise and salary-wise, which was why I left there and have been enjoying a brief break before seeking out a new opportunity.

This place feels like I have found just what I am looking for.

But have I?

'Husband and kids?'

Edwin's next question is very personal, and I pause for a moment, but he quickly fills the silence.

'I'm only asking because I'll need to tell Amy, my personal assistant, so I don't forget any birthdays,' he tells me. 'I like to send a card and a little present to my employees' families on their big day.'

'Oh, that's lovely,' I say, because it is. 'But no. No husband or kids. Not yet. Well, not ever, maybe. I don't know.'

I'm rambling, so I shut up, but Edwin doesn't seem perturbed.

'Well, whether you stay single or go on to have lots of babies with some lucky guy, one thing I do know is you sound like my kind of employee,' Edwin says with that devilish smile of his still on full display. 'So, with that said, I'd be more than happy to give you a start here, and we can see how things go. Sound good?'

'Yeah, it sounds great!'

'Good. Now, there's still fifty minutes left of this interview. What do you say we go and grab a coffee from across the street, and you can tell me more about that Christmas party you think I'm going to be throwing in December? The one with the free bar.'

And that was it. That was how easy it was to get a job working under Edwin van Dekker. Sure, it must have helped that I was friendly, funny, and attractive enough to pique his interest. But really, I just thought he was a cool guy who had a very laid-back approach to running his own business.

Alas, as I soon discovered, the approach he actually took was nothing short of criminal.

14

PRESENT DAY

After finishing my first day back at work after Natasha's death, I have made plans for this evening, though they are not the kind of plans I had wanted to make. I'm going to see a friend, but it's not about socialising, and the main topic of conversation certainly won't be fun. I'm on my way to see Bev, and when I get to her, I will be telling her all about my little chat with the man who was following me earlier.

I'm sure she'll be all ears because she has just as much to lose as I do in all of this.

That's because that man is just as dangerous to her as he is to me.

I have spent the afternoon wondering if he has also been following Bev or if it is just me he has taken such an interest in, but there's no real way I can know for sure, so it was pointless to keep dwelling on it. I've only just discovered he has been on my tail, so I'm hardly likely to know if he's been on Bev's too, though I will be asking her if she has noticed anybody watching her recently and, in particular, anybody who matches the description of the man who has been after me.

Because I have been followed, I have decided to take extra precautions tonight as I go to meet Bev. I've already messaged her and told her to meet me at a pub neither of us have been to before, and my reason for that is because if we can break a habit, we're more likely to lose anybody who might be trying to plot our next move.

I've also told Bev to take an unusual, elongated route to the pub in question, and that is with the intention of losing any potential followers too.

If that man is hoping to follow me tonight after he spooked me during our conversation in the side street this morning, I'm not going to make it easy for him by walking in straight lines and taking conventional routes. I'm going to zig-zig, get lost in the crowd, use different modes of transport instead of just being predictable like I've always been. Anything to shake him off my scent, and providing Bev does the same to anybody who might be following her, it will mean the pair of us can have our discussion tonight without anybody else watching it.

The man who followed me earlier must be keen to know what I am going to do next, so it's imperative that he doesn't find out. What I plan to do is tell Bev everything that has happened, and then, together, I'm hoping the pair of us can figure out who this man is, how he could possibly have some clue as to what we did, and then, from there, we can make sure he never gets the evidence he needs to see us punished. It's not likely to be as simple as that, but all I can do at this point is try and stay calm and remind myself that I'm still a free woman, so nobody has anything on me yet that I cannot get myself out of.

Walking past my usual bus stop, I cut through a crowded lane full of cafes and small shops and then double-back at the next street, essentially walking in one big circle whilst checking over my shoulder as often as I can. I'm looking for that man, but I can't see him, though if he is out here somewhere, he'll have a hard time keeping up with me, and once I have made it around another corner, I run across the road and jump into the back of the taxi at the front of the queue in front of the hotel. I knew there was always a long line of cabs here and now I'm in one, I don't waste any time telling the driver to get us on the move.

After giving him an address, I turn around and look out of the back window of the taxi as we get moving, and I'm checking to see if any of the taxis behind are on the move too. If so, that man might have just hailed his own cab and told the driver to follow behind this one, but so far, none of them have moved. But all the way, I keep checking for any other kind of vehicles that might be behind us. Thankfully, there are none of interest, and after ten minutes, the journey is complete, and I get out of the taxi after paying the quiet, rather bored-looking driver.

Once out of the vehicle, I jog down the street that is just around the corner from the pub where I'm planning to meet Bev. But just before I go in, I duck down the side of a building and find a doorway to linger in, and my reason for doing that is because I want to see who might walk past this doorway in a few moments' time. If that man has managed to follow me here then he will walk past this point any second now, and if he does, I can jump out, tell him I've caught him and then at least gain some kind of minor victory in the war that has started to rage between us.

But ten seconds go by, and nobody walks past. Another ten. Then thirty. It's been a minute now, and there is no sign of him. That's a good thing, and I breathe a sigh of relief because at least that's one less thing to worry about tonight. Now I can just focus on giving Bev some very bad news.

Leaving my little hiding place, I walk straight into the pub and order myself a drink, and after seeing that Bev isn't here yet, I take a seat at a table where I can put my back to the wall and keep my eyes fixed firmly on the door. From this position, I'll see everybody who comes in, and while I'm expecting to see Bev enter, I also have to be on the lookout for that man walking in as well, under the guise of being just another customer in this busy pub.

The door doesn't open for the first five minutes that I'm watching it but when it does, two women walk in, chattering away loudly before reaching the bar and ordering themselves a couple of cocktails. But they are immediately followed by Bev, and when I see her, I give her a wave to alert her to my location.

She gives me a wave in response before ordering herself a drink, and as I wait for her to join me, I think about the best way to say to her what I have to say without causing her to panic. It won't be easy, but we have to stay calm, and I can increase our odds of doing so by not spooking her when she sits down.

'Hey, you okay? Sorry I'm late. It took me ages to get here. Why this pub?' Bev says as she sits down at the table with me.

'Somebody recommended it,' I reply, but as Bev looks around at the dated décor and just-as-dated clientele in here, she can't quite see why anybody would recommend this place.

'Thanks for coming,' I say as I nurse my drink. 'How have you been feeling since, you know?'

'Rubbish,' Bev replies with a simple shrug. 'I've not slept much.'

'Me neither.'

'I just keep thinking about Natasha's poor family and what they must be going through.'

This seems like a good point to mention that Natasha's mother paid me a visit yesterday and when I do, Bev is surprised.

'Oh my God, that must have been so hard. What did she say?'

'She just wanted to know what happened when we found her.'

'What did you say?'

'I told her everything except the part about the note.'

'And she believed you?'

'Yes. Why wouldn't she?'

Bev doesn't answer that.

'She hasn't come to see you?' I ask her, and Bev shakes her head whilst looking pleased about it.

'I guess we'll just see her at the funeral now then,' I add, and the thought of that awful occasion looming on the horizon is enough to keep us quiet for the next minute or so as we sip our drinks and watch a few other people in this pub do the same. But Bev breaks the silence when she asks me why I urgently wanted to see her tonight.

'I've got something to tell you but when I do, you have to promise me that you'll stay calm because it's under control,' I say to her.

'What are you talking about?'

Here goes.

'Somebody has been following me.'

'What? Who?'

'Some guy. I don't know his name, but I saw him at the canal yesterday, and then he followed me to work this morning.'

'The canal? What were you doing there?'

It's not surprising that Bev is disturbed by me mentioning the place where she helped me dump Edwin's body six months ago.

'I'd just gone for a walk. I needed to get out of the house after Natasha's mum called around.'

'But why did you go there, of all places?'

'I don't know. I just did.'

'So what happened with this man? How do you know he was following you?'

'Well, I didn't know then. I just noticed him looking at me, so it struck me as a little odd. But it was only when I saw him standing outside the coffee shop near my office this morning that I realised he was watching me again.'

'Why?'

'I didn't know. That's why I chased after him to find out.'

'You chased after him?'

'What else could I do?'

'I don't know. Go to the police? Tell them you have a stalker.'

'I think you and I both know the police are the last people we should be speaking to about anything, if we can help it.'

Bev can't argue with that, and I go on.

'I caught up with him and asked him what he was doing. I was hoping he'd just apologise or even try and deny it. But he didn't. Instead, he told me he knew my name and everything about me.'

'Everything?'

Bev now looks as pale as the white beer mat that her drink sits on.

'He didn't mention Edwin,' I say. 'But he did hint at it.'

'Oh my God.'

Bev looks like she could be sick, but I grab her hand and give it a squeeze.

'Relax, he doesn't know anything. If he did, we'd have been arrested by now.'

'But you just said he hinted at it!'

'And that's all he did. He doesn't have any evidence. He's following me because he wants to get it. But I'm not going to give it to him, so there is nothing to worry about, alright?'

'But how does he suspect? How could he possibly know?'

'I have no idea, and I'm hoping to find out, but until then, we have to not do anything stupid because he could be watching. Do you understand?'

Bev looks around the pub then as if she is expecting to see a team of undercover cops staring back at her, but nobody is paying us any attention, although I won't say to her that if there are any undercover cops in here, it's their job to blend into the background.

'I made sure I wasn't followed tonight,' I say, trying to ease her worries. 'But I'm going to need you to start doing the same. Be more conscientious of who is around you. Keep an eye out for anybody following you. Anybody suspicious. Hopefully, he is just watching me, but he might have help and be watching you too.'

'What are you talking about?'

'I'm saying we have to be super careful now. Don't do anything that makes us look guilty.'

'Like going to the canal?'

'That was a mistake, and I won't be going back there again.'

'You should never have gone back there at all. We promised each other we'd never return to the scene of the crime.'

'I know what we promised.'

I take a deep breath and try to summarize all of this in a positive way.

'No one knows Edwin is at the bottom of that canal but us because the police haven't searched it, so don't worry about that. As for this man, he clearly isn't that good, or I wouldn't have caught him following me. So he's an amateur, and whatever he is up to, it's unlikely there is much substance to it.'

'Then who is he, and why is he following you? He must know something.'

'Maybe, but knowing something and proving something are two very different things,' I say, as I feel the wall against my back and think about how it is a relief to not have to be looking over my shoulder in this position. But as soon as I leave this pub, all that will start again.

Noticing that Bev looks very anxious now, I lean in closer to her and put a hand on her shoulder. Then I remind her of something positive.

'Remember how you looked after me on my first day at Van Dekker?' I say to her, and she nods her head. 'Well, I'm going to look after you now. Whatever this problem is, I'm going to make it go away. Trust me, all this will be okay. Now, before we go home and carry on like everything is normal, how about one more drink?'

Bev nods her head, so I get up to go to the bar, but when I look back at her, I see her sitting uncomfortably in her seat with her head bowed and her shoulders hunched.

She looks nervous. Very awkward. Unsure.

She looks just like I did on the day we first became friends.

15

ONE YEAR AGO

After being offered, and then gratefully accepting, the role of new accounts assistant at Van Dekker Logistics, the time has come for me to experience my first day in my new job. After Edwin asked me how soon I could start, I didn't want to disappoint him by giving him an answer in weeks, or even days, for that matter. That's why I told him I was ready and raring to go whenever he wanted me, and that is why I am now walking through the doors of this office for the second time.

However, this time, I am doing it as a paid employee.

After greeting the receptionist, who was so kind to me the last time I was here, I am handed my new access card that Edwin assured me would be ready and waiting for me when I arrived. It's a simple thing, but it's a good start because I've worked at places before where they almost seemed to have forgotten they hired me, based on how unprepared they were for me when I turned up for duty.

Pleased that this place seems to be a slick operation, I use the access card to summon the elevator, and again, just the fact that the card actually works and doesn't need resetting by someone in I.T. is another plus. Anyone who has ever worked in an office knows how frustrating it is when your access card stops working.

Disembarking on the second floor, I am initially a little unsure where to go next because while I was told to report to Amy, Edwin's assistant, I'm not sure where she sits. But once again, any potential problem is snuffed out quickly because Amy has come to find me, and after calling out my name, she walks over to me and welcomes me with a handshake.

'Okay, let's get you settled in,' she says, helping put me at ease further. 'I'll show you the kitchen, and then I'll take you to your desk.'

The few nerves that were jangling around inside me soon dissipate when I'm introduced to a couple of friendly colleagues in the kitchen, and once I know where to go to make myself a cup of tea and store my lunch, I am taken to what will be my new workstation. When I see it, I also see who is based at the desk next to me, and that's what makes this part of my initiation tour so important.

Nobody really cares about what desk they will be given in an office.

What they really care about is who they will be sitting beside for eight hours a day.

When I see who my nearest colleague is, I recognise her as the woman Edwin spoke to just before I followed him into the meeting room for my interview. However, I can't recall her name, although that doesn't matter because we're about to be introduced anyway.

'Liz, this is Bev,' Amy says, and I quickly extend my hand out towards my new colleague, hoping she is going to be as friendly now as she seemed to be when I first saw her. Thankfully, she is, and after we shake, Amy hands me a piece of paper with my log-in details on, and then tells me that Edwin will be here to see me soon. Until then, I'm to get myself settled in before the real work starts, and that all sounds fine by me, so I thank Amy and then take a seat in what is now my new home for forty hours a week.

'Welcome aboard,' Bev says to me. 'Or should I say, welcome to the madhouse.'

I laugh. 'It's not that bad, is it?'

'No, I'm only joking. It's alright. I've certainly worked in worse places.'

That sounds promising.

'How long have you been here?' I ask Bev as I wait for my computer to load up with the log-in screen.

'Almost two years now,' she replies.

'Well, it can't be that bad if you've lasted that long,' I say with a smile, but Bev doesn't return it. All she does is lean in closer to me and lower her voice.

'It's okay, or at least it is if you just keep your head down and do your job.'

I'm not sure what prompted the sudden change in tone, or the slightly ominous statement she just made.

'What do you mean?'

'I'm talking about the boss,' she replies, still speaking quietly.

'Edwin?'

Bev nods.

'What about him?'

'Let's just say he can be difficult.'

Bev looks like she is being honest, but I'm confused because as far as I could tell when I met him, Edwin seemed like a great guy, and I imagined him being a wonderful boss.

Is he not?

'Difficult? How do you mean?' I ask, hoping it's nothing too serious.

'Let's just say you'll do well to keep things totally professional with him,' Bev tells me before turning back around in her swivel chair and leaving it at that. But she can't leave it there because I have more questions than answers, so I wheel my chair over to her and ask her again.

'What are you saying?'

Bev sighs and takes her hands off her keyboard before looking at me, but when she speaks, her voice is practically a whisper.

'Look, all I am trying to tell you is just try to do your job here. Nothing more, nothing less. Edwin is the friendly type, but he can be too friendly, if you get what I mean.'

It takes me a couple of seconds to understand but when I do, I raise my eyebrows.

'You've slept with him?' I ask, fascinated that I might be getting such a juicy morsel of office gossip so soon after starting here. I thought it would be weeks before I was settled in enough to be told all sorts of interesting stories about the lives of my colleagues, but it seems not.

'No, I have not!' Bev says, the volume of her voice suddenly rising as she shoots that notion down.

'Oh, I'm sorry. I just thought that's what you were hinting at by saying he was too friendly. I didn't mean any offence.'

I'm worried now because, in less than five minutes, I might have just annoyed the person who will be sitting beside me for the duration of my career here.

'It's fine, I'm not offended,' Bev tells me, her voice low again now. 'I didn't sleep with him. We just kissed after an office party. It was stupid, and I apologised the next day, assuming he would do the same.'

'Did he?'

Bev shakes her head.

'No. He just told me he wouldn't mind if it happened again.'

'What did you say to that?'

I'm thinking how I would get quite a thrill out of having a man like Edwin interested in me, but judging by the look on Bev's face, it's not all it's cracked up to be.

'I just made a joke about how drunk we both were and left it at that. But that wasn't where he left it.'

'What do you mean?'

Bev looks unsure about saying any more.

'Doesn't matter. It's nothing, really. I was just saying that you'll be fine if you just focus on your work here. I made things complicated with Edwin when it didn't need to be, and while it's okay now, it could have been worse.'

I'm just about to ask Bev for more details when I hear a voice behind me and when I do, the pair of us shut up immediately because we both know who is coming.

Turning around, I see Edwin walking towards me with a big grin on his face, looking just as suave and sophisticated as he did when he interviewed me. His appearance has put a swift end to my conversation with Bev, and after noticing her burying her head in her work, I see she's not particularly keen to have a chat with her boss. But he is keen to talk to me, and as he reaches my desk, he has his hand out towards me.

'Welcome! How are you settling in? Everything's okay, I hope. I trust Bev is looking after you?'

I see him wink at Bev then, but even though she looks up, she just offers a faint smile before putting her head down again and pretending to be hard at work.

'Yes, everything's great, thank you,' I say, and Edwin likes the sound of that.

'Fantastic! Well, I'll let you get settled in, but if you knock on my office door at 1 p.m., there's just a few things to go over with you. Nothing major, just how I see your role panning out over these next few months.'

'1 p.m. Sure. See you then,' I say, and with that, Edwin turns and strides away, occasionally pausing to say something to one of his employees seated at the other desks around here but eventually making it back to his own desk, which is more private than the rest.

As he closes the door to his office, I look back at Bev, but she doesn't seem interested in engaging with me at the moment, so rather than push it and risk irritating a woman who I hope will become a good friend soon, I leave it and try to get on with my own work.

My log-in credentials work, so now I'm inside the company system, and I see there is already an email waiting for me in my inbox in which there are a couple of links to health and safety videos I need to watch on my first day here. It's enough to keep me occupied for the next hour or so, though it's not boring admin tasks that dominate my thoughts for that duration.

It's what Bev said to me about Edwin.

"It could have been worse."

What was that supposed to mean?

I can only hope Bev and I get closer to one another, in terms of friendship, to the point where she fully enlightens me as to what she was getting at there. Until then, I can only imagine what she meant.

Worse? How could it have been worse?

If only I knew just how bad things could get...

16

PRESENT DAY

After smoothing out the black blouse against my skin and picking off a speck of dust from the sleeve of my left arm, I look up and spot the person I've been waiting to see arrive ever since I got to this funeral parlour.

Like me, and everybody else here, Bev has come dressed in all black, and the dark colour on show reflects the sombre mood my friend appears to be in. This is the first time I've seen Bev in a few days, and she doesn't look like she has slept much since then. She doesn't look like she's eaten much either, if her loosely fitting blouse is anything to go by, although that could just be an item of clothing she purchased back when she carried a little more weight around her midriff.

Bev used to be bigger than she is now, but she managed to lose the weight she accumulated over a period of several months when she seemed to neglect healthy food choices and just piled on the pounds. I noticed a change in her after I'd been working with her for a while. While reasonably slim when I met her, her dietary habits began to resemble that of a person not exactly living with their waistline in mind, and when she wasn't snacking at her desk, she was loading up on carbs during her lunch hour at the café around the corner from the office or taking on plenty of calories in liquid form at one of the many pubs in the area too. However, I always knew the change in Bev came down to a specific reason rather than just a vague sense of letting herself go a little, and that reason was the reason for so many other things too.

Edwin.

It took me a while to fully understand why Bev had given me a slightly ominous talk about him on my first day at his company but once I had, I understood why she had felt the need to say such things. I also understood why she lost a lot of confidence in herself and let her health suffer as a result of that. Impressively, Bev made the commitment one day to suddenly making healthier choices and cleaned up her diet, and the extra weight gained dropped off accordingly. She felt better for it, and it was nice to see her happier. But while she was eating better, her appetite for an extra drink or two had remained, and it was during one of our visits to a pub one Friday evening after work when she told me the main reason she had committed to taking better care of herself again.

She told me it was because she didn't want to let that bastard win.

As Bev makes her way towards me through the sea of mourners who have come out today for this funeral, I think about how that attitude, that decision to not let Edwin get the better of her, is one of the reasons we are both here today. It's an attitude I came to share with her once I truly got to know what kind of a man our boss was too, and it was also one Natasha shared, with even more reason than I ever had. Yet somehow, with Natasha lying in a coffin inside here somewhere and Bev and I here to attend the service that marks the final event of her life, it doesn't feel like we have done a very good job of not letting that man win.

Sure, he might be dead.

But what good is that when he has left such a mess in his wake?

'Good afternoon,' I say to Bev once she is beside me, more out of politeness than any deep thought behind it. But I've already said the wrong thing.

'Is it?' she replies quickly.

'No. I mean, I was just saying hello.'

It seems silly to have to justify my use of a common greeting a person makes to another person once the clock has passed midday, so I leave it there, and Bev and I have a quiet, slightly awkward moment before she speaks again.

'Ruth looks quite well considering,' Bev says, and when I see what she is looking at, I realise she is right.

Natasha's mother is several feet away from us, in the midst of the mourners, and is chatting with a few of them in between receiving condolences from several others. But considering she is here to lay her troubled daughter to rest, she does look quite well, although I suspect it is firmly a case of her putting on a brave face in public and not letting her real emotions make what is a difficult day even harder. I dread to think what Ruth is like behind closed doors at the moment, but she is clearly a proud woman and obviously prefers to do much of her grieving in private. But there's no getting away from the fact that this funeral is a very public event, and as the doors open and several mourners start to file inside, I steel myself for what is set to be a very difficult next half an hour or so.

Entering alongside Bev, the pair of us find ourselves a seat and get as comfortable as we can while we wait for everybody else to take their place. Then, once we are all inside and reasonably confident everybody who wishes to be here is in place, the doors are closed, and the service can begin.

Having read the notice informing Natasha's family and friends of her funeral, I was already aware that it would be a member of Natasha's family who would be running the service today, and as I watch her uncle take his place at the lectern before us all, I am wondering what kind of service he has in mind. Anybody can oversee a funeral in the UK, and seeing how Natasha was not religious, it seems more apt that this event will have a less traditional feel to it. It certainly starts off that way because after introducing himself as Greg, Natasha's second-favourite uncle, which gets a laugh from the crowd, the brave family member gets proceedings underway with a few more jokes.

Befitting of the woman she was and the life she led, the funeral service is one that passes by in a flurry of good humour, interesting anecdotes and, of course, a couple of cheesy pop songs from the early 2000s, songs that anybody who knew Natasha knows were her favourites and songs that she spent plenty of time dancing to whilst getting ready for a night out. It's one of those songs that is played as the service ends, and everybody rises up out of their seats before leaving and making their way to the venue for the wake.

While Natasha's closest family members lay their beloved to rest, everybody else at the funeral piles into the Dog & Partridge Pub, a venue that is a five-minute walk away, and when we get there, we see there is already a table full of refreshments laid out for us to tuck into. After helping ourselves to a couple of small sandwiches and a few crisps, as well as a drink each from the bar, Bev and I find ourselves a corner of the pub to have a quiet word with each other in.

'Have you seen him again?' Bev asks me, and I know she is referring to the man I told her was following me, so I shake my head quickly because it's important to put her mind at ease.

'Nope. No sign of him,' I reply before taking another bite of my tuna and sweetcorn sandwich, though the casualness of my reply does not convey the fact I still feel nervous about that man. However, Bev is far too smart to misread my response for me thinking our problem is over.

'I can't live like this. Knowing somebody out there knows what we did to Edwin,' she says, not having touched her own sandwich since she put it onto her paper plate.

'They don't know what we did, or at least they can't prove it, so try not to worry.'

'How is that possible? Aren't you afraid of the police coming to your door? I'm jumping out of my skin every time the phone rings or my doorbell goes. I'm looking over my shoulder everywhere I go. Even today, instead of just remembering Natasha, I feel like I'm constantly scanning the crowd for anybody who seems to be paying me a little more attention than usual.'

I see Bev means what she just said because she is looking around the pub to see if anybody is looking back at her, though fortunately, they are not. But I've been doing the same thing, both here and back at the funeral parlour earlier, just to make sure that the man who followed me, or anybody else, for that matter, is not watching my every move now.

'Emotions are always going to be heightened today,' I say, stating the obvious. 'Let's just get through this and move on.'

'But it's not just today, is it? What about tomorrow? What about the next day? How long can we go on, waiting for somebody to expose what we did?'

'That's not going to happen.'

'How can you be so sure?'

'How many times do I have to tell you? Because nobody knows what we did besides us three. We're the only ones. The secret died with Natasha, and it will die with us too, okay? Forget about that man. I wish I'd never told you about him. He was just some weirdo, no doubt taking a morbid curiosity with Edwin's disappearance and looking into anybody he used to work with. I bet he's read all the rumours online and made up some fantastical theory in his head. You know how many rumours there are online, right? But that's all they are, and that's all they will stay.'

I don't want to give Bev another chance to voice her concerns because it's no good for the mood of either of us, so I quickly leave her under the guise of going to get another drink from the bar. But really, I am just giving the both of us a little break from each other, although given the stress I am under, another drink won't hurt.

Ordering another wine from the busy barman, I wait patiently to be furnished with my drink and while I do, I look around the pub at all the people here. There's plenty of chatter in the room, and it's clear that lots of light-hearted tales are being told about the deceased, considering all the smiling faces, which is nice to see. But what is not nice to see is the one person I hoped I would never see again.

It's him, the man I followed into the side street near my office after I caught him following me.

He's here.

He's in this pub.

It looks like he's talking to some of Natasha's friends as if he fits right in here, but he doesn't, and now I have seen him, I feel like I don't belong here either. Forgetting all about the drink I just ordered, I walk away from the bar and plan on making my way back to Bev before telling her that we need to leave. But before I can get there, the man sees me making a move and when he does, he breaks off from his conversation and starts heading my way.

Unable to go any quicker due to the volume of bodies inside this section of the pub, I am trapped, and that is how the man is able to reach me and speak to me before I can leave.

'Hello, Liz. My condolences for your loss,' he says. 'Natasha was very popular, I see.'

'What the hell are you doing here? Did you even know her?' I reply.

'No, not personally. But don't pretend that's why you are upset to see me because we both know that's not the real reason now, is it?'

'What are you doing here?' I ask him again before noticing that Bev has spotted me talking to this man, and I wonder if she realises who he is.

'I told you, Liz. I'm on to you and your friend over there.'

He nods towards Bev in the corner before returning his steely gaze to me.

'We've not done anything wrong,' I try, hopelessly.

'Really? You're entirely innocent? Never made a mistake in your life? Never committed a crime and gotten away with it? A crime like, let's say, oh, I don't know…murder?'

My entire body turns cold, and all I can think to do is keep on the defensive and tell this man to stay away from me, an order which he surprisingly heeds, though not without leaving me with an ominous message.

'Okay, but do me a favour,' he says. 'Give my condolences to Bev too. Also tell her that she'll be seeing me very soon, although I'm sure you've warned her about that already.'

With that, the man turns and leaves, and despite me calling out to him, my shaky voice is lost amongst the din of all the chatter in here. By the time I return to Bev, she has already guessed who that was.

'Was that him? The man who followed you?'

When I nod, Bev panics a little more.

'What did he say? What did he want?'

But I don't answer that. Instead, I just look around at the busy pub I am standing in and register all the faces around me. All these people drinking, eating, conversing. It's not quite a party because to call it such would be inappropriate, given the circumstances, but surrounded by this many people, all of whom have a drink in their hand, it makes me think of a simpler time.

A time when the social gatherings I went to were fun and were actually parties.

A time when the innocence I once possessed slowly started to be eroded away.

17

NINE MONTHS AGO

As I hear the dulcet tones of Michael Bublé coming from the speakers, hot on the heels of a very famous Mariah Carey track, I know it can only mean one thing.

It's Christmas.

If I need any more signs of that then I only have to look around the pub I'm standing in to get them because this place is heavily decorated in tinsel, and there is a pot of mulled wine available at the bar for anybody who wishes to indulge in that traditional festive drink.

Yep, there's no doubt about it; it's that time of year again.

The time when everybody seems extra friendly, or at least extra lubricated.

Certainly extra fed.

It's the evening of December 22nd, just a few days out from the big one, and as such, the mood is high. There's no doubting it; it's reached that point where work professionals around the world begin to down their proverbial tools and relax as the holiday season begins, and boring things, like fulfilling employee responsibilities, can be forgotten about for a few days, or preferably, until the new year. But before my own holidays begin, there is one employee obligation I am obliged to fulfil before I disappear home to gorge myself on chocolates for the next several days.

It's my office Christmas party, and like everybody else I work with, I have made the effort to be in attendance on the request of the man who pays us all to work for him.

Spotting the boss across the bar, I chuckle to myself because to see Edwin as he is tonight is a far cry from how he is every other time I have seen him. No longer is he sporting the fitted suits with the crisp white shirts and smooth ties. Instead, he is now wearing a very quirky Christmas jumper to match the occasion he finds himself attending.

On the front of his woolly jumper is emblazoned the image of a snowman who looks like he's had one too many drinks at his own Christmas party, and if that wasn't enough, Edwin has a red Santa hat on top of his head, covering his neat hair and further transforming his look. But despite his seasonal outfit, there is still plenty of evidence of the usually presentable man on show, like his smart stubble, his nice jeans and shoes, and last but not least, those dazzling white teeth of his, his smile capable of allowing him to pull off any outfit, no matter how ridiculous it looks.

Speaking of looking, Edwin catches me with my eyes on him and makes his way over to me, making me wish I hadn't been so obvious in how much attention I was paying him. Then again, that's been a battle I've been constantly fighting ever since I started working for him because since I've known him, I've found myself attracted to him in a way that is not exactly appropriate for an employer/employee relationship.

They say workplace romances are a bad idea, and I tell myself that is why I have not made a move on Edwin yet. But in reality, the only reason I haven't initiated anything even remotely romantic with him is because I'm far too scared to.

What if he doesn't feel the same way?

What if he rejects me?

I could lose my job, and that would be a disaster. It would also be hugely embarrassing. That's why I've not let Edwin know that I like him in such a way, and as he reaches me and asks me if I'm having a good time tonight, I simply smile and say yes, harbouring the secret that really, all I want this Christmas is a kiss from him.

'What do you think of my outfit?' Edwin asks me before giving me a twirl, and I laugh.

'It's great. A big improvement on what you usually wear.'

Edwin returns the laughter, and I feel the warm buzz inside that comes from having the man I like show a strong sign that he enjoys my company. Or maybe that warm buzz is just from all the mulled wine I've drunk this evening. I have had a lot of it.

But 'tis the season and all that.

'So, tell me, Liz,' Edwin says, and his use of my name gives me another thrill. 'How does this Christmas party compare to the ones in your old jobs? Is it better or worse?'

'Oh, this one is much better,' I say, not wanting to disappoint him. 'Trust me, I've been to some terrible parties in my time, but this is definitely one of the better ones.'

'That's good to hear. I didn't want you being disappointed and thinking you would have to find somewhere else to work in the new year.'

'No chance. I love my job!' I say, perhaps a little too enthusiastically, but at least I manage to stifle the burp that threatens to escape my lips a second later. That would have been most embarrassing.

'Great! I love having you with us,' Edwin says, flashing me that smile of his. 'I know it's only been a few months, but I have been impressed with your progress so far, and I can see big things for you at this company, that's for sure.'

'Wow, thank you,' I say, genuinely flattered because as much as I'm looking to get some encouragement from this man in a much more personal way, it's never bad to hear that your boss thinks you're doing a great job.

'I mean it. I've been really impressed with both your work ethic and the content of your work,' Edwin says, continuing to shower me with compliments, all of which I will gladly accept. 'And I know it's not very interesting of me to be discussing work matters at a party, but if you will indulge me for one moment, I have a proposal for you.'

'A proposal?'

Stop imagining a wedding, Liz. He's obviously not talking about that, you silly woman.

'Yes,' Edwin says, totally oblivious to me and my nonsensical thoughts of walking down the aisle towards him in a white dress. 'I can see your role increasing greatly with the company in the near future, and I just wanted to check if you would be interested in such a thing, if I was to make you a more formal offer.'

'Yes, of course!' I say, committing to something I'm still not entirely sure I know all the details of. But what else can I say? No thanks, go and give this opportunity to one of my other colleagues? I'm not going to do that and not just because there might be a chance of a pay rise coming my way soon. It's because I don't want to say or do anything that would make Edwin think I wasn't the kind of woman he clearly thinks I am.

'Excellent. Well, like I said, it's a party, so I won't bore you with all the details of what I'm thinking yet, but how about we have a meeting the first day back after the holidays, and I'll discuss this further with you then. Sound good?'

'It sounds great,' I say with a big smile, and Edwin seems satisfied with my answer.

I'm hoping he might want to linger around and talk to me a little longer, but a man like him always has somebody else waiting to speak to him and even more so here because while this party consists mostly of his employees, there are a few clients and customers here too, so it's important he shows them plenty of attention in order to potentially get future business from them in the new year.

'Enjoy your mulled wine,' Edwin says to me with a wink. 'And I guess I'll see you later.'

With that, Edwin moves away from me and is soon chatting to somebody else, but I keep watching him and thinking about how the only place I want to see him later is under the piece of mistletoe that hangs above the bar to my left. But any fantasies I might be entertaining are quickly ended when I'm joined by my best work buddy.

'What were you two talking about?' Bev asks me, and with her eyes on Edwin, I guess she is referring to the conversation I just had with him.

'Not much,' I reply, opting not to mention there might be a potential promotion in my future just in case Bev gets envious that no such opportunity has come her way lately. As my best friend in the office and someone who I have become close to outside of it, I really want her to keep liking me, so I won't go bragging or doing anything to suggest I might be popular with Edwin. But it turns out that I don't need to because Bev must have been watching us speak, just like she's been paying attention to us in the office whenever we've spoken, and that's why she has a word of warning for me.

'Don't even think about it,' Bev says with a shake of the head. 'I know you are, and it's only natural because he's a good-looking guy, not to mention rich and charismatic. But don't, Liz. Don't get involved with Edwin beyond being his employee. I'm begging you.'

Begging? That's a bit of a strange word to use, isn't it?

'He's single. I'm single. It's Christmas. It wouldn't be the worst thing in the world to happen, right?' I ask, checking to see just how much Bev is against this idea.

'It would be the worst thing to happen to you,' she replies without skipping a beat. 'Trust me on that. Do you know how many women I've seen come and go at this company, all of them leaving abruptly, just gone one day? And you know what they all had in common?'

'What?'

'Do I really have to spell it out for you?' Bev asks me, but I nod my head so that she does.

'They all slept with the boss,' she says with another shake of the head.

'What? So he makes a habit of sleeping with his employees?' I ask, on the one hand feeling disappointed because I thought we had a genuine connection. On the other hand, I feel a little thrill because it seems there is a very good chance that I can be intimate with Edwin if he has a history of doing such things with the people who work for him.

'A habit?' Bev retorts. 'No, a habit would be something that could be changed. I'd say it's more of an addiction. That's much harder to cure.'

'Let me get this straight,' I say, wondering if Bev is just chatting nonsense because she's had as much mulled wine as I have this evening. 'Edwin sleeps with everyone in the office? Is that it?'

'Not everyone.'

'He hasn't tried it on with you?' I ask Bev, intrigued.

'Oh, he did. More than once, as well,' Bev tells me. 'But I shut him down, at least I did after we had shared a kiss.'

'What did he say to that?'

'He didn't like it, but I also think he respected me for it too. Not many women say no to a man like him.'

'Wait! So you're saying he has gotten rid of women he's slept with but kept you because you said no?'

Bev shrugs her shoulders by way of an answer.

'Nice try, but I'm not falling for it,' I say with a laugh as another Christmas classic begins to blare out from the speakers. 'You're trying to wind me up, aren't you? But I'm not that easy to fool.'

'I'm not joking,' Bev says without the slightest hint of a lie. 'If you sleep with Edwin, it'll be the biggest mistake of your career. But not only that, it might be the biggest mistake of your life.'

Bev seems to have finished what she came over to me to say and goes to get another drink from the bar, telling me she'll grab me one too. But I couldn't care less about another drink, not after that ominous warning.

The biggest mistake of my career? That would be unfortunate, but it also seems unlikely, considering Edwin just hinted that I was in line for an exciting new opportunity within his company.

But what about the biggest mistake of my life? Surely that seems a bit drastic.

Looking back at Edwin, I see he is now chatting to Monique, a twenty-five-year-old new member of the marketing team, and by the looks of it, there is a lot of flirting going on.

Am I jealous that Edwin might be stealing a kiss with a younger colleague of mine tonight rather than me?

A tiny bit.

But am I also worried about what might happen to Monique if she takes things any further with the boss based on what Bev just told me might happen?

A tiny bit too.

I guess this can be the test. If Monique sleeps with Edwin and Bev is right, she won't last long at his company. So I'll play it safe and let her have whatever fun she wants with Edwin this evening.

If nothing weird happens, then I guess Bev was wrong.

But if it does?

Maybe the woman bringing me a drink back from the bar was right all along.

If so, that will spell trouble for Monique and, maybe one day, trouble for me too.

18

PRESENT DAY

It's not often I'm glad to be at work, but I'd take today over yesterday anytime. Less than twenty-four hours ago, I was dressed in black and helping mark the final chapter in the life of Natasha, but now, normality has resumed. Colour has returned to my outfit in the form of the navy blue trousers I'm wearing to go with the black shoes and white blouse with a thin red trim around the neckline, a fairly standard type of look I go for when in the office these days. The time for low-cut tops and short skirts has passed for me, not because I'm too old to pull them off now but simply too aware that I'm worth so much more than just looking sexy for whichever members of the opposite sex I might encounter that day. But whilst my outfit has some colour in it, my mood is still just as dark as yesterday, not that any of my colleagues have noticed.

Not a single one of them has asked me how yesterday was, despite them all knowing I was attending a friend's funeral because I had to explain it in an email, which I sent to them all to say why I wouldn't be able to be at the weekly staff meeting. I wasn't exactly expecting to be greeted with a wave of sympathy cards or bouquets of flowers, but it would have been nice to at least have been offered a few polite condolences by the people I work with five days a week. But such a thing would require any of these people to possess positive characteristics like empathy, sensitivity, and affection, and I think that might be asking a bit much from this crowd.

With the average age of my colleagues here so low, I doubt any of them possess the life experience to truly understand why yesterday was so difficult for me because I presume none of them have watched a friend be buried. Of course, I hope that is the case because I wouldn't wish grief on anybody, but it's just yet another example of how I have failed to make any kind of a connection with the people I work with, making me almost long for the time when I used to sit beside Bev every day and chatter away to her, whilst also having numerous other good friends seated at desks nearby, Natasha amongst them.

Almost.

After enduring a tedious morning of lots of work punctuated by a distinct lack of conversation, it's a relief when lunchtime comes around, and I make sure to get away from my desk to spend the next sixty minutes anywhere but here. After grabbing my sandwich from the staff fridge, I leave the office and head for the park around the corner, looking forward to the temporary distraction that the change of scene will provide. It's always nice to be in nature, but the way I feel right now, I really do need the calming effects of green vegetation, and after securing myself a spot on one of the benches that are dotted around this pleasant green space, I unwrap my sandwich and tuck in.

As my taste buds get a load of the ham, cheese, and pickle filling between the two slices of brown bread, I use my free hand to scour the internet on my phone.

But I'm not whiling away this time with some light relief of reading about which celebrity is now in trouble for doing something they shouldn't have done. Instead, I'm putting the name 'Edwin van Dekker' into my search engine, and, as always, I'm intrigued as to what the results will be.

It wasn't so long ago that a search like this one on the internet provided the user with links to Edwin's company website, as well as numerous photos of him looking resplendent in suits and various links to newspaper articles about some of the charity work he had done in the area. But these days, the same search throws up very different results.

Each and every link now talks about his disappearance.

Clicking on the most recent article to reference his name, I see that it is a report from a Dutch media outlet and, as such, is written in a language I do not speak. That would usually present a problem, but in this day and age, all I have to do is click the 'Translate' button, and it converts the entire article into English for me. Able to read it now, my eyes scan across the text while my jaw keeps working on my sandwich.

Dutch National Still Missing After Six Months – What We Know About Edwin van Dekker's Mysterious Disappearance In The UK

As the six-month milestone since he was last seen passes without any news, only questions remain regarding the vanishing of a successful Dutch man who was living and working in England. Edwin van Dekker, 51, founder and CEO of Van Dekker Logistics, was last seen on Monday 14th March leaving his place of work, but since then, there has been no more information as to what might have happened to him. Despite repeated requests for progress in the case from the Dutch Foreign Minister, Martin Rijker, the British Police remain as dumbfounded by the disappearance as those who knew Edwin and, as of yet, there have been no arrests in connection with Edwin's vanishing, nor any evidence discovered to back up the numerous theories that abound about what might have happened to the missing man.

But while this is frustrating to the Dutch Government as they seek answers overseas, it pales in comparison to the difficulties being endured by Edwin's only child, Phillip, who simply wishes to know what has happened to his father and best friend.

I scoff on my sandwich then because as far as I knew, Phillip and Edwin were not best friends. I heard that Phillip had once requested a top role within his father's company after completing a long and expensive trip around the world, presumably funded by his old man, yet Edwin had said no. He had been willing to give his son a position within his organisation, but he wanted his offspring to learn about the business from the ground up, starting off in a lesser role before gradually working his way up under the tutelage of his father. Perhaps unsurprisingly, Phillip had not taken too kindly to being told he would have to slot in amongst all the other lowly workers under Edwin rather than be given a plum job on a big wage right up there beside his father at the top of the company's organisational chart. That was why Phillip had chosen to go and work with a competitor in the city, no doubt to try and make his father feel bad for what he had done to him, not that Edwin seemed to care too much. A man as selfish as him hardly tended to worry about other people for too long, even his own child. While the pair were on speaking terms, Phillip and Edwin were definitely not best friends, though Phillip is clearly keen to portray a different image in this article.

"I just want to know where my father is. Is he safe and well somewhere, or has he come to harm? Does he need my help? There must be somebody out there who knows where he is, so I implore you to get in touch with the authorities either in England, where my father was last seen, or here in his native Netherlands. Please, help in any way you can."

Since his father's disappearance, Phillip van Dekker has assumed the role of leading Van Dekker Logistics, though it remains clear his priority is finding Edwin and restoring him to his rightful position. However, such a move has been met with scepticism in some parts of the media, as there are those who suspect Phillip of being involved in the mystery of what happened to Edwin, a claim the worried son firmly denies.

"I do not wish to give any credibility to those people who think I would wish harm on my father. I am simply trying to make sure the company he spent his life building does not falter during his absence, and I am very much praying and hoping that he is back soon to carry on the great work he was so talented at."

The rumour of Phillip van Dekker potentially having orchestrated his father's disappearance so he could take over the reins at the company is false but very useful for me because it helps deflect attention away from where people really should be looking. Do I feel bad that an innocent man like Phillip is being accused of certain things by strangers on the internet? A little bit, though Phillip is hardly angelic, and the apple hasn't fallen far from the tree there either. Like his dad, he has been known to be rude and selfish, so that makes me feel a little less guilty about having him mentioned in the news as a possible cause of his dad's disappearance. But mainly, it's just a relief to have the media tying themselves up in knots trying to figure out what happened to Edwin because so far, not a single thing they have reported has been anywhere near close to the truth. There has been no mention of his three colleagues who hated him, nor has there been any mention of what really happened to him, including being hit over the head and then stabbed to death.

Most of all, there has been no mention of his final resting place.

The canal remains out of the news for now.

The canal that holds my deepest, darkest secret.

19

SIX MONTHS AGO

You might think three people could move a body between them, but it's way harder than it looks. It's difficult to distribute the weight evenly, it's almost impossible to do it without getting blood all over your clothes and, most of all, it's tough to do anything illegal when you're utterly terrified that somebody will see you and tell the police. There are no lessons on this, no teachers telling their pupils how to move a corpse, and if there are any videos on YouTube about such a thing, they are quickly removed and whoever uploaded them is in serious trouble.

It turns out that the only way to figure out how to do it is to gain practical experience. Learning on the job, as it were. That's what Bev, Natasha and I are doing right now.

Or rather, we are failing on the job.

It's been half an hour since I stabbed Edwin to death and, in that time, all the three of us have managed to achieve is making a mess of getting Edwin out of Natasha's house and into the back of my car. After killing him, I knew we needed to move quickly, not just because there was a danger someone might visit this house and see what we had done, but because I knew the longer we delayed the next step, the more chance there was of us losing our nerve.

I'd already stood by and watched Natasha fail to inflict the deadly blow on Edwin, a blow she had told

Bev and I that she was more than ready to deal out, when we were planning tonight. But the moment was too much for her, and while it's understandable that she found it difficult to stab a man to death, it's not very helpful to have an accomplice who has already shown signs of freezing at an important moment. Bev has also displayed evidence that she's starting to doubt we can pull off what we so carefully discussed beforehand, and that's why, after killing Edwin, I've also been the one who rolled him up inside the plastic sheeting we bought last weekend.

With the corpse wrapped in the sheeting and tied tightly by several pieces of cable ties, I then draped a large cut of carpet over the top of it. That way, I'm confident that if anybody saw us taking this out of the house and putting it into the back of my car, they would just think it was three friends working on a home renovation project. But what I'm not confident about is actually getting this body out of here in the first place.

'Guys, please. We need to hurry up,' I say, as Bev and Natasha look far less prepared for this as I thought they'd be at this stage.

'Why? He's not coming back to life,' Bev says rather sarcastically.

'Just come on. Grab hold of one end, and let's go,' I say, and I'm pleased when Bev actually helps me this time. But Natasha doesn't move.

'What have we done?' she asks us both as she stares absently at the carpet beside Edwin's body.

'We've done what needed to be done,' I tell her firmly. 'Now come on, let's get him in the car. We can't do it without you.'

'Are you sure?'

I'm thrown off by Natasha's question, but it's not the action at hand that I think she is referring to, nor is that why it troubles me. I think she is hinting that I've had no problem doing what I've done so far, despite how gruesome it has been.

If I'm honest, I did surprise myself with my ability to stab Edwin without so much as a second thought. Who knew taking a life could be so easy? It helps when the victim deserves it, just like it helps that there was really no way we could have ever let him go without him telling the police what we'd already done to him. What choice did I have? Having always been a very practical person, as many an accountant is, I've quickly been able to process what I've done and move onto the next item on the To-Do list. But Natasha is not so practical, though I should have known that because she worked in marketing, and those creative types are often very different people to the ones who keep tabs on the finances.

Note to self – if I ever have to kill anybody again, find another accountant to help me.

Bev is pretty useful and uses enough of the logical part of her brain on a daily basis to know that I'm right when I say we have to move this body quickly. The two of us are ready to get this carpet out of the door and on the way to the canal, but we still need Natasha to assist.

Realising that most of what I have tried so far with her this evening has not worked, I change tact.

'Fine. Don't help us. Edwin's body will have to stay here then, and we'll have to think of some other way to get rid of it. Chop him up, maybe. Put him in the bins. Hope nobody peeks inside the bags when they come to collect them next week.'

As I expected, my alternate plan does not go down well with Natasha, and she realises she really has to help me, so she reluctantly does so, and once all three of us have hold of the heavy carpet and sheeting with the even heavier body inside it, we begin to transport it. Whereas before we dragged Edwin's body, now I am forcing myself to lift it off the floor because I'm afraid we might be smearing blood on the carpet if we drag him across it. But lifting him is much harder for me, as it is for my accomplices, which is why we are moving more slowly than we were when we moved Edwin into here in the first place.

'All clear,' Bev says, after checking the street for any pedestrians, and we use that bit of luck to hurry to my car as quickly as possible and load the carpet into the back. I'd already moved my vehicle closer to Natasha's house after killing Edwin so we'd have less far to travel, and while it was tempting to just drive away and leave the whole horribleness of the dead body behind, I knew I couldn't leave until the job was done. Now the carpet is in the car, we're over halfway there.

'Let's go,' I say, heading for the driver's seat, and while Bev and I get inside my car, Natasha locks her front door before joining us. Now the car has three occupants, or is it four? I'm not sure Edwin counts, although he most certainly will if the police are to stop us and ask what we might have in the back.

As I drive in the direction of the canal, I'm finding it impossible not to think of how many times I have seen a similar scenario play out in movies or TV shows. This would be the part where I get stopped because one of my taillights is out, or some other such nonsense that leads to a very unlucky encounter with an officer of the law. But after telling myself that my luck isn't that bad, I start to say a silent prayer that the section of canal that we are going to will be just as quiet as Natasha's street was a few minutes ago. If it is, this will all be over in a few moments.

Arriving at my pre-determined parking spot, a spot I scouted out beforehand and chose on account of it being as close to the canal as a car could feasibly get, I'm relieved to see that the banks of the canal look deserted. I expected as much because who wanders around beside a canal after sunset? Well, besides criminals looking to hide some evidence, of course.

'One last effort, and then this is over,' I say to my accomplices as my final pep talk before I get out of the car, trying to convince all of us that this last part will be easy. But there's something so final about disposing of a body. It's one thing to create a dead body but to hide it in a place where it will hopefully never be found? That seems almost as bad as the killing part, or perhaps even worse, because to hide it is almost saying that this person never existed, and the thought of someone hiding my body is a terrifying one.

Vanishing off the face of the earth without a trace? How frightening. But that is what must happen to Edwin, and as Bev and Natasha join me at the back of the car and the three of us pick up the carpet again, we're suddenly interrupted.

'Good evening.'

The male voice behind us causes each of us to drop our section of the carpet and spin around, shocked to learn we're not the only ones here and terrified as to who might have just spoken to us.

With it being dark, it takes me an extra second to see him but when I do, I observe a man in his fifties in a long, grey coat.

And he has a dog with him.

I immediately start to fear that the dog is going to smell what we are hiding and alert his owner, barking wildly or jumping up at us or doing whatever it is a dog might do when they think they are in the presence of something interesting to them. I had a sniffer dog paying me extra attention whilst walking through an airport in Australia once, and while I knew I was innocent and carrying no contraband, it was still a nervy experience, so multiply that feeling by a million now that I really do have something to hide.

But so far, the dog, a yellow Labrador, has not reacted to the carpet and remains by his master's side, although trying to predict the behaviour of a canine is impossible, so I'm not going to relax until the dog and its owner are out of our way.

'Oh, hi. Good evening,' I say, managing to offer a response.

'Are you ladies okay? We're not used to seeing too many people around here at this time of night - isn't that right, Reggie?'

The man looks down at his dog then, and I presume his companion is Reggie. I also get from what he just said that they must make a habit of walking this section of the canal at this time of the evening, and that grates with me because it means I missed something very important when I was doing my reconnaissance work for the best place to ditch Edwin's body. Either that or I have just been very, very unlucky. If we parked here thirty seconds later, this man and Reggie would have already passed this point, and I wouldn't be forced into having this conversation now.

'We're fine!' Bev replies way too abruptly.

'What have you got there?' the man asks us as he looks from our three nervous faces to the carpet that lies in the back of my car. He's either genuinely curious, just making conversation, or starting to think that we might be up to something we shouldn't be.

'What, this? Just an old carpet. My friends are helping me redecorate,' I say, pleased that I'm able to come up with some kind of plausible excuse so quickly. But while the redecorating might explain why I have a carpet in my car, it doesn't explain what I'm doing with it here down by this canal at this time of night.

'Oh, I see,' the man says, and he suddenly looks rather sad.

What's he thinking? Does he know? Is he worried for his own safety now? Or dismayed that these three women are not as pleasant as he thought we might be when he approached us.

'I know it's not really any of my business, but I do hope you are not planning on dumping that carpet in the canal,' he says then, letting us know what he is most worried about, and thankfully, it is just a bit of fly-tipping.

'Oh, erm,' I begin, scratching around for a good answer for him, but there is none. That's when Natasha jumps in.

'Sorry. You've caught us. We were going to put it in the canal,' she says, admitting to our plan, though only a fraction of it, really.

'That's a shame,' the man says. 'I wonder if you might reconsider. I know this canal isn't exactly a beauty spot, but it would be even worse if everybody in town decided to come down here and dispose of their waste in the water, don't you think? Couldn't you take it to the recycling centre tomorrow? That seems more proper.'

I look at my two accomplices, and when Natasha shrugs, I can't see any reason why we would say no to this man.

'You're right. We shouldn't put the carpet here,' I say with a shake of my head. 'We're sorry.'

'It's okay. I'm sorry for the preaching, but I'm a councilman, you see. The name's Terrence Andrews, and because I work for the council, I know just how much work can be caused by people leaving things in places they shouldn't do. Is that okay?'

'Absolutely fine,' I say, nodding my head enthusiastically. 'We'll take the carpet to the recycling centre tomorrow.'

'Wonderful. Have a good evening, ladies,' Terrence says, and with that, he is on his way down the canal with his trusty companion, Reggie, by his side.

That was a close call, and it's annoying our plan was thwarted, but at least the body beneath the carpet remains undetected.

Now we just need to figure out what to do with it now our first idea has been scuppered.

Fortunately, Bev has a suggestion.

'We wait until he's gone,' she says with a shrug. 'We're not driving back through town with this. Give it five minutes and that busybody will be far enough away so we can stick to the original plan.'

I guess Bev is right and as I watch Terrence disappearing into the darkness as he gets further away, I think about how he'll never know what we were really doing here.

He almost stumbled upon the biggest crime this town has ever seen.

As it is, he'll simply go to bed tonight thinking he did a good deed for the local environment.

Meanwhile, Edwin's body will become fish food at the bottom of this canal and the three of us will get away with what we've done.

Hopefully.

20

PRESENT DAY

There are plenty of things I expect to keep me occupied tonight as I arrive home from work. I need to cook my evening meal, there is a basket in my bedroom full of dirty laundry that needs to be put into the washing machine, and it certainly wouldn't hurt if I was to get the vacuum cleaner out of the cupboard and run it over the carpet in my home for the first time in a while. On top of all those tedious tasks, there is the small matter of still having to deal with all the paranoia, guilt, and sadness that comes from what has happened with both Edwin and Natasha, so all in all, I'd say it's going to be another 'fun' night in my life.

But then something new is thrown into the mix no sooner than I have taken off my coat, kicked off my shoes, and recalled what ingredients I have in my fridge to help me make a meal. I don't know if it's something that is going to add to my woes, because initially, I am pleased to see the friendly face at my front door, but very quickly, I come to realise that an even bigger problem has just landed on my doorstep, one that will soon make me long for the torturous night I had planned before it arrived.

'Hey? Is everything okay?' I ask Bev after opening the door to find her looking pensive on the other side of it.

'Can I come in?' she asks, but it's a silly question because of course I'm willing to let my friend in, so once I've stepped aside, Bev enters. But it quickly turns out that she is not here for a cup of tea. Instead, she has something troubling to tell me.

'He's a private investigator,' Bev says, though it takes me a few more seconds to catch up.

'What? Who?'

'The man who has been following you. He's a PI, and he's being paid to find out what happened to Edwin.'

My entire body turns cold because while I already knew the man who had been following me could be a problem, I didn't realise it was as serious as this. He's been hired to get the truth? He's a professional? If that's the case, he's more than incentivised to not stop until he unravels this whole mystery, and I assume he comes with a stellar track record of already having done the same thing in other cases, otherwise why would anybody hire him now?

'His name is Jack Ferdinand,' Bev says, before handing me a small business card, and when I take it, I see that exact name printed across the front of this grey card in small, silver lettering. It's neat, but I couldn't care less about where the owner of these cards had them printed. What I do care about is the job title listed just below the name.

Bev is right.

Jack Ferdinand is an investigator.

And he's investigating us.

'Where did you get this?' I ask Bev as I turn the card over and examine every inch of it as if there might be some more clues on it somewhere.

'He gave it to me,' Bev replies calmly. 'When he came to my house.'

'What? He was at your house? When?'

'He was waiting for me when I got home from work.'

'Tonight?'

'Yes.'

'And you came straight here after he visited you? He could have followed you here! How's it going to look if he's seen you come running straight to me after he spoke to you. It'll look like we both have something to hide.'

'Oh, that ship has sailed,' Bev says with a shake of her head. 'Jack knows we have something to hide, and he's not afraid of letting us know it. He must be confident he'll find it if he's given me his card.'

I keep studying the card again, trying to make this all make sense.

'Why would he do this? Why would he let you know he was investigating us? For a private investigator, he's not very private!'

'He says that whole idea of private investigators hiding in the shadows is just in the movies. Real investigators like him have no issues approaching their targets and asking them questions directly, as we both know.'

'So what did he say to you?' I ask, handing the business card back to Bev as if that will somehow make this problem leave me alone.

'He was very polite. He introduced himself and then said he knew all about me because he had been talking to people who knew me. Friends. Former work colleagues. Even someone I used to go to the gym with. He seems to know my entire life history.'

'Oh my God. And you didn't know about any of this?'

'No. From what Jack told me, he'd only spoken to them very recently, but yeah, not a single one of them had bothered to get in touch with me and let me know someone was going around asking questions. Maybe they were worried they might interfere with an investigation or something. Jack seemed very slick. I bet he told them they weren't to say anything or they might get in trouble for hindering any investigation, and they must have believed him.'

Well, it's either that or the people whom Bev calls friends aren't actually as close to her as they would like to think they are. After all, I told her the second somebody was snooping around into our affairs and not just because we're linked by what we did to Edwin; it's because that's what friends do. They tell each other things. But nobody told Bev that Jack Ferdinand was running around town asking about her, though I wish they had because then she might have been more prepared for him accosting her on her doorstep.

'What did he ask you?' I want to know then.

'He asked me what my relationship was like with Edwin. He knew I worked for him, but he wanted to hear what it was like on a daily basis. He said he wanted to hear it in my own words.'

'Why would he say that?'

'I guess because he already has some idea of what it was like, and he was checking to see if my story matched what he'd already heard.'

'So what did you say?'

'I confirmed that he was my boss and said that we got on as well as a boss and a colleague could, and I was shocked when I heard he had gone missing.'

'Why did you mention him going missing? Does it not draw attention to it?' I cry, ever fearful of one wrong word from either of us catching us out.

'I think it would draw more attention if I didn't mention it, what with it being in the news and all,' Bev replies, and I suppose she is right.

'What else did he ask you?'

'He asked about secret agendas. Grudges that I or any of my other colleagues might have towards Edwin. Of course, I denied knowing about anything like that, but he told me he knew about issues with several employees who had left Edwin's company recently. He mentioned Natasha, of course. And then he mentioned you.'

'What about me?'

'He said he knew you left under a cloud of suspicion. The fraudulent accusations. He called it a bit of a cover-up. Said you'd gotten away with doing something you shouldn't have.'

'He's got it all wrong. I was innocent!'

'That's not the point,' Bev says, forcing me to calm down for a second. 'The point is he knows everything that happened at Edwin's company. Everything. How is that even possible?'

I'm not sure either, so I think about it until I have a suggestion.

'You said he'd spoken to people who knew you, right? So he must have spoken to people we worked with. They must have told him about us and Natasha and everything that happened when we worked there.'

I think that's it, but Bev shakes her head.

'No, surely not. The company made them sign non-disclosure agreements, remember? Just after Edwin went missing and his case was in the news. All employees still at Van Dekker had to sign a contract to say they wouldn't speak to anybody about what went on there unless it was the police. As far as I can tell, Jack is not with the police, he's some freelance investigator. So the employees can't have spoken to him. It has to be somebody else.'

'Who?'

'The only person I can think of is Phillip.'

It makes sense that Edwin's son would be the one to have hired Jack, and it would also explain how Jack knows so much. Phillip could have told him every little detail of Van Dekker because, as the new company boss, I bet he didn't make himself sign a non-disclosure agreement, only his employees. Phillip must be convinced that whatever happened to his father is based on something that happened in that office in the past, and unfortunately, he would be right.

A lot did happen there.

But it really only started to affect me the first day back after that Christmas party.

21

NINE MONTHS AGO

Returning to the office after the Christmas holidays usually involves having lots of conversations about the annual event that has just passed.

'Did you have a good Christmas?'

'What presents did you get?'

'How was your turkey dinner?'

'Did you watch anything good on TV?'

'I ate way too much. Diet starts now.'

'It all went too fast, didn't it?'

As I enter the office after a seven-day break, I'm prepared for all that, and more, as I rejoin the rest of my colleagues now the festivities are out of the way. The last time I saw them all, we were dancing the night away after our Christmas party had moved on from a pub to a club. It's a good thing there was a break from work after that because it took a couple of days for my hangover to subside, and I doubt I was the only one. Everybody I work with certainly made the most of the whole evening being on Edwin's company expense account, and why wouldn't we? It's one of the perks of being an employee – when the boss gives you a treat, you take full advantage. However, I certainly overdid it even more than I've been known to before at Christmas parties in my past, though much of that was because I ended up being very envious that it was one of my colleagues who was getting close to Edwin instead of me.

Seeing Edwin flirting with Monique at the party was one thing, but finding out that the pair of them had left the party at the same time and failed to reappear again was another because it was pretty obvious what must have happened. They had either gone back to her place together or his, and they had most likely given the other one an early Christmas present in the form of various physical intimacy acts that two single people are entitled to do without having to explain themselves to others. But having had a crush on Edwin, a crush that still remains even if I am disappointed in him potentially sleeping with one of his employees who is almost half my age, I can't lie and say I didn't spend a lot of my Christmas break wishing I had been the one he had left the party with.

Unable to do much about it and not wanting to spend my entire Christmas holidays feeling jealous, I had pushed the thought of him out of my mind as best I could, and as I re-enter the office today, I'm feeling confident I can put on a brave face around him and carry on being as professional as my job requires me to be. There is also the not-so-small matter of the 'opportunity' he mentioned to me when we spoke at the party, and I have spent the last week looking forward to finding out much more about that.

Making my way to my desk, I see a few remnants of Christmas decorations still visible around the office. Some of my colleagues decided to put a little tinsel around the place, as well as a few baubles on a small tree in the corner, and so far, nobody has bothered to take them down, even though Christmas has passed.

That's always the way with decorations, isn't it? It's easy to get excited and put them up but not so much fun to take them all down again once the fun is over. Assuming the task of removing the now-outdated decs will fall in the lap of the young office administrator who seems to get all the rubbish tasks, I reach my desk and smile when I see Bev already seated at hers and looking ready for her own return to work.

'Morning,' I say with a smile, before dropping my first sarcastic joke of the day. 'Isn't it wonderful to be back here again?'

I expect Bev to roll her eyes and smile before agreeing with me that she would much rather still be sat at home watching Christmas movies and eating leftover turkey sandwiches. But she doesn't do that. Instead, she just looks pensive, and I get the impression it is about much more than just post-holiday blues.

'What's wrong?' I ask her, and that's when Bev tells me to check my emails.

I frown and ask her again, but she just repeats the instruction, so I do as she says, although first, I have to wait a few seconds for my computer to load up. Once it has, I open my inbox, but all I see is a whole stack of unread emails that I will have to spend this first day back sifting through to see what is important and what isn't. But Bev helps me narrow my search down.

'Look at the email from Amy this morning,' she tells me, so I do just that and find it at the top of my inbox as the second most recent email I have received. It was sent at 08:02 this morning, and when I open it, I see that it went out to everybody in the office. But it's only when I read the content of it that I see why Bev is looking so dismayed.

Staff Update – Monique Brown has left the company with immediate effect, due to a private matter. All business matters relating to her role are now to be discussed with her team manager, Sarah. Any questions, please speak to me.

Best regards,

Amy.

Turning around so that Bev can see the expression on my face, it doesn't take long for my friend and colleague to give me a knowing look before she utters those famous words that nobody likes to hear.

'I told you so.'

However, I can see that Bev is taking no pleasure in being right about what she told me in the past. She predicted this. She warned me it might happen. She enlightened me all about what tends to happen when a female colleague here gets a little too close to Edwin and the relationship strays from professional to personal.

She told me about the trend of employees leaving quickly and unexpectedly.

And it seems it has just happened again.

'A private matter? What is Amy talking about?' I ask.

'That's just a simple way to stop people asking any questions. If it's a private matter, Amy can just hide behind that and not answer any questions, or rather her boss can.'

'But she can't just go without anyone knowing why. What about her friends here? They must know what happened.'

'Oh yeah, they will know what happened, alright,' Bev says, and she looks across the office at the row of desks where Monique used to sit. There are three employees over there sitting beside the one empty desk that Monique previously occupied, and those are the three workers who will be missing her the most now she is gone. But they are also the three who might be able to tell me what has actually happened, so I get up out of my chair to go and ask them.

But just before I can, Edwin appears, and when he does, he wants me to follow him. Aware that his need to speak to me probably has something to do with what we discussed at the party, I decide not to delay our chat, so I do as he says, and after following him into his office, he closes the door behind me and invites me to take a seat.

Sitting down on one side of his huge desk, Edwin occupies the opposing seat before showing me a broad smile.

'How was your Christmas?' he asks me. 'I trust you had a good one?'

'Err, yeah, it was great, thanks. You?'

'Can't complain, although my waistline certainly could,' he says with a chuckle whilst patting his stomach. 'But back to business now, and I'm very much eager to get a jumpstart on things as the new year begins. Do you remember what we discussed at the party? It's okay if you don't because we'd all had a lot to drink that night.'

Edwin winks at me, but I assure him that I remember.

'You mentioned an opportunity,' I say, and he nods his head.

'That's right, I did, and I bet you're eager to hear what it is, so I'll get on with it. I'm having a bit of a reshuffle here amongst my staff. You might have already heard that Monique has left us, and between you and me, she most likely won't be the only one. You see, I like to keep things fresh around the office, so staff turnover is not unusual here. People might have all sorts of theories about why that is, but I can assure you that it's just business. You don't get to be the head of a company like this one without making some tough calls.'

That could all be true, and I nod my head to show Edwin that I understand and believe what he has just said, but another part of me also thinks that all sounded like a very good excuse to get rid of certain people for reasons that might not be strictly business related. People like Monique, who seems to have been let go not long after she fell into Edwin's bed.

'So, as part of this reshuffle, I am promoting you to my head of finance. How does that sound?'

I'm stunned because to me, that sounds like a very big promotion.

'Wow, really?'

'Yeah, sound good?'

'It sounds great! I'm just shocked.'

'Don't be. I've been impressed with your work here, and with your prior experience, I think you're ready for this.'

'Erm, okay. But what about Jonathan? I thought he was head of finance?'

'He's going to be moving on to another company very soon. He handed in his notice a few weeks ago, but I haven't told anybody yet. But there's a job that needs to be filled when he's gone, and I think you're the person to fill it.'

'Thank you. I'm flattered.'

'No problem. Of course, we'll have to get the contract sorted, and Amy will speak to you about that. But for now, I just wanted to make you this verbal offer, and I'm glad you have accepted it. Now, if you would accept my apologies, I have a nine o'clock meeting, but we'll chat more about this later, okay?'

'Yeah, sure,' I say, and Edwin leaps out of his seat to show me to the door. But just before I leave, I have to ask the question that has been playing on my mind ever since I read Amy's email. 'Sorry, I was just wondering because I liked working with her - what happened with Monique?'

I notice Edwin's smile falter for a second then, before he composes himself and returns to his usual positive ways.

'It was a private matter. I can't say anything more than that. Now, have a good morning, and make sure you celebrate at lunchtime. It's not every day you get a promotion, is it?'

Edwin shows me out of his office then, and I do leave, though I can't help feeling like he tried to deflect away from Monique by reminding me that I should be grateful to have just received a better role in his company. It's almost as if he thinks he can keep anybody sweet just by showering them with a pay rise and a promotion. Maybe that works for him and others. I'm certainly excited about my new position here. But as I make my way back to my desk, I glance over at Monique's empty one, and the mystery of what really happened with her still remains.

It was a mystery that, once explored, changed the way I felt about my new boss forever.

22

PRESENT DAY

Against my better judgement, I have decided to be proactive and try to talk my way out of the difficult situation I seem to be in at the moment. It might be a terrible idea, but it has been my best idea out of a bad bunch of them, and ever since Bev came to see me most recently, I've known I have to do something.

Having Jack, the investigator, snooping around and asking people about Edwin's former colleagues, as well as interviewing a few of them, is a problem, but like any problem, the only way it can be solved is by cutting straight to the heart of the matter. That means trying not to deal so much with Jack and, instead trying to deal with the person who is paying him.

I'm going to see Edwin's son because it must be him behind this.

It's time for me to have a chat with Phillip van Dekker.

While such a thing will be difficult any time, it's made even harder by the fact that the only place I know I could find the young man is in the one place I never wanted to set foot in again. It's the offices of Van Dekker Logistics, and this is the first time I have been back here since I was able to entice Edwin to my car and drive him to Natasha's house, where he met his doom. Now I'm here to try and convince his son that I had nothing to do with his father's death.

This is going to be fun.

Realising that the best way to approach this situation is to do so by acting with the boldness of a person who has absolutely nothing to hide, I stride right through the entrance doors to the office and then smile when I see the receptionist behind the desk. Like most other roles, this one has seen great turnover, and this is not the same receptionist who worked here when I did. I can only imagine what reasons the previous one had for no longer working here, but that's not important right now. What is important is that I get to speak to Phillip, and I know he is here somewhere because his car is out there in the car park.

He's currently driving his dear daddy's old vehicle, although he's had the license plate altered so it reflects his initials now rather than his father's.

I guess he's not too grief-stricken to see a good car go to waste.

'Hi. Good morning. I'm here to see Phillip van Dekker,' I say, keeping the smile on my face because I want this receptionist to just think I'm some friendly woman coming here on business and not an ex-employee here to discuss a missing man, a private investigator and the mystery surrounding it all.

'Good morning. Do you have an appointment?' is the obvious response.

'Not exactly. But I was hoping Phillip might be able to spare me five minutes of his time. If you could just call him and let him know that Liz is in reception, thank you.'

I go to take a seat on the sofa then, and while the receptionist says something about her not being sure if he is in meetings, I see her eventually pick up her phone and make a call. When it's answered, she does exactly as I asked of her, relaying my name and location before putting the phone back down.

This is it. The moment of truth. Am I going to get to see the man I need to speak to, or will he be too much of a coward to talk to me and hide away upstairs, leaving his investigator to carry on doing his dirty work for him?

'Phillip will be here in a moment,' the receptionist says surprisingly.

'Thank you,' I say, the smile on my face this time not a fake one because I am genuinely pleased that I'm going to get to have my next conversation.

Sure enough, it does only take a moment before Phillip appears, and when he lays eyes on me sitting on the sofa in his reception area, he does not look particularly happy to see me. But like the business professional he is, he knows better than to start conducting business in this public place, so he invites me to follow him upstairs. When I do, I spot several familiar faces in the open-plan part of the office and many of them look interested to see me, but I try and avoid eye contact as much as I can, and only when we are in the privacy of a meeting room do we speak again.

'What are you doing here? You know ex-employees are not permitted back on these grounds without good reason.'

'Well, it turns out I have a good reason,' I say, before looking around at this meeting room and almost chuckling at the irony of this situation.

'You know, this is the exact room I sat in when your father interviewed me for my job here,' I go on, wanting to let Phillip in on what is almost amusing to me, considering the present set of circumstances we find ourselves in.

'If only he hadn't been charmed by you, then he might still be here now,' Philip says and, to give him credit, that line has quickly cut me down.

'What?'

'I'm just saying. Who knows what might have happened if my father hadn't hired you. What do you think?'

I decide not to say anything to that, though it doesn't exactly help me.

'That's what I thought,' Phillip says with a smirk. 'Best not answer that question. Not yet, anyway. Wait until you have a lawyer present.'

'Why would I have a lawyer present?'

'Isn't that what people do when being interviewed by the police?'

'But I'm not being interviewed by the police,' I say, and I'm already regretting my decision to come here.

'Not yet,' Phillip says, before smoothing out his tie in exactly the same mode and manner as his father used to smooth out his own.

'What's that supposed to mean?'

'I presume you came here for a specific reason, and it wasn't to reminisce on your first interview,' Phillip says, ignoring my last question. 'So what are you here for?'

I take a deep breath before deciding I've come this far so I might as well just say it now.

'Have you hired an investigator to follow me around?'

I study Phillip's face carefully for the answer, aware that the next few words out of his mouth may not be honest ones. But to his credit, he doesn't even try to deny it.

'I am paying someone to look into a few things, yes,' he confirms.

'Why are you looking into me?' I cry, doing my best to sound incredulous because that's how an innocent person would be if they had an investigator on their tail.

'Why wouldn't I?' comes the rather chilling response.

'Excuse me?'

He knows.

'As you well know, my father is missing and has been for half a year now. While I would like to be optimistic, I am a realist. I don't buy the theory that he ran away to start a new life abroad, not because he wouldn't leave without telling me but because there's absolutely no evidence to suggest any of his bank accounts have been used in the last six months. I think that, unfortunately, my father is dead, and that means there is a killer, or killers, at large, and they are most likely right here in this town, considering that this was the last place my father was seen alive. More so, this office was the last place he was known to be, so that might mean the killer could have a connection to this place. Hence my reason for looking into a few of his ex-employees.'

Phillip gets up and walks over to one of the glass walls of the meeting room, and as he looks out at his team of employees beavering away on the other side of it, he gestures with his arm towards them.

'The killer could be right out there now under my nose. Or they could be even closer than that.'

He turns to look at me then, and I get exactly what he is hinting at. He definitely suspects me, and unless I want to add more fuel to his suspicions, I better start saying things that could help throw him off my scent.

'If you think I had anything to do with Edwin's disappearance, then you are wrong,' I say clearly.

'Well, of course that is what the killer would say,' Phillip says, not entertaining any second thoughts that he might be going down the wrong path with me. 'But let's look at the facts, shall we? You used to work here with my father. You and he were close. Some would say much closer than two employees should be.'

'Your father did not care about getting personal with his workers. He slept with half the women in the office.'

'Including you.'

Wow, he really does know a lot about me.

'So what? That makes me a suspect in his disappearance?'

'No, what makes you a suspect in my eyes is the fact that your relationship with him ended badly. I know you left here, and I know about the rumours about why you did. The dodgy accounts, right? As you were the finance manager, that seems disturbing, does it not? But if you maintain you were innocent, that must mean you bore a grudge towards him. So, did you?'

'No, of course not!'

'I find that hard to believe. I would have done so in your position. You can be honest here. Tell me what you really thought of my father.'

'Why should I? It sounds like you think you already know everything. But guess what? You don't know a damn thing and neither does your investigator.'

Getting up out of my seat, I decide to try and ride the wave of false bravado that my last statement has just given me, and as I approach Phillip by the glass, I force myself to keep eye contact with him so he sees that I am not backing down in the face of his harassment of me.

'I understand that you are worried about your father, and you are desperate for answers. Everybody who ever knew him is. But believe me when I say this - I did not have anything to do with him going missing. I'd moved on from this place. I'd moved on from him. Sure, you might think I had a motive to want to hurt him but so did multiple people. I'm not saying any of them did anything to him, but if you are hiring investigators to look into me, and Bev, for that matter, then you might as well hire them to look into everyone he ever knew because I'm sure we all have a story about how he screwed us over at one time or another.'

With my piece said, I can only hope that it has gone some way to make Phillip reluctant to keep his investigator poking around into my life, and Bev's, for that matter, too. I decide to leave it there before I say something that could trip me up, so I turn for the door, but just before I can walk through it, Phillip has something he wishes to leave me with.

'Nice try, Liz. But you'll have to do better than that. I have a feeling I'll be seeing you again very soon. I sure know Jack will be. So be on your best behaviour, as remember, we're watching you. Unless you want to go to the police and tell them you feel I'm harassing you. But I have a feeling you won't want to do that, will you? Something tells me you'd prefer it if they stayed out of all this.'

I wish I had something clever to say back to the man behind me. Some words that would go a little way to allowing me to walk out of here with a little of the power in this dynamic back on my side. But I dare not utter another word because it's already abundantly clear that me coming here was a complete waste of time.

Phillip is not planning on discounting me as a suspect at all, and perhaps I've just made myself look even more suspicious in his eyes.

What a mess.

But at least I'm out of the meeting room now and heading for the elevators. But I can't get there without passing the desk I recognise so well.

My old workstation.

The place I sat when Edwin first became more than my boss.

23

EIGHT MONTHS AGO

'Five o'clock. Finally! Fancy a drink?'

The suggestion of a little liquid refreshment after a long day in the office is normally one I would jump at, but it's not possible for me to accept tonight, so I turn to Bev and let her down gently.

'Sorry. I have to work late,' I say, slightly envious that my colleague is free now to go and spend her evening as she pleases but also feeling a little proud of myself that I'm so important here to have such a heavy workload to keep me occupied.

'Really? That sucks! Just you or anyone else?'

'Just me. Well, Edwin as well.'

Bev's eyebrows shoot up then, but I quickly dispel whatever idea is percolating in her mind.

'We're just working. He asked me to help him go over some of last quarter's figures with him, and as the new finance manager, I can hardly say no, can I?'

'He couldn't do this with you during normal office hours? He had to suggest you do it when everyone else has gone home?'

'He's busy,' I say. 'We all are. This is the only time we could do it.'

Bev looks sceptical, and a second later, she looks worried.

'Just be careful, okay? I love working with you, and I'd hate to come in one morning to find you've had to leave because of a private matter too.'

I get what Bev is hinting at, or rather who she is referring to, and after she has logged off and wished me a good night, I turn back to my desk with thoughts of Monique on my mind. My former colleague, the one who so mysteriously ceased to work here after the recent Christmas party, had been a puzzle I was eager to solve, and ever since learning that she was gone, I'd endeavoured to do just that. Aware that the company line was simply 'left due to a private matter', I realised I wasn't going to get many answers at the office, but who knew what I could get somewhere less formal, like the pub, for example. That's where I ended up after managing to tag along with a few of the workers in Monique's team when they were going for drinks the first Friday night after she had left the company, and once there, I started to get a little more information.

As expected, the hot topic of conversation was Monique and why she had left so suddenly under such a shroud of secrecy, but I started to be enlightened when one of our group proposed a theory, which quickly turned out to have some evidence to back it up. She said that Monique had slept with Edwin that night of the Christmas party, but something had happened between them that shouldn't have, and very quickly, Edwin had made her an offer to not come back to work for him. This theory was told to me by Alexa, a young marketer who was just as pretty as Monique and, therefore, potentially just as much at risk of falling victim to the same thing her former colleague had.

Alexa told me that she had called Monique as soon as she heard she wasn't coming back to work, and whilst initially coy about her reasons, she did hint that Edwin had made her an offer to not come back.

'A financial offer?' I had asked Alexa. 'Why would he do that?'

'Because he'd done something he shouldn't have and was desperate to cover it up,' had come the response.

'Like what?'

'Think about it,' Alexa had said. 'He was drunk after the party and so was Monique, so it might just seem natural that the pair of them fell into bed together. But if you really knew Monique, you'd know one-night stands were not her thing, no matter how much she had to drink.'

'So what are you saying?' I'd asked then, feeling more apprehensive by the second as I'd listened to this.

'I'm not saying anything. Well, nothing that Edwin can find out about and sue me for. But all I will say is think about what I've just told you. Monique did not do one-night stands. The question then is, did Edwin accept that and leave, or did he force her into doing something she didn't want to do?'

It had taken me a few seconds to realise what Alexa was getting at and when I had, I had been horrified.

'You think he hurt her?'

'I'm not confirming or denying anything, and I hope you know this conversation did not happen, okay?'

'Of course. I'm not going to tell anyone what we're talking about. I'm just trying to understand what happened. What do you think he did?'

Alexa had not said a single word after that, but she hadn't needed to. The expression on her face had said it all, and even though I tried to get more out of her, whilst also suggesting that if Monique had been hurt, surely she wouldn't just accept a pay-off to stay away from Edwin and his company, no more was said on the matter, and I had left the pub that night with more questions than answers.

They are questions that still remain to this day, nearly two weeks on, but everybody seems far too afraid to talk about it now and probably for good reason. If Monique won't tell anyone what happened, all that is left is speculation and allegations, and without proof, they are the kinds of things that can see a person not just lose their job but be sued by the person they are accusing.

With all that having already happened, it might seem foolish, possibly even dangerous, for me to willingly accept staying back late in the office with Edwin tonight. If I think he is capable of dangerous acts, I would make sure I was never alone with him, right? But that's the thing. I'm not sure I think he is capable of such an awful crime. Having known him for a few months now, he seems nothing but polite, charming, and caring, and while I'm aware he wouldn't be the first predator to appear normal on the outside, surely I can only go off the evidence I have been witness to and from that, nothing Edwin has done has made me concerned.

The more I think about it, the more I think what Alexa said in the pub that night was just the over-zealous and rather naïve ramblings of a woman who had one too many glasses of wine to drink and missed her old friend,

Monique. Unless Monique actually said she was hurt, and as far as I know, she hadn't, there was no basis for the rumours Alexa was propagating that night, and I almost feel bad for even listening to her tell me about it. If Edwin is innocent, and there seems to be no police officer in town who has any reason to think he isn't, then saying such things about him is truly awful.

Overall, I believe that if Monique had been made to do something she didn't want to do, she wouldn't have just taken hush money from Edwin and left her job. He wouldn't get away with it that easily, right? That makes me think there was actually nothing for him to get away with, and really, Monique's reason for leaving really was just a private matter that had nothing to do with anybody she used to work with.

'Wow, everybody certainly made a quick exit around here. It's literally only just five o'clock.'

I turn around to see Edwin standing behind me, and he's referring to how empty the rest of the office is around us. Looking at the rows of empty desks and chairs, I see we are the last two here.

'Thanks for staying behind. I really appreciate it,' Edwin says then. 'Now, if you're ready, come to my office, and we can get started. The sooner we do that, the sooner we can finish, and I imagine you're as eager to get home as I am.'

Edwin strides away in the direction of his office, leaving me to gather up a few of the things I think I might need for when I rejoin him, namely my notebook, a pen, and the file in which I keep all the information I have on the last quarter's profits. Most of it is stored digitally, but the most salient information can be printed off and kept to hand, and I like to have it because it's handy to peruse whilst sitting in a meeting. It also makes me look more conscientious if I turn up with some paperwork in my possession, and I'm all about looking like a hardworking pro, if I can do.

Walking into Edwin's office, I find him sitting behind his desk, but instead of the second chair in here being opposite him on the other side of that desk, I see he has pulled it around so that it sits right beside him.

'Have a seat, and we'll get started,' he says, and it's obvious I'm supposed to just sit down next to him. It wouldn't normally feel like a big deal but considering we're alone together in the office, it seems like us being so close might be a little too intimate, given the circumstances.

'Chop chop, unless you don't want to go home tonight,' Edwin says with a laugh when he notices that I'm still standing by his desk, and I ease myself into the seat before he begins.

Noticing that I've brought my file of facts and figures with me, he quickly tells me I won't need them because he has all the information he needs to show me on his computer, and after I watch him access a part of the database that I've not been in before, he enters a password, and then I see an unfamiliar spreadsheet on the screen.

'What's this?' I ask him as I lean in a little closer to get a look at the information on the screen, but in the process, I can't help getting closer to the man sitting beside me, too.

'This, Liz, is the real report for the last quarter,' he says, as if that's not a terrifying thing for a finance manager to hear.

'Excuse me?'

'Look, I understand you're going to have lots of questions, but before you begin, let me just explain. This is how I actually have to keep account of the profit and expenditure here because otherwise, there is simply no other way to assure its privacy, and I can't have information leaking out. But I'm allowing you to see this now because I trust you. Okay?'

I'm still concerned, but hearing that I have Edwin's trust is enough to keep me quiet for a moment.

'The thing is, Liz. I don't just trust you as an employee. I trust you much more than that,' Edwin says, and his eyes are off the screen now and on me instead. With his gaze lingering on me, he apologises if he is being inappropriate before he tells me that he wouldn't be showing me this if he didn't see me as more than just a colleague.

'You're a smart, beautiful, and talented woman, Liz,' he says to me with that undeniable smile of his so close to my face. 'And I was wondering if you saw me as more than your boss. I do hope so.'

That was when he put a hand on my leg and left it there for a second.

A short moment after that was when I realised he was looking at my lips, and from there, I realised he was just about to go in for a kiss.

It turned out to be a kiss I was unable to resist.

24

PRESENT DAY

After leaving Phillip and my old office behind, I was planning on going back to work. But whilst driving through town and mulling over everything about the investigator in my mind, I realised I was playing this all wrong. Because he suspects my guilt, Phillip assumes I will not involve the police and tell them he is unnecessarily harassing me. He has been right about that so far, and it has never actually occurred to me that I could do anything other than stay away from anyone wearing a police uniform. A murderer does not willingly enter a police station, or at least not unless they want to get caught out of some strange desire to get attention. But the sudden realisation that I was acting like a guilty person instead of an innocent one is what made me alter my route and end up in the one place Phillip and I never thought I would end up in.

As I wait to be seen by a police officer, I am telling myself this is actually the right thing to do. I have to project innocence, and if I was truly innocent, I'd be stressed out about having an investigator sniffing around and would seek any help I could in changing that situation. So here I am, at the police station, seeking help, and while I feel incredibly nervous about this, I know I have to file a report that says I am being targeted over a crime I did not commit.

While I wait to be seen, I notice that Bev has sent me a message asking me how I am whilst also telling me that she is struggling to sleep, and she now understands why Natasha was in such turmoil before she did what she did. Frustrated at Bev for putting more evidence of us having something to hide out into the world, I tell her that I am fine, urge her to just get on with what she needs to do today, and then I delete her message. I'm not expecting a police officer to ask to see my phone while I am here, but I'll still feel better knowing the message is not just sitting there in my pocket while I'm talking all about how I have done nothing wrong.

The officer who has been assigned the riveting task of speaking to me about my problem is a fair-haired man in his thirties with a strong build and a friendly look in his eyes that instantly helps put me at ease. Following him into the room we will talk in, I am glad I've got this guy and not some grizzled, thirty-year veteran of the force who could read me like an open book and realise that what I am about to say is all lies. However, I'll still have to be on my guard because this officer might be more experienced than he looks.

'So what seems to be the problem?' PC Rose asks me, and after thinking what a nice surname he has, I get straight to the point.

'You're aware of the case of Edwin van Dekker?' I begin with, and PC Rose nods, so I continue. 'Well, he's my former boss, and I knew him quite well.'

'Okay. His disappearance must be quite upsetting for you.'

'Yes, it is. But what's making this whole thing worse for me is that Edwin's son, Phillip, has hired a private investigator who is going around town talking to all sorts of people who knew Edwin as if he thinks one of us had something to do with him going missing.'

'Oh, I see.'

'Yes. But he's not just talking to us. He's following us around. I've caught him stalking me at least twice, which I think is unfair and possibly illegal, considering I have done nothing wrong.'

'Do you have the name of this investigator?' PC Rose asks me then, and I give him the name, not expecting it to get much of a reaction, but it does.

'Ahh, Jack Ferdinand. Yes, I've heard that name before,' the police officer says as he leans back in his seat. 'He has a few unorthodox ways of conducting his business.'

'Unorthodox? It's downright disgraceful! He's been following all sorts of people who used to know Edwin, but I don't know what he's trying to find. Nobody knows what happened to him, and I do not appreciate being made to feel like some sort of criminal.'

I'm laying it on thick, but the man across the table from me seems to be falling for it.

'You say Phillip van Dekker is the one who has hired the investigator? How do you know that?'

'It was a guess,' I reply. 'I figured it was him because who else might be so desperate to find out what happened to Edwin than his own son? While I appreciate that, I do not appreciate his methods, and after I went to his office to see him, he did not deny that he was the one who has got Jack Ferdinand poking around in my business and the business of other people I know. Now, what I want to know is, what are you going to do about it?'

I hold eye contact with PC Rose until he gives me what I hope will be a satisfactory answer. Anything like him telling me he will go and speak to Phillip and get him to call off Jack Ferdinand would be just fine. I think if he was to do that, Phillip would hopefully assume I was really innocent if I'd involved the police and then at least leave me and Bev alone. But that remains to be seen.

'I am willing to speak to Mr van Dekker,' PC Rose tells me. 'And I will definitely make sure that Jack Ferdinand is not doing anything he shouldn't be. But in terms of Phillip hiring Jack to look into matters, there is not much I can do there. Jack is a licensed investigator, and if Phillip wishes to employ his services, then he is free to do so.'

'What? Didn't you listen to what I just said? He is harassing me, and if he's doing it to me, I bet he's doing it to others. You can't just let him bother innocent people. What has happened with Edwin going missing is terrible, but we're all just trying to get on with our lives, and we shouldn't be subjected to this just because we happened to know him in the past.'

'I understand that, but if you have nothing to hide, it shouldn't be too much of a problem, surely?' PC Rose responds with, and that shuts me up.

Is he testing me now? Does he think I might be protesting a little too much about this? Maybe I have overplayed my hand. I knew it was a stupid idea to come here. Oh no, what have I gone and done?

'Look, I'm sorry,' I say, trying to calm down a little bit. 'I just want you to see this from my point of view. I have done nothing wrong, so how do you think it feels to have to keep looking over my shoulder to see if Jack Ferdinand is behind me?'

'I understand, and I will go and speak to Mr Van Dekker and see what I can do about that,' PC Rose says, and while I get that he is just trying to show that he wants to help me, the thought of him sitting down in Phillip's office and having a chat does make me nervous. What if Phillip gives him his theory that I have something to do with his dad's disappearance? What if Phillip has already amassed some evidence, with the help of Jack, and decides to present it to prove that he is justified in his interest in me? That would make my situation worse, not better, but it's too late now because I've already brought this to the attention of the police, and I can't take it back.

Unless…

'Never mind. Forget I said anything. I'll just hope it all goes away on its own,' I say, and I stand up to leave then, but PC Rose assures me that he will take this seriously. Unfortunately, that's what I'm worried about now, and I fear things might be about to get worse.

'I'm innocent,' is all I have left to say, and in my tired, sleep-deprived state, it's actually very easy for me to force a few tears into my eyes, tears that must make what I have just said to PC Rose seem even more true.

As I leave the police station, I squint in the bright sunshine and reach into my handbag for my sunglasses. But as I do that, I see Bev has messaged again, and just like the last time, she has left another ill-advised piece of evidence on my phone.

I really think they're onto us. We need to meet and discuss this again. Maybe we need to take action. What do you think?

What I think is I wish Bev would call me if she has something like this to say, but just before I can ring her myself, I stumble down the last step outside the police station and fall to the floor, groaning loudly as I do. When I look up, I see PC Rose standing over me, and he has already picked up my phone. He wants to know if I'm alright, and I tell him I'm fine before taking back my handset as quickly as I can before he can read the message that's still open on the screen. Thankfully, he hasn't seen it, but I can sense him watching me as I make my way to my car and get in behind the wheel. Only once I have left the car park do I feel better, but not much, and with so many things to stress me out, I wonder how I am ever going to cope.

To think that it wasn't so long ago that I thought I had my life sorted. I was earning good money in a job I liked. I had Bev as my best friend, and the most stressful thing we ever discussed was which bar to get a drink in that weekend. And most of all, I was in love, or at least I thought I was.

But just like everything else, it all went wrong very, very fast.

25

EIGHT MONTHS AGO

Just one quick peek at my digital calendar for the day reminds me that I have a very full schedule, but as the finance manager, I could expect nothing less. My role requires numerous meetings with all the different heads of department to ensure that everything is being run within budget, and then from there, I provide my reports to the man who oversees us all.

It's that man I am on my way to see now because I have a stack of documents to deliver to him that all need to be signed by the end of the day so I can file our latest tax returns. It wasn't always the case that I had a spring in my step so early in the morning, but I certainly have one now as I head for Edwin's office, fuelled not just by the cup of coffee I had on the way into the office a short while ago but by something else much more powerful than caffeine.

Love.

Okay, so it might be a little too soon to be feeling so strongly about my boss, and it's certainly too soon for me to actually tell him the depth of my feelings, but I'm not going to lie to myself. I have fallen for Edwin, hook, line, and sinker, and because of that, it's getting increasingly difficult to keep my private life separate from my professional one. I get a perfect example of that when no sooner have I entered Edwin's office then he pulls me aside and plants his lips on mine.

The serious business professional in me melts away in an instant, and I do not even bother fighting it, instead kissing Edwin back whilst being amazed that I could ever be this happy at nine o'clock on a Monday morning.

As our lips finally part, I see Edwin's warm eyes and dazzling smile, and if it wasn't for the pile of paperwork in my hands to remind me, I'd completely forget what I came in here for. Fortunately, I compose myself enough to tell him that I require his signature, and after handing him the papers, I plan to walk out of his office before I have another moment that would be best saved for when we're alone together at his apartment. But just before I can leave, Edwin reaches out and grabs my hand, and then he pulls me in for another kiss, and just as before, I'm powerless to prevent it.

This is how it has been recently. Edwin and I stealing little moments of affection in amongst our busy day while all our colleagues are only a few yards away on the other side of his office door. Of course, we're far more affectionate after office hours, but we certainly don't waste the forty hours a week we are in this building either, although we have stopped short of having sex in here. I drew the line at that, even though Edwin was more than keen to, because that felt like taking things a little too far. But it was still a tough thing to turn down, and I'm not entirely convinced I'll be able to resist it forever.

'I have to get back to work,' I say, after our second kiss has ended. 'And you have an interview to conduct.'

'You're right,' Edwin says whilst rolling his eyes. 'Damn our work here. Why must it always come in between us?'

'Because we both need the money,' I say with a laugh, before reminding Edwin about his need to sign those papers today and then walking out of his office. It does feel good to know that I have left him wanting more because I certainly don't want him to start getting bored of me, not that he has shown any signs that such a thing might happen. He's been incredibly attentive with me since we became close, not just physically but emotionally too, and we've spent just as much time having long conversations over lovely meals in restaurants as we have falling into each other's arms. That's important to me because I don't just want to feel like I am just somebody he is having a brief fling with. I really want this relationship to go somewhere, and it will get to that somewhere much quicker if we're talking as well as kissing.

Returning to my desk, I believe I have composed myself enough after my little rendezvous in Edwin's office to not have anybody know that I have just been smooching with the boss. However, the way Bev looks at me as I retake my seat suggests she knows exactly what I have just been up to, and based on the things she has been saying to me recently, I have no doubts that she does. But she doesn't say anything this time, leaving it at just a sceptical expression for now, which I appreciate because I don't have time today for another one of her lectures.

It's no secret that Bev thinks me getting closer to Edwin is a very bad idea, and while I'm confident that no one else in this office knows the true extent of my relationship with the boss, Bev certainly does. She can read me like a book, not just because we sit beside each other five days a week but because we talk and message all the time outside of work, and while that's nice, the downside is she can easily tell when I'm lying. That's why she shook her head at me recently when she asked me if I was sleeping with Edwin and I told her no.

She didn't buy it.

And she was worried for me.

But as I have also told her, I am not Monique, nor am I any of the other women who might have worked here once before but left prematurely after they may or may not have become too involved with Edwin. I believe the reasons for those people leaving this company came down to something else beyond Edwin, and I am not buying into any of the rumours at all. If I honestly believed Monique had been hurt by the man I am currently with, then there is obviously no way I would have allowed myself to get close to him, but I do not. It's a shame Bev doesn't share the same high opinion of Edwin that I have of him, but I can't do much to change other people's minds, and I certainly don't have time to try and change that today.

Turning away from Bev and her silent judgement of me, I focus on the task at hand, which today is all about making various checks and balances of the company's accounts, more specifically, doing a quick audit of supplier invoices to make sure everything is as it should be. I do this once a month just to keep on top of it and also to make sure there are no nasty surprises should we ever get audited by a third party because no accountant likes surprises. However, surprises have been a part of my new role here since I accepted it, and I'm not just talking about the surprise of ending up sleeping with the boss.

I'm talking about the secret spreadsheets he showed me in his office last week, which was also the night we started to become more than just colleagues.

It's never nice for an accountant to learn that there are other numbers beyond the ones they've already seen and analysed, but that was exactly what Edwin had shown me, and I was worried at first. However, he quickly dispelled those worries by explaining why he had a need for secrecy and when he did, I was flattered to have been allowed in on that secret.

Edwin told me that he liked to keep certain things fully under his control without all his employees knowing about them, but as the finance manager, I was qualified to be shown things no one else at the company knew about. Things like income from bigger suppliers I wasn't even aware of, as well as outgoings on things I didn't know about before. Edwin told me that when he had been starting out in business, his mentor had advised him to keep such things secret so not every single facet of his business was laid bare for anybody to see, and I suppose that made sense. However, I did tell him that it was all well and good keeping secrets from his employees, but there could be absolutely no secrets when it came to the government and those he owed his taxes to.

Edwin assured me that there was not, and after that, we had got to work, although not before he had sworn me to secrecy about what he was showing me. I agreed, of course, because he's the boss, and other than me and him, nobody else at this company needs to see these figures. What I do wish is that I could understand them a little better, because the more time I spend looking into them, the more questions I have.

They are questions that Edwin has been a little vague in answering so far, but there has been no rush quite yet because it's still a while off before we file the returns for the current quarter. But he'll have to be far more transparent when it comes to the time for that, and he assures me that he will. Or at least his version of assuring me is to just kiss me again and tell me how beautiful I am.

But I'm not stupid, and while I'm loving all the extra attention I'm getting from my boss, I'm not going to let it come between me doing a good job here. I have a professional reputation to uphold, so I will ensure all the finances are in order at this company without compromising a thing.

As I play around with the numbers on my screen and try to reconcile them, I hear Edwin across the office and turn to see who he is talking to. When I do, I see a very attractive woman in her late twenties shaking his hand, and I realise she must be who he is interviewing this morning.

'Oh, she's pretty,' Bev says as she sees her too. 'Better watch your back.'

'What's that supposed to mean?' I ask, but Bev doesn't answer that, telling me not to mind and going back to her own work. But I don't go back to mine because I'm keeping my eyes on the woman Edwin is showing into the meeting room now, and just before the door closes and they have full privacy, I see him flash her the smile I thought he mainly reserved for me.

At the time, I thought that woman might end up being a potential love rival.

But I was very wrong.

What she ended up being was my partner in crime because that was the first day I ever laid eyes on Natasha.

26

PRESENT DAY

'Graveyards are just so depressing, aren't they?' Bev says to me as we make our way past the rows of headstones in search of the one we have come to visit today.

'I don't think they're meant to be fun places,' I reply, not trying to be witty, just stating a fact. There really is nothing fun about a setting like this.

A person's final resting place. The home of the dead.

And now the home of our late friend, Natasha.

We find her headstone in a more maintained part of the graveyard, and there are plenty of visible signs that the burial here has been more recent than many of the others that surround it. The flowers are fresher, the soil is still showing signs of being disturbed, and the headstone itself looks clean and crisp as opposed to some of the others around here that look much more dated. This cemetery houses graves that date back over a hundred years, but the one we are looking at now is not even a week old.

I'm not quite sure what to say at this juncture, so I just let my actions do the talking for me and crouch down in order to be able to place the bouquet of flowers I brought with me beside the headstone. Bev is just as lost for words, and after putting down her own flowers, the pair of us stand back and share a quiet moment of reflection. But, as always with my best friend, it's not long until she has something to share.

'At least that bastard doesn't have this,' she says, referring to our old boss with her usual level of affection. 'No official burial for him means nowhere for people to leave flowers or come and pay their respects, and that's just what he deserves. I like that he's still rotting at the bottom of that canal.'

I know Bev has never liked Edwin, so her level of vitriol towards him and his experience in the afterlife is not surprising, and I do share many of the same sentiments. But I always find it a little tougher than her to voice them quite so earnestly because it's still not that long ago when I was in love with him.

The thought of all the times he ran his hands over my body in the past still sends a shiver down my spine, and I'll always hate how much I was a fool for falling for him, just as much as I hate him for what he did to me and others. It's never nice to know you loved an evil man, but I did it, and while I feel like I redeemed myself by ultimately killing him, I still can't erase that portion of my life where I harboured hopes of settling down with Edwin and maybe even having a child with him.

'I wonder what she would be doing today if she was still here,' Bev says, returning my thoughts to Natasha, a person who is far more deserving of my contemplation. 'You know, assuming she was a healthy, vibrant woman who had never encountered Edwin and, therefore, had no reason to fall into a depression and end up locking herself away at home all day and feeling suicidal.'

'I don't know,' I say, and I expect to leave it at that because none of us can predict such things as the life of another person. But Bev has a good go at it.

'I bet she'd have been thriving,' she says. 'I bet she'd have a great job at a big company with a boss who respects her and treats her right. She might also have met a nice man by now, someone she might have gotten engaged to one day. Kids probably would have been on the way at some point, and she would have made a great mum, don't you think? Instead, she's lying here, six feet underground, and all that future happiness will never exist now.'

I don't need Bev to remind me of what Natasha's death has deprived the world of because she was a vibrant, wonderful woman, or at least she was when she turned up at the offices of Van Dekker Logistics for her interview with Edwin. Yet Bev seems intent on reminding me of all this, and then she explains why.

'I'm telling you this because I want you to think about what it feels like to stand here should you ever start having doubts about what we did.'

'Doubts? What are you talking about?'

'A guilty conscience can be a devastating thing. You might not think it now, but in years to come, you might start to feel bad about what you did to Edwin. But don't, and if you do, just come here and remember what he did to her.'

'I don't have a guilty conscience,' I insist, but Bev believes that about as much as she believed me back when I used to tell her that nothing was going on between me and Edwin in the office.

'I'm just saying that we have many years ahead of us, or at least I hope we do, so we can't afford any slip-ups.'

'Slip-ups? I'm not the one who has been sending text messages giving ourselves away!' I cry loudly, though there is no one else around in this graveyard to hear me, beyond the dead, of course, but they can't eavesdrop, or at least I don't think they can. 'How many times have I had to tell you not to text me saying you're worried about getting caught and asking if the private investigator is going to catch us out?'

'Excuse me for being worried about getting caught! I'm entitled to not want to spend the rest of my life in prison!' Bev retorts.

'So am I, but you panicking as much as you have been recently is not helping things!'

'I haven't been panicking. I just need reassuring.'

'And I have reassured you, have I not?'

'I suppose so.'

'Well, there you go then.'

I shrug at Bev and allow her to relax a little bit. But, like me, she hasn't felt relaxed for a while, and she's only been even jumpier since I told her about what I did the other day.

As I expected, Bev was not at all happy about the fact that I went to talk to the police about Phillip and the private investigator he had put on us. She immediately panicked and feared I had just made a terrible mistake, one that would lead to Phillip, Jack, and the police paying us more attention, not less. But I assured her it was a very calculated move, and so far, I appear to have been proven right. As he said he would, PC Rose has spoken to Phillip and Jack and made sure their interest in me, Bev, and anybody else is not crossing the lines of legality. Because neither of those two men were able to provide any shred of evidence that those they were looking into had done anything to make Edwin disappear, PC Rose has instructed them to leave us all alone, and, so far, they have done just that.

I have not seen Jack following me at all since my first conversation with PC Rose, and I can only assume Phillip has told him to cool off. Of course, I thanked PC Rose after he had given me this update, and now I feel assured this matter is at rest. Bev is not so convinced, but as I have said to her many times over the last few days, there was a problem, but I dealt with it, and while there may be other problems in the future, we have at least tackled the most pressing one.

'You know, I find it a little offensive that you would feel like you have to remind me of the woman Natasha could have been to stop me ever regretting killing Edwin,' I say to my friend as we remain standing by the grave. 'I will never forget what he did to her. Just like I'll never forget what he did to you.'

My reference to Bev's own suffering at the hands of Edwin draws a sharp intake of breath from the woman beside me because, for all her outside strength and bluster, I know Bev is still healing on the inside from what she went through herself.

'We're a team, and we're in this together,' I say, taking Bev's hand and giving it a squeeze. 'We couldn't save Natasha, but we can save each other, okay?'

Bev squeezes my hand back and nods her head, and a moment later, the pair of us leave the resting place of our late friend and head back to our cars.

If only these headstones could talk, they would have an interesting story to tell about the two women who just visited here. As it is, the only ones who can tell our story are us, and that's the way we need to try and keep it.

27

SEVEN MONTHS AGO

As the days have gone by, my days at the office have become more difficult. I was expecting an increase in both workload and difficulty when I accepted the promotion to become the finance manager, but as I've been exploring the depths of Edwin's accounts and the covert way in which he appears to have been storing some of his company's income, it's become clear there is a lot to do.

I've never been shy of hard work, but I have been shy of doing any work that I feared might start straying into murky waters, or even the kind that may be downright illegal. Having raised my concerns with Edwin that there seemed to be an awfully large amount of income previously unaccounted for, he told me that I was mistaken and that I would see that everything was fine once I'd fully worked through all the figures. But the problem is, the more I do for him, the more I worry that I'm unravelling a problem that is far bigger than he seems to think it is.

Unpaid tax bills. Hidden income. Overinflated invoices. Grey areas where there should be clear, documented paperwork.

It all came to a head yesterday when, after yet another afternoon of tying myself in knots trying to decipher all of Edwin's accounts, I demanded a meeting with him in his office so I could clearly voice all my concerns for the record. I had tried to include Amy from

HR in the meeting, not simply to cover myself but to show how seriously I was taking matters and my desire to ensure this company was diligently doing everything expected of it, should we ever be questioned in future. But when Amy had failed to show up for the meeting, Edwin had inexplicably told me he had not seen any need for her presence and had cancelled her attendance himself. Then, whilst I was launching into my well-rehearsed speech about the need for this company to do a far better job of reporting its various incomings and outgoings, Edwin did something entirely unprofessional.

He stopped me from talking by kissing me.

Okay, so I've been guilty of behaving inappropriately around the office ever since my romance with Edwin began but only in the form of a few stolen moments here and there between us, in and around work. I'd never just come right out and kiss him in the middle of an important meeting, especially not when he was halfway through a sentence. But Edwin had no qualms about doing such a thing, and after I had pulled back from him and asked him what he was doing, he had simply told me that he had been unable to resist and that I looked gorgeous that day.

While a younger, more naive version of me might have bought that and just been flattered at the compliment and attention, the more experienced me saw it for what it clearly was, and that was a distraction tool to stop me talking about a very awkward subject. Edwin would rather try and be intimate with me instead of acknowledging that there are some worrying discrepancies in his company's accounts, discrepancies that could lead to all manner of nasty surprises for this company if they aren't rectified soon.

Fines. Restrictions. Maybe even criminal charges. Yet here was the manager of that company acting like an impulsive teenager, thinking a quick snog was all that mattered in life.

To show my displeasure at how he had acted, I had voiced a concern to him that I had been harbouring for a little while by that point, and it was one that made me angry and upset to think about in equal measure.

I asked him if he was simply pretending to like me so that I would help him cover up any wrongdoing within his organisation.

Edwin had appeared shocked by my suggestion, before denying that was the case at all, but after again failing to listen to my concerns, he did little to put my mind at ease. All he did do was take my hand, tell me he didn't want any confusion over the accounts to come between what we had and that he would take a look at things himself, and then we could discuss the matter together again shortly.

I'd accepted that answer at the time and left his office, though I didn't feel particularly good about it, and that's still the same way I feel today as I sit at my desk and try not to give into my paranoid thoughts about what the potentially dodgy accounts here could mean for me in my position as finance manager.

The last thing I would want is for somebody to think I was complicit in the unorthodox and potentially illegal accounting, but how would it look to an outsider if I was in charge of those accounts? I'd seem just as guilty as Edwin. He assures me there is nothing to worry about and that he would never put me in a position where I could get into trouble for anything he had done himself, but can I really trust him? I thought I could, at one time, but now I'm not so sure, and my confidence is not helped by my fear that he is faking his personal interest in me just to keep me on his side. The truth is, with some of the things I am discovering in his accounts, I should already be raising these concerns with other people. But I haven't done that yet, and Edwin must know it's because I have feelings for him and would, therefore, try to protect him, if necessary.

But for how long? If he is using me, then I have been played for a fool, and I would deserve to get my own back on him. But acknowledging such a thing would also mean Bev was right, and I have been an idiot to get involved with him. It might also mean career suicide because not only would Edwin most likely terminate my employment here if I referred him to any financial board, but would any future employers I might have really believe me when I tell them I had no idea what Edwin was doing? Or would they err on the side of caution and decide that rather than hire me, they would just go with another candidate, one who had no links to a company that had been found to be fraudulently reporting its accounts?

What a mess. I can't believe I'm in this position. But maybe I have no one to blame but myself.

Turning to look at the desk next to me, I wish Bev was in her usual seat because I sure could do with seeing a friendly face and having a brief chat about something other than work to try and take my mind off things for a moment. But she is not here today, and, so far, I am not exactly sure what the reason is for her absence. I presumed she was sick, so I sent her a message to ask if she was okay, but I have received no response yet. After that, I went and spoke to Amy because I figured Bev would tell HR why she wasn't in today, right? But there were no answers there either because Amy just told me that there was a matter being looked into, and we would know more soon. I demanded to know what the matter was but was told it was private for now, which immediately set alarm bells ringing in my head because it was a "private matter" that spelt the end of Monique's time here at this company.

Seeing Monique go was one thing but to lose Bev as a colleague would be something else because she is my best friend in the office, and I must spend at least half of every day here either talking to her myself or listening to her talking to somebody else down the phone. I need her around, especially now when I've got so much on my mind about Edwin, but she is nowhere to be seen, and from the vibe I got in Amy's office, it doesn't sound like she will be back either.

There is a new colleague here who is friendly, though, and as I see Natasha pass my desk, I give her a smile, and we chat briefly for a few minutes. She makes a few jokey references to the late night we had after work the other evening whilst I beg her not to remind me because I was very drunk, and I spent the preceding twenty-four hours recovering from said night. As she leaves my desk, I think about how I felt jealous of her when I first saw her and even worried she might be a threat to come between me and Edwin, though now I do not see her that way at all. Despite her stunning good looks, she does not carry herself in a way that would make other females despise her. She is very sweet, loves self-deprecating humour, and, from what I can tell since she has been here, is simply keen to just do a good job at work.

She's already become a friend, but whilst that's nice, she's not Bev, and her absence is still keenly felt here today, so much so that I'm planning to go and see Bev as soon as the clock hits five and I can leave. Once it does, I turn off my computer and get up from my desk, grabbing my coat from the back of my chair and preparing to make a swift exit. But just before I can do that, Edwin approaches me and tells me he needs me to work later tonight.

'No can do, sorry. I have plans,' I say, not usually one to defy the wishes of any of my bosses, but I'm not in the mood for extra work today, particularly after this boss is the reason for my current mood.

Edwin seems surprised by my response, before telling me that it was less of a question and more of an order, though I still decide to defy him and say I need to leave. That's when Edwin's demeanour darkens, and as the last of my colleagues around the office leave, he steps closer to me and lowers his voice.

'Don't be silly, Liz. I treat you well here, don't I? I'd say you're one of the best-paid finance managers around, certainly in this town. Is it too much to ask for me to need you to stay back late tonight?'

'Yes, I'm paid well, and I appreciate that, but what I don't appreciate is you giving me last-second orders to work late when I've got plans for this evening that I cannot cancel,' I reply, standing my ground. 'I also don't appreciate you not listening to what I had to say in the meeting I tried to arrange with you. And finally, I don't appreciate not being told what has happened to Bev because, as one of my close colleagues, I deserve to know where she is and why she wasn't at work today.'

Edwin seems surprised, possibly even a little impressed by my show of strength, but quickly returns to his darker side.

'Fine. You're right. Come into my office, and I'll tell you everything you want to know. Finances. Bev. Monique. You name it, I'll answer all your questions.'

It sounds good, but there's something in Edwin's eyes that makes me sense he is not being as sincere as he might want to seem, and I get the strange feeling that whatever I do next, I should not go into his office with him, especially when everyone else has left the office now. That's why, after telling him I will stay back, I pretend to need to visit the bathroom before we begin. He says he will see me in his office in just a moment and walks away, but as soon as he has, I make a quick dash for the elevator and get the hell out of the office as quickly as I can. Once out, I hail a taxi and instruct the driver to take me to 52 Birchwood Close, which is Bev's address, and we make quick progress through town until we get there ten minutes later.

Rushing to the front door after paying the driver, I knock on it several times whilst wondering if I am going to get an answer from within. But I do, and after the door is unlocked, I get to see the person inside the house, though when I do, I get a shock.

It's Bev, but never as I have seen her before.

She looks exhausted. She has been crying. She might even be drunk.

What the hell has happened to her?

It takes half an hour and a lot of tears before she tells me. When she does, she begins with only one word.

'Edwin.'

28

PRESENT DAY

After saying goodbye to Bev at the gates to the graveyard, I have come home to try and have a somewhat normal evening. But having had to remind Bev that I would always be on her side and would never forget what Edwin had done, not only to Natasha but to her too, it is not so easy to remove some uncomfortable memories from my mind.

The night I went to Bev's house, only to find her upset and drunk, is one I will never forget because it was that, rather than anything else, that really was the catalyst for what eventually ended up happening with Edwin. Things got worse after that night, but seeing Bev in such a state was the first moment I truly had my eyes opened to the danger that Edwin posed to women, and as such, things were never the same again.

After I had refused to leave Bev's house until she gave me an explanation as to why she was upset and why she had not been at work, I had managed to get myself inside her house and continue urging my friend to open up to me. It took a while, but eventually, as we had sat beside each other on her sofa, Bev told me what had happened, and it had begun with the name of the man I already had plenty of concerns about.

'Edwin.'

'What about him? He did this to you?'

Bev had taken a deep breath before starting from the beginning.

'I was out for a drink last night with a friend from school,' Bev had begun, stifling sobs whilst also picking up a glass of red wine that sat beside an almost-empty bottle. 'We catch up once a month and always go to the same pub. We usually stay out until around ten, then I get a taxi home. But last night was different.'

I'd gathered that night must have been different, but I said nothing and had allowed her to go on.

'It was just after ten, and I was getting ready to leave when he walked into the pub.'

'Who?'

'Edwin.'

'What was he doing there?'

'I don't know. I'd never seen him in that pub before, but when he saw me, he seemed happy and offered to buy me a drink. I told him I was going home, but he insisted, and stupidly, because I'd already had a few to drink, I gave in and agreed.'

'So what happened?'

'We sat down and had our drink. Edwin was in a good mood. He told me about how he had just been out with a client and closed some big deal with him. He was clearly drunk himself, but I just sipped my drink and listened enough to be polite. The truth is, I didn't really have to say much because Edwin was doing all the talking.'

'Okay, so then what happened?'

'He wanted to buy me another drink, but I told him no and said I wanted to get back because I had a busy day at work tomorrow. I figured reminding him that I was one of his employees with duties to fulfil for him might make him happier about me leaving. But he just said he better be getting home too, so he left the pub with me.'

'Okay,' I had said, nervous as to where this was going.

'I had ordered a taxi on my phone, but the driver cancelled on me at the last minute, and I was struggling to find another one,' Bev went on. 'That's when Edwin propositioned me.'

'What?'

'He told me that I was beautiful and that while he knew he had a bit of a reputation for being a ladies' man around the office, I was really the only one he had wanted to be with.'

I had felt sick at hearing he had said such a thing because obviously, at that time, he was supposed to be in a relationship with me, although it's now a relationship that, in hindsight, was a complete joke. No, a joke would be funny. The right word to describe our relationship would be toxic, and that is correct because it ended up poisoning us both.

'Then he tried to kiss me,' Bev had said, her eyes having appeared both teary and vacant at the same time. 'I pushed him away and told him that I wasn't interested in him like that and that our previous kiss a while ago had been a mistake. But he told me not to be a tease and tried again, so I had to get more forceful. I slapped him and then told him what I really thought of him.'

'What did you say?'

'I told him about how I knew every woman who ever got close to him seemed to end up worse off than before. I told him that I knew he was dangerous and that he should stay away from me or I would go to the police. He laughed at that and said he had done nothing wrong and even if he had, I had no evidence, which was true. But at least he had stopped trying to be physical with me. Or so I thought.'

I'd waited with bated breath to hear the next part of Bev's sorry story.

'He forced himself on me then, but he was firmer than the first time. He didn't just try and kiss me. He pushed me against a wall. I screamed and if I hadn't been able to knee him between his legs, I dread to think what would have happened.'

It had been a sickening thing to hear, and I had gasped as Bev had continued to recount her night with Edwin.

'After I'd kneed him, he stepped back and I was able to get away. I ran all the way home.'

That explained why she was upset, but what it didn't explain was how Edwin had been at work that day and seemingly walking free when he should have surely been at a police station being questioned over this.

'Please tell me you've gone to the police about this,' I had said, but I was already pretty confident what the answer was there, based on how Edwin seemed fine at the office that next day whilst Bev had been struggling when I'd gone to see her.

After shaking her head, Bev had explained what had happened next.

'I got home and just wanted to go to bed,' she had told me.

'But Bev! You should have reported him,' I had cried, but it had already been too late for that.

'I know! I just wasn't thinking straight. I was in shock. I still am!'

I'd felt so sorry for my friend at that moment that I stopped berating her for not doing the right thing and going to the police because the truth was, after an experience like that, there was no right thing to do. She had just done what she had needed to do to get through those awful first few minutes, and I could never blame her for that.

'So you didn't come into work today,' I had said. 'Edwin must know why. What does he think? That you'll just stay away, and he'll get away with this?'

Bev had shaken her head at my summary because she knew better.

'After I'd got out of the shower last night, I heard a knock at the door. I wasn't going to answer it because it was late, and I was scared it was Edwin. But it wasn't. It was Amy.'

Hearing our HR manager had turned up at Bev's house had been yet another surprise.

'What the hell was she doing coming to see you?'

'What do you think?' Bev had asked. 'Edwin had obviously contacted her and told her she needed to pay me a visit to sort out what had happened.'

'Sort it out? There is no way to sort it out,' I had cried, before realising that Bev had looked a little sheepish. 'Is there?'

'I'd opened the door to hear what Amy had to say and when I did, she told me she heard there had been a misunderstanding with Edwin.'

'A misunderstanding? That's not what happened at all!'

'I told her that, but she kept calm and said she was aware I was upset and passed on that Edwin was also upset about what had happened.'

'He was upset? You've got to be kidding me.'

Bev had clearly not been kidding and went on to further prove just how serious it all was.

'Amy said that because he felt bad, Edwin was willing to offer me something by way of an apology. He accepted that I wouldn't want to return to work for him, but he was willing to give me something to make up for that. Six months' wages upfront and a glowing reference for my next employer, as long as I didn't tell anybody what had happened.'

'Wait, what? He offered you hush money? Please tell me you didn't take it!'

'Of course not. I said no and told Amy to leave and said that Edwin would be hearing from the police. But Amy seemed prepared for that because she then came back with a counteroffer. She upped it to a year's wages upfront and then said Edwin would pay off whatever I had left on my car payments too.'

'But it's just money! He can't go around hurting people and then expect to just pay them to be silent,' I had cried, but Bev had simply looked sorry before telling me that she had done the unthinkable.

She had accepted the money.

'No,' was all I had been able to say to that before I had urged Bev to reconsider and still go to the police. But it was already too late for that.

'I signed an NDA,' she had confessed. 'I can't break that now.'

'An NDA? Amy had one with her? Oh my God, how many times has he done this before?'

I had almost been as sick at the thought of what Amy had done as I had been about what Edwin had done because it sounded like she was enabling her boss to get away with things like this. It also made much more sense of what had happened to Monique too. She must have done the same thing as Bev had.

I'd held Bev as she had cried then, whilst trying to tell her that she didn't have to honour the contract she had signed and that she could still make Edwin pay for what he had done, but she wouldn't listen to me. She refused to go to the police, and when I said I would do it for her, she begged me not to until I had no choice but to do what she wished.

That was a very dark night, and the memory of it will stay with me until the day I die. But Bev moved on from it much better than I did. She got on with her life, spending some of the money she had got from Edwin, whilst finding another job, and whilst it could never make up for what she went through, she seemed like she was dealing with it.

But she was just papering over the cracks, and we both knew it. We also both knew Edwin was likely to do something like that again, but what could we do about it?

I had an idea.

I was going to catch him out and expose him for the man he really was.

I was going to destroy him before he could destroy anybody else.

Or so I thought.

As it would turn out, I was already well on the path to my own destruction by then.

29

SEVEN MONTHS AGO

With Bev's telling of her sorry story still ringing in my ears after hearing it the previous night, I have returned to the office with a grim determination to do something I possibly should have done already by now.

Expose Edwin.

However, I'm aware it's going to be tough to catch a man like him in terms of his crimes towards people like Bev, Monique, and any other former employee he might have mistreated, what with his armoury of hush money and NDAs at his disposal. But I believe they are not the only crimes he has committed, and with full access to Edwin's company finances, I know I can garner him a lot of legal attention that way instead. All I need to do is get to my desk, download all of the secretive spreadsheets onto the USB drive in my pocket, and then deliver them to somebody with a keen interest in making sure British companies are operating fairly and, most importantly, paying the tax they owe.

The spreadsheet that holds all of Edwin's dodgy accounts is password protected, but he has trusted me with that password, and that is going to be his downfall. He'd never suspect that I would betray him, not with him seeing me as some lovesick puppy eager to do anything to appease him and keep him close to me. He must think he is so clever, making me fall for him like I did so he could use me, but my eyes have been fully opened now, and it's time to redeem myself.

It's time to bring down Edwin van Dekker once and for all.

My plan is to avoid Edwin as best I can whilst in the office this morning because after hearing all about his despicable actions towards Bev, I'm not sure I'll be able to keep my feelings towards him private, if I am forced to interact with him. Fortunately, my plan seems to be going well because I make it through the office and to my desk without encountering my boss, and I am hoping he will be busy in meetings for the next hour or so, leaving me with ample time to take as much evidence off the company hard drive as I can and be gone before he is any the wiser.

Confident that my acting as a whistleblower is the best way to destroy Edwin's reputation, I'm fully prepared to have to sit and be interviewed by police about what my roles and responsibilities were here, as well as attend any court hearings, if necessary. Whatever it takes to see Edwin's financial crimes unravelled and the man responsible for them severely punished. Losing his company, perhaps the only thing he actually cares about other than himself, will be a given, along with losing most of his wealth, but I'm also hoping there will be a substantial prison sentence coming his way too, and there's almost a better chance of him being severely punished for falsifying accounts than there is for hurting others in this country, sadly enough.

White-collar crime always seems to be treated the most harshly, while dangerous criminals roam the streets daily with not so much as a slap on the wrist. As it is, Edwin falls into both categories, so he'll surely get his comeuppance either way, and I'll be the one to expedite it.

With thoughts of Bev firmly in my mind, I navigate my way to the part of the internal database where I'll find the spreadsheet that is password-protected. Then I enter the password and press ENTER, the USB drive in my hands and ready to be plugged into this computer to download all manner of incriminating things.

But there's an unexpected problem.

My password is incorrect.

Trying it again, I assume I just mistyped a letter, but I get the same result. The password is not working, and it's only on the third try that I start to realise I'm not getting it wrong.

The password has been changed.

Before I can figure out what might have happened, I hear a voice behind me asking me to step away from my computer. When I turn around, I see it is Amy, and she looks very serious.

'What's going on?' I ask her, but she just repeats her order and not only that but after spotting the USB drive in my hands, she asks me to hand it over. When I decline, she tells me not to make this any more difficult than it has to be.

'Amy, what are you talking about?' I try again, but then I get some form of an answer when I look over the HR manager's shoulder and see Edwin watching me. His arms are crossed, and he is not smiling, instead looking like he is carrying the sort of grim determination I entered here with a moment ago.

Getting up out of my chair, I decide to hand the USB drive to Amy simply because I haven't actually used it yet, so there is nothing I can get in trouble for having on there anyway. Then I follow her as she leads me to Edwin, and ignoring some of the pensive looks from my colleagues seated around me, I walk into the meeting room. Once there, Edwin asks if Amy will give us both a moment alone.

Like the loyal lapdog she seems to be, Amy does as she is told, and once she has left and closed the door behind her, Edwin turns to me and shakes his head.

'Oh, Liz. I really thought we had something special, you and I.'

'What's happening?' I ask, noticing a solitary piece of paper and a pen on the table between us.

'I'm sorry, but I'm going to have to let you go. I simply can't trust you anymore.'

'Let me go? What? You're firing me?'

'I wouldn't put it that bluntly. In fact, I think once you've had a chance to consider my offer, you will see that I am actually taking good care of you. Here, have a look for yourself.'

Edwin picks up the piece of paper and holds it out for me to take, and I very reluctantly do so. Examining it, I see that it seems to be some kind of financial offer, and the figure in question is considerable. But I also know better than to just accept such a thing from a man like Edwin.

'You're paying me off? What for? Because I know all about those secret accounts you have?'

'That's not all you know, is it?'

'What?'

'After you so quickly left the office last night when we were supposed to be having a meeting, I followed you and saw that you went straight to Bev's.'

'You followed me?'

'I wonder what it was you were talking about inside her house? I imagine she was telling you all sorts of lies about me. The question is, did you believe her?'

'Lies? I think she was telling me the truth! You hurt her!'

'That's a strong allegation. What proof do you have?'

'How about her story? That's plenty of proof.'

'No, it's not, especially when she already signed an agreement preventing her from talking to the police about it.'

'But I haven't signed anything,' I remind him, and it feels good to have some power here, not that Edwin seems perturbed in the slightest.

'Not yet,' he says calmly. 'But you will if you know what's best for you. It's either that or you go to prison, and I'm pretty sure you don't want that, am I right?'

'Prison? What are you talking about?'

'Oh, come on, Liz. It's not that difficult. As my finance manager, who do you think I'll blame if the police come to me and tell me that my company has fraudulent accounts? I'd point them in your direction and tell them that you had full reign over my finances. Sure, I might not get away with it all completely, but you sure as hell will be dragged down with me. Forget losing this job - you'll have a criminal record and will most likely never work again.'

'Nice try, but they'll believe me, not you,' I say defiantly. 'This is your company. I was just an employee. You oversee everything - you can't just blame things on your staff.'

'I guess that's a risk you're going to have to take then,' Edwin says with a smirk. 'But I'd go and get yourself a lawyer as quickly as you can if I were you because with the mountain of evidence that I'm going to bring down on you, you'll need a damn good one.'

'Evidence? What evidence?'

'Oh, I don't know. How about all the secret payments that have left my company and gone into an account registered to your name.'

'What are you talking about?'

'Did you really think I'd let you in on my little secret regarding my finances here and not give myself a back-up option? I've framed you, Liz, plain and simple. I've funnelled several sums of money out of this company, not huge amounts, but enough, and if the police investigate, it will look like you have been embezzling from me.'

I can't believe this! He's set me up in case I ever turned against him?

'I'm innocent! I've done nothing wrong!' I cry, but Edwin just rolls his eyes.

'Yeah, like it's that simple,' he says with a smirk. 'Why not put it to the test then? Go to the police. Tell them you think I'm dodgy and let them come here. I'd be more than happy to give them access to everything, but, of course, I've made it look like you were fiddling the figures, not me.'

'You can't get away with this.'

'I've been getting away with it for years,' Edwin says with a laugh. 'What's really funny is you thinking you can come in here with your USB drive and try and take some evidence. So what? You can help get some form of justice for your friend? Trust me, she isn't worth it. Nothing is worth you going to prison. So stop wasting time and sign that NDA, and then we can get you paid, okay?'

I look back at the figure on the piece of paper, and while it is sizeable, easily enough to help me pay my mortgage for the next couple of years and still have a little left over for a holiday or two, I cannot comprehend doing what this man wants me to do. To sign this would not only ensure he beats me but further condemn Bev, Monique, and any other women he has hurt, to defeat too.

'No, I won't do it,' I say before changing tact. 'I thought we had something special. I thought you loved me.'

'Well, now you know the truth,' Edwin says without skipping a beat. 'Here, take this pen. I think you're going to need it.'

He holds out the pen towards me, clearly keen for me to use it to sign the paperwork and then leave him and his company alone forever.

It's at that moment that I curse myself for not being prepared for something like this. Naively, I thought I could bring down a man as powerful as Edwin by just strolling in here and taking whatever evidence I needed from the database, but I should have known it wouldn't be that easy. Why didn't I have a Plan B? If only I was secretly recording this conversation, then I'd have everything that I would need to destroy him. But I haven't done that, and now I seem to be running out of options.

It's either sign this piece of paper or have the police investigate me, and based on what Edwin has said, he's certainly had his Plan B in place.

I'm screwed.

He's played me.

And now I have no choice.

I have to take the pen and sign this.

But as I do, I think to myself that while he has won the battle, I will still find a way to win the war. I have enough money here to tide me over until I can figure something else out, and as I walk out of the meeting room and go to gather my things from my desk, I am already scanning my brain for ideas as to how I could get back at Edwin some other way. Little did I know it but the answer was staring me right in the face when Natasha came to see me before I could leave the office and asked me if I was okay.

I told her I was going, and she seemed upset. I was upset too because she was a friend, and now it meant I wouldn't see her as much anymore.

Or so I thought.

If only Natasha had left the office with me that day.

She would still be alive now.

So would Edwin.

He had no idea what was coming as he waved me goodbye that day and went to put my NDA alongside all the other ones he'd already managed to acquire from his innocent victims.

Sure, he'd got me to sign that awful piece of paperwork but in doing so, he had signed something himself.

His own death warrant.

30

PRESENT DAY

A lonely breakfast is made a little more entertaining by the video I watch on my phone of a popular television presenter grilling a member of parliament about some video that has leaked out, and whilst I watch the politician squirm, it makes it a little easier to forget about my own problems. But by the time I have finished my bowl of cereal and left my phone lying on the kitchen table to put the bowl in the dishwasher, I am back to feeling glum about my predicament.

Wearily trudging through my monotonous routine as I prepare to leave the house and start another day at work, I'm thrown off course slightly when I hear a knock at my door. Thinking about it, I'm half expecting it to be the postman coming to deliver the package of beauty products I ordered for myself online last night. Feeling low, I decided that a little retail therapy was in order, and with the wonders of the modern world, it seems my goods have already arrived at my doorstep. But then I open the door and do not see the postman.

All I see is the investigator who has been paid to potentially unravel my lies.

'What the hell are you doing here?' I ask Jack Ferdinand, before nervously looking past him to see if he has brought any members of the police with him too. He hasn't, but I'm still wary because for him to be so brazen as to approach me at my home, there must be something he is feeling confident about.

'Can I come in?' he asks me politely, as if he is not some massive imposition on my life.

'No!' I reply firmly, surprised he would even bother asking such a stupid question.

'I think you might be interested in what I have to say,' Jack goes on, not put off by my desire to refuse him entry.

'Why don't you just say it here, and I'll be the judge of that.'

'Fine,' Jack says with a sigh. 'I'm here to let you know that Phillip van Dekker is no longer paying me to look into you or any of your associates.'

I was not expecting that.

'Really?'

'Yes,' Jack replies with a nod, but as quickly as I felt hope, some scepticism returns.

'Wait. Why have you come here to tell me that?' I ask, wondering what benefit there would be to Jack in doing such a thing.

'Because I'm an investigator, and as such, I can sense when there is a story to be told. Phillip has had me looking into you and your story, as well as numerous others who worked at Van Dekker Logistics. But what I've started to realise is that it's not your story that is the one that needs to be told. Rather, it's Phillip's and his father's.'

'What do you mean?'

'Oh, come on, Liz. I'm not so stupid as to think that only innocent people hire private investigators. I know guilty people do too, and while Phillip has been keen for me to try and pin some guilt down on you, I've been wondering what is it that he is trying to hide. And what did Edwin do before him? Maybe they are the real criminals here, and I've just been looking into the wrong people.'

'Why has Phillip told you to stop investigating me?' I ask, still unsure about all of this.

'Because I'm not getting anywhere. I've not found a single shred of evidence that links you, or anyone else, to what might have happened to his father. But what I have found is plenty of people telling me that they are innocent, and that, coupled with the fact that it's obvious there was a high turnover of staff at Van Dekker, makes me think there is a big cover-up somewhere. What is it exactly that Phillip is trying to disguise? His father's crimes? His own? Did Phillip hurt Edwin and is trying to make himself look innocent by appearing desperate to find out the truth?'

Whilst Jack is right about Phillip and Edwin being guilty of various things, he is mistakenly leading himself away from one very juicy crime, and that is the one in which I killed Edwin and hid his body. But I'm hardly going to help put him back on track, and with Jack seemingly back on my side now, I am more receptive when he asks me if he can come in, for a second time.

Once he's in my house, I offer him a drink, and as we go into the kitchen, I'm feeling eager to find out how this man and his investigative skills could further get Phillip and the spectre of Edwin off my back. But what Jack says next gives me second thoughts about this.

'I need you to tell me everything about your time working with Edwin,' Jack says, after taking a seat at my kitchen table. 'And I mean everything. As his finance manager, you must have been very close to him. Perhaps privy to some interesting information. Anything to share?'

There is a lot I could share but before I do, I remind myself that I am dealing with a very slippery character here. This is a man who has no qualms about following people around, and it wasn't so long ago that he was working against me.

So can I really trust him now?

Having been filling up the kettle with hot water to make us both a cup of tea, I suddenly change my mind, and, turning back from the sink, I change my demeanour.

'I'm sorry. I don't really want to talk about all of this. I have to go to work. Please can you leave?'

'What?' Jack asks, surprised, but I'm not sure he should be when we were enemies not so long ago.

'I'd rather not dredge up the past,' I tell him, feeling that is my safest option here rather than having someone like him know more than he already does about me.

Jack protests a little longer, but I stand firm, and without wanting to push it to the point where I call the police and tell them I have a trespasser in my house, he reluctantly leaves. Once he's gone, I can return to what I was doing before I was interrupted, and I finish getting ready for work, before going to leave myself. As I'm just about to make my exit, I have a thought that Jack might be lingering outside my house, waiting for me and hoping to have another go at talking to me. But that thought is quickly pushed aside for another one when I realise that I haven't got my phone with me.

Remembering that I had it with me while I was eating breakfast earlier, I return to the kitchen and expect to find my device sitting on the kitchen table where I left it, but it's not there. Frowning, I look around the room, well aware that this was the last place I had it before Jack interrupted my morning.

Oh no.

As I am unable to locate my phone anywhere, I suddenly have the awful thought that Jack may have taken it while he was here. He was sitting at this table, for a couple of moments anyway. Did he see my phone sitting there in front of him and sense an opportunity? Is he now trying to find out if there is any incriminating evidence on there in relation to Edwin?

If so, there just might be.

I think I deleted all of Bev's messages that referenced what we did, but did I really get them all, or is there still one there lurking amongst our numerous conversation streams? She texts me so much, there could be. What if I missed one? I told her not to be so stupid and create evidence on both our phones, and now look what's happened.

I feel sick at the thought that Jack could be out there now with my mobile, but hoping I can catch up to him, I run out of my house and onto the street, praying I'll see him still nearby. But there's no sign of him, and why would there be because if he does have my phone, he won't be hanging around long enough for me to catch him with it.

As another wave of nausea washes over me, I turn back, but instead of going into my home, I head for my next-door neighbour's. The person who lives next to me is a sweet lady called Betty, but I'm not going to see her for one of our semi-regular chats. I'm going to her because I know she possesses the one thing I do not.

A landline telephone.

Knocking on her door, I hope she is in, and as she is retired, there should be a good chance that I will catch her at home because she won't be rushing to leave the house this morning and join the unlucky people who have soul-destroying commutes to make. I'm right because Betty is here, and as she opens her door, she looks surprised but pleased to see me.

'Hello, Elizabeth,' she says with a warm smile, using my full name because she's that polite. 'Is everything okay?'

'I'm not sure,' I say, speaking honestly. 'I think somebody has just stolen my mobile phone.'

'Oh no! That's terrible!'

'Yes, it is. I was wondering, if it's possible, please could I use your telephone? I just need to make a call, and that was the only phone I had.'

'Of course, dear, come in,' Betty says, and she invites me inside before leading me to her landline phone, which sits on a small table in the hallway at the bottom of the stairs. The phone, and the location of it, reminds me of my childhood home because my parents had their landline telephone in a similar position, and I used to spend many a minute as a child sneakily trying to make calls on it and thinking I was very grown up as I pretended to have conversations with somebody at the other end of the line.

'Here you go. I do hope the police are able to help you with this,' Betty tells me as she hands me the receiver to the telephone, and I thank her but decide not to mention that it won't actually be the police I am about to call now.

'I'm really sorry, but it's been quite a stressful morning. Is there any chance of a cup of tea?' I ask, needing some way of getting Betty to leave my side so she won't stand next to me and hear the conversation I am about to have.

'Of course, dear. I'll put the kettle on,' Betty says with a smile before going into the kitchen, and once I'm alone, I make my call.

Entering the digits to Bev's mobile number, I pray my friend will answer her phone and not miss my call while undertaking her commute. I need to tell her what happened, but most of all, I need to make sure she doesn't have another crisis of confidence and send a guilt-laden message to my phone, talking about what we did to Edwin, because if she did that, then Jack would see that message flash up on my phone's screen, and they would have us bang to rights.

'Bev! It's Liz! Listen to me!' I say quickly as my friend answers, and before she can ask any questions, I explain exactly what has happened and why I am now having to call her off a number she doesn't recognise. As

I thought, once she knows the story, Bev is just as anxious as I am.

'You need to find him. You need to get your phone back!' she tells me, and while I wholeheartedly agree with her there, it's easier said than done.

'I don't know where he is,' I lament, as I hear Betty pottering around in her kitchen, the tinkle of a teaspoon against a cup telling me that she will be finished making my tea soon and will then be back to overhear what I am currently saying. 'I don't know what to do.'

'You need to figure it out and fast!' Bev replies, surprising me with her sudden order. I presumed she was going to be as frightened and paranoid as me once I passed on the troubling news, but she seems surprisingly focused. 'If you know Jack is working for Phillip, you need to go and see him because if they are planning to do anything with your phone, Phillip will be the one who decides what that is, right?'

Bev is making sense, and I know what I have to do now. I have to go and see Phillip and tell him that we have to talk. It's either that or go to the police and report my phone being stolen, but what good would they be to me if they help me find it, only for Jack to tell them what kind of messages I have on there?

I have to sort this mess out myself. I let Jack into my home and gave him the opportunity to steal my phone, so I'm going to have to be the one who fixes this mess. Nothing else can help me now. Certainly not a cup of tea from the smiling Betty, which is why I thank her for letting me use her phone before I run from her house, and I don't stop running until I make it all the way back to my old workplace.

When I get there, I see Phillip's car parked outside the building.

But that's not all I see.

I also see the police car parked right beside it.

Should I go inside or not now? I have no idea what I might be walking into, but I won't get any answers if I stay out here.

As I ponder my next move, I stare at the prominent markings on the side of the police car and as I do, I can't help but think how the more I try and do things to avoid the police, the more I seem to end up attracting them. But before I can decide whether to try and go in and see Phillip or walk away and tell Bev that I couldn't risk talking to him with the police around, I see something shocking.

I see Phillip being led out of the office.

In handcuffs.

31

PRESENT DAY

I was able to stay out of view as I watched Phillip being put inside the back of the police car and driven away, presumably to the station where I imagine he is currently being questioned.

But what about? What have the police arrested him for? Do they have something on him? Something that he won't be able to talk his way out of? If so, it might not necessarily be good news for me to have him out of the picture. That's because a desperate man will do anything to save himself, and if Phillip really is in trouble, he won't hesitate to try and drag Bev and me down with him.

I never thought I'd be so upset to see one of my foes in handcuffs, but witnessing Phillip's arrest has left me fearful that my own arrest might be imminent. I still don't have my phone; Jack Ferdinand has it, and for all I know, the one phone call that Phillip is allowed from custody will be to him, and when they talk, who knows what Jack might have found on my mobile by then. I need to speak to one of the men, but if Phillip is clearly occupied, it will have to be Jack.

But how to track down a man like him?

After going home and giving it some thought, it comes to me that if the PI can deceive me so easily, what's stopping me from giving him a taste of his own medicine? Using my laptop, I find his website online, and I decide to send him an email posing as a potential customer. It only takes me a few minutes to create an email address that doesn't have my name in it, so Jack will have no idea it is me behind the message, and once it's sent, I impatiently wait for a reply. But is he going to be checking his inbox, or is he too busy trying to find something incriminating on my phone?

I get my answer when I receive an email back thirty minutes later.

Jack has thanked me for contacting him, and after I asked if he would possibly be able to help me look into my fictional husband and any potential fictional affair that he might be having, the PI confirms that he can be of service to me. Now all I need to do is arrange a suitable place for us to conduct our 'business meeting', so I reply and ask him if he can be at the park at twelve-thirty today, and when he says yes, I feel relieved that I'll know exactly where he is going to be and when. Then all I need to do is call Bev and pass on the good news, but to do that, I have to return to Betty's because I still don't have a damn phone of my own.

I plan to change that very soon, but for the time being, Betty's landline is my best bet, and after she graciously allows me the use of her telephone again, I contact Bev.

'I'm meeting Jack in the park at half-past twelve,' I tell my friend. 'I think you should come with me, just in case he has found anything on my phone, and we need to try and explain ourselves.'

'I'm not meeting him,' Bev replies. 'It'll make us look more suspicious if we both go. You have a reason to want to see him. He has your phone. But I don't. Me going just makes me look guilty.'

I'm not too happy that Bev won't be offering me any support for my meeting later, but there's not much I can do to change her mind. But I keep her talking when we move on to discussing what I saw earlier, that being Phillip's arrest.

'I still don't know what's going on with him,' I tell her. 'But Jack might, assuming he knows that Phillip is in custody. But it might also be news to him too.'

'Just be careful,' Bev warns me. 'Don't say or do anything stupid when you meet Jack.'

Unfortunately, while I can assure her that I won't, I might be lying because I can't commit to anything until I know exactly what I'm walking into when I see Jack soon.

After calling Bev, I contact my employer to explain why I failed to show up for work this morning. I keep it vague but mention that there was a theft at my home, and I've been dealing with the police ever since, and they seem to buy it. They seem to understand, or rather they don't care enough to pry too much, and I end the call by telling them I'll be back at work tomorrow. That might be optimistic of me because, for all I know, I could be in handcuffs, like Phillip already is, by then instead. But one thing that does make me hopeful is that there have been no police officers arriving at my house during the course of the morning, giving me optimism that Jack has found nothing on my phone, nor has Phillip mentioned my name yet during whatever questioning he is being subjected to.

By the time I leave my house and start walking to the park, I'm telling myself that this might all turn out well in the end. My plan is to surprise Jack, but before he can walk away from me, I will ask him to give me my phone back, or I will report his theft to the police and get to work on ruining his career as a PI. Nobody will hire a thief, so surely, it's in his best interests to cover up what he did and just give me my phone back. With one of his clients currently in police custody, he may have just lost that income source, so I doubt he is in a position to risk further work by refusing to give me my phone back and risking me damaging his reputation.

As I reach the park, I see that it's not quite as busy as I was hoping it would be. I want there to be enough people around so that it will be harder for Jack to say or do anything too bad because people are always on better behaviour when they're in a public place. But instead of this park being full of parents and children sitting on the grass enjoying their morning, there is just the occasional dog walker ambling around, and I think the weather is to blame for it. It's overcast and blustery, so hardly perfect park weather, but there should still be enough people around to make it difficult for Jack if he decides he doesn't want to give me my phone back and tries to run. All I will have to do is call out to one of these dogwalkers and tell them this man has my phone, and they will come to my aid. Jack won't want that, so all he has to do is say sorry for stealing from me and give me the phone back, or take me to where he currently has it, and all of this will be over.

One good thing about there not being lots of people here at the moment is that it will make it easier for me to see Jack, and vice versa, and as I stand on the path that runs through the centre of this park, I look in all directions for any sign of the PI. I want to make sure I spot him early so that he can't turn around and make a quick exit before reaching me, but as I keep searching, I fail to spot him.

As the clock ticks past our arranged meeting time, I hope he is just running a little late, which wouldn't be very professional of him when he's supposed to be meeting a new customer, but it is forgivable as long as he gets here in the end. But after twenty minutes have passed, I start to fear he isn't coming at all.

Where is he? Has he figured out I'm the one behind the email, and now he has rather wisely stood me up? Or is he lurking in the trees around here somewhere, having got here early, and having been peeping out from his hiding place, has now seen it's actually me who has shown up and is opting to remain hidden until I've gone? At thirty minutes past our rendezvous time, I'm about ready to give up and go home, but then I see a sight for sore eyes.

Jack is walking along the path towards me and not only that, but he has something in his hand that I was hoping he would have with him.

My phone.

'Ahh, Liz, what a pleasant surprise,' he says, clearly being sarcastic because he doesn't look at all like a man who was expecting to be meeting somebody else.

'How did you know it was me?' I ask him, but I almost wish I hadn't when he gives me his answer.

'I didn't just take something from your house,' he tells me as he holds up my phone rather brazenly. 'I left something too.'

'What?'

'It's a rather clever little device,' Jack tells me. 'It's very discreet. So discreet that you clearly haven't noticed it. I left it on top of your fridge while your back was turned in the kitchen, and what it does is it automatically connects to your Wi-Fi and picks up everything you do on your internet connection. It also shows me the history of your IP address, and as such, I saw that you had created a fake email account and visited my website today, making it rather obvious that it was you who had messaged me about meeting here.'

This man and his means of conducting business become even more disgraceful and illegal by the minute, and I'm so shocked I can barely speak. But Jack just takes my silence as an invitation to carry on talking himself.

'Don't worry, I forgive you for tricking me into coming here, just like I hope you can forgive me for taking this.'

Jack holds out my phone, and I quickly swipe it back before he can withdraw it. But even though I have it back now, it doesn't mean my worries are over because I still don't know what he might have found on there.

'Why did you take it?' I ask him. 'Why steal from me?'

'I think you know why,' Jack says calmly as a man walking a Labrador strolls past us, totally oblivious to the fact that he and his cute canine are currently sharing the park with two criminals because Jack and I look perfectly respectable to the untrained eye.

What is that answer supposed to mean? Did Jack find something on there? Does he have evidence now? If so, I have to presume he has downloaded it, which is why he's so happy to just hand my phone back to me. Just like that fancy gadget he left on top of my fridge, he must have some other way of seeing what I have done, and it's already too late for me to pretend it hasn't happened.

'What did you find?' I ask him, ripping off the proverbial band-aid because I'd rather just know if he has seen a text message in which it's clear Bev and I are guilty.

'That's not for me to answer,' Jack replies.

'What's that supposed to mean?'

'I think you're better having that conversation with Phillip.'

Jack's reference to that man makes me think he doesn't know Phillip is currently in custody.

'I saw Phillip get arrested at his office this morning,' I tell Jack, expecting that I'm enlightening him. But as always, he knows more than I give him credit for.

'Don't worry, it was just a little misunderstanding. Phillip is out now, and he has some business to attend to. Speaking of that, check your messages. There's a new text in there that you haven't read yet.'

Frowning, I look at my phone and when I do, I see that there is indeed an unread text message waiting for me. Opening it up, I get a chill when I read it.

The fun's over, Liz. I know exactly what you and Bev did. Stop playing games and come and meet me so we can talk about what you did to my father. Meet me at my office tonight at seven pm. Bring Bev but no one else. No police, Liz, I mean it. Otherwise, you'll be the next person they take away in handcuffs.

The message is a frightening one, and I look back to Jack to see what he has to say about it.

But he's gone.

Looking around, I see him several yards away, clearly having decided to walk off while I was reading the message, and while I call after him, he doesn't turn back and look at me. He just leaves, the same as the man walking the Labrador, and suddenly, I'm the only one left in this chilly park.

Reading the message again, I've never felt so alone in my life.

Phillip knows what I did to his father, and tonight at seven o'clock, I get to find out what he plans to do about it.

This is it. The culmination of everything I have been trying to cover up.

I got myself into this mess, and I'm not sure I can get myself out of it. But I was only trying to do the right thing.

I was only trying to help a friend in need.

32

SIX MONTHS AGO

It's probably most people's dream to have enough money in the bank to not have to go to work for a few months. Have a lie-in instead of commuting. Put your feet up with a cup of tea and watch television in the afternoon instead of listening to a boss telling you what to do. Enjoy an extra glass of wine in the evening without worrying about having to wake up early and be presentable.

I'm in that enviable position right now, and like most people, it should be a dream come true.

But it's not, and the reason for that is very simple.

The money in my bank account that affords me that pleasant lifestyle is dirty money.

Having signed the NDA and accepted Edwin's pay-out in exchange for me keeping quiet about the financial wrongdoings within his company, I am free to take my time before I need to go and find work again. But rather than being able to enjoy having my weekdays to myself and making my monthly mortgage payments without much effort for a while, it's not a fun time in my life. I feel ashamed for taking the money rather than exposing Edwin and not just because he has effectively bought me and my silence. It's a shame because I know what he did to Bev and Monique and what he will most likely do to somebody else too, whenever he gets the chance.

He hurts women.

He leaves them worse off than before they met him.

And so far, nobody has been able to put a stop to it.

As I sit here on my sofa after another easy weekday at home, I so desperately want to be that person who stops Edwin from hurting anyone else. But I already fear I have missed my chance because by signing that NDA, I allowed him off the hook for crimes that could have seen him go to prison and therefore, be unable to hurt any women, at least while he was in custody anyway. I should have gone to the police, told them what I knew, and then seen what happened. It might not have worked out, but at least I could have rested easier knowing I tried my best. There's not much peace for me here knowing that I didn't do the right thing, and no amount of money in my bank account will make me feel better about that.

The guilt I am feeling over not doing more to try and stop Edwin is the main reason why I have slowly withdrawn myself from some of my friends' lives. I haven't cut anybody from my past at Van Dekker Logistics off yet, but I am making a conscious effort to see and speak to them less, and that is obviously because that's the only way I can feel less guilty about things. It's why I don't message Bev as much as I used to, as well as why I make up excuses whenever she suggests we meet up for a drink and a chat. I tell her that I'm busy, that I have a new job, that there's stuff going on in my family that requires my attention. Anything to make her think that I really am just a little preoccupied with other things in my life and not just a friend of hers who took the easy way out and, ultimately, is helping contribute to her attacker being free to potentially attack again.

The same goes for Natasha, another person who was a good friend when I worked in my old job but who has become just another person who I make up excuses not to have to see much of anymore. I turned down her invitation to go for a drink a couple of weeks ago, and I haven't even replied to her last message, which she sent me last night at ten in the evening. I'm assuming she had a bit to drink before sending it because she told me how much she missed me and that the office wasn't the same without me around. It was nice of her to say so, but instead of feeling able to send a nice message back of my own, in which I thanked her for her kind words and told her I missed her too, all I could think was that I hoped she would leave that same office before anything bad happened to her there as well.

Unfortunately, five seconds later, I realised it was already too late for that.

Having not been expecting any visitors, the banging on my front door startles me, and it's so aggressive and constant that my first thought is that I'm not going to answer it. It could be trouble, possibly a drunken youth from the area playing games or worse, wanting to get inside and burgle me. There have been a few stories like that on the news recently, and I wouldn't want to become another statistic. Then again, I wouldn't want whoever this is to give up here and go next door to try Betty's house instead because I don't want her to be put at any risk. That's why I decide to open the door and confront whoever this is myself, fully expecting that I'm going to have to tell whoever it is to get lost before I call the police and report them for causing a disturbance. But when I open the door, I am stunned to see Natasha standing there.

But I'm not stunned because my old friend has decided to come to my place unannounced.

I'm stunned because of what she looks like now she is here.

Her hair is scraggly, and her face is red and blotchy, her mascara smeared and tear-stained and her red lipstick smudged. She's wearing a dress and heels but is still far from presentable, and when she sees me, she lets out a noise that can only be described as a whimper.

'Natasha! Oh my goodness, what's happened?' I cry, before stepping forward and wrapping my arms around her, clearly aware my friend is in desperate need of comforting. As I embrace her, Natasha's body feels weak and fragile, and as she cries onto my shoulder, I can't recall ever seeing someone look as broken as this.

It takes a lot of effort just to get her inside my house and sitting on my sofa because she seems disoriented, which is strange because she obviously found her way here, although now she has arrived, it's as if she has used all her energy and has now given up.

'What's happened? What's wrong?' I ask her again, but I'm still not getting a decipherable answer, and starting to feel overwhelmed, I decide to call for back-up. Leaving Natasha on my sofa while I go out into the hallway, I call Bev on my mobile, and when she answers, I tell her exactly what is going on.

'Natasha has turned up at my place, and she's in a bad way,' I explain. 'Can you come over and help me talk to her? I don't know what's happened, but it can't be good.'

Despite me hardly being the best friend to her lately, Bev does not hesitate in telling me that she is on her way, and as I wait for her to arrive, I keep trying to talk to Natasha and get to the root of the problem. But I'm no nearer by the time Bev arrives, though at least by then, Natasha has stopped crying, so there seems a better chance of her actually giving us some words now. But before she does, Bev pre-empts what she might be about to say by asking if this has anything to do with Edwin.

Natasha's eyes go wide at the mention of his name, which gives us our answer, and suddenly, I'm feeling even more guilty about accepting that man's payoff instead of trying to ruin him.

Oh no, has he hurt Natasha? If so, how badly?

Bev, perhaps understandably with her experience with him, is treading carefully now, holding Natasha's hand and slowly persuading our distressed friend and ex-colleague to open up to us, and eventually, she does.

'He attacked me,' is the short but stinging sentence that rips through the room and causes Bev and me to stare at each other in horror.

'Were you able to fight him off?' I ask nervously, but Natasha sadly shakes her head. But before Bev or I can feel even more guilty for not stopping him,

Natasha delivers another statement that might be just as shocking as her last one.

'I want to kill him,' she tells us.

But maybe that's not the most shocking part at all. Maybe that would be the fact that as Bev and I look at each other, neither one of us has the inclination to try and talk our friend out of it. All we do is share a look that says that shortly, we are going to make a plan that will see the three of us get our own back on the man who has done us all wrong.

And that's exactly what we did.

33

PRESENT DAY

It's hard not to feel like I have a date with destiny as I make my way to my old office to meet with the son of the man I murdered.

While I might be feeling like a condemned woman, at least I'm not alone. As per Phillip's request in his text message, I have brought Bev with me, not that it was easy to convince her to come along. Why would she? There's surely nothing good going to come out of this meeting, but what other choice do we have? Do I not go and then just reside in a place of paranoid anxiety while we wait to see what Phillip's next move might be? At least this way, we can find out tonight, although we might quickly wish we didn't know what he plans to do next once we hear it.

According to the message he sent me, he knows what we did. If that's true and he does know we murdered his father, he's hardly going to be welcoming, is he? It's already crossed my mind that he might be wishing a fate on us that is even worse than getting the police involved. He might want cold-blooded revenge.

An eye for an eye.

He might be preparing to kill us both.

That's why Bev and I have made sure that we will not be walking into tonight's meeting totally unprepared. If Phillip does wish harm on us, and he certainly has good reason to, then we are not going to make it easy for him. I am carrying a knife that is tucked into the waistband of my trousers, and Bev also has a blade of her own hidden away should we need to fight and defend ourselves at any point during this meeting. Not only that, but we have both made sure to tell other people where we are going tonight, so if anything happens to us and we go missing, the police will have an idea of our final movements and location. I told a few friends that I was attending a reunion at my old office, so it's a plausible excuse for me going there tonight, certainly preferable to telling them that I'm going to discuss what happens next with the offspring of the man I stabbed and dumped in a river. I'm hoping that my friends won't have to make any phone calls to the police in a few days' time when I've failed to show up anywhere but if they do, at least they can point the police in Phillip's direction, not that it will do Bev or me much good if we're already dead by then.

'Just park at the front door. There's no point trying to be discreet when he knows we're coming,' I tell Bev as she slows her vehicle down outside Van Dekker Logistics, and taking my advice, she steers us into the car park, where we see just one other vehicle residing.

Bringing us to a stop beside Phillip's car, I wonder if we will all be driving out of here again shortly or if one of these cars is fated to be removed by a third party at a later date as part of a criminal investigation. That remains to be seen, and as Bev and I exit her vehicle and look towards the front door, we know this will all be over, one way or another, very soon.

'I have a bad feeling about this,' Bev says to me, not that such a comment helps matters.

'The fact he wants to talk to us is a good thing,' I say, rather hopefully. 'And I'd rather talk to him about this than the police.'

With that, I march towards the front door with grim determination, and Bev follows me. Stepping into the reception area, our footsteps echo on the marble flooring, and the place has an eerie feel to it. It doesn't get much better once we have ascended to the relevant floor because as we leave the lifts, I see all the empty desks, and despite being with Bev, I feel incredibly lonely right now. Philip must be up here somewhere, and as we walk past all the desks whilst looking for him, I see where I used to sit. Bev sees her old workstation too, as well as Natasha's, and being back here is a sobering reminder of the women we used to be.

The office is still deadly silent, and I'm just about starting to think that Bev was right and we shouldn't have come here because something about this doesn't feel good. But it's too late to change our minds when we see Phillip step out of his father's old office and when he does, he is holding a glass of whiskey.

'Right on time. Come this way, ladies,' he says as he beckons for us to enter his office, and after exchanging a puzzled look, Bev and I follow him in. When we do, he invites the pair of us to join him with a drink, holding up the bottle on his desk.

'No, thanks,' I say, but Bev clearly needs something to calm her nerves because she accepts, which is not the best thing to do, seeing as she is supposed to be driving us away from here shortly, but I have a feeling that's the last thing on her mind. Phillip pours her a hearty measure before doing the same for me, even though I declined, and then he invites the two of us to take a seat on the other side of his desk.

We sit down, nursing our drinks while Phillip finishes his and pours another before he is finally seated as well.

That's when our meeting begins.

'Well, how about this? Who would have thought I would ever be sharing a drink with the women who killed my father?' Phillip starts with, and it's enough to make me want to guzzle my whiskey down, if only to numb some of the nerves that are jangling around my body.

'What are you talking about? We didn't kill your father,' Bev says, but it's more for show, at this point, because Phillip doesn't seem like he was speculating there, rather speaking from a place of certainty.

'Oh, come on, Bev. Drop the façade. I know you two did it. Well, you and Natasha, although she is no longer here to answer for it.'

'How do you know?' I ask then.

'You mean besides the messages that Jack found for me on your mobile phone?' Phillip replies with a smirk. 'You know, you two should have been a little more careful than to send each other texts about what you did. Your phone could have fallen into the wrong hands, though I'm sure you deleted the worst of them. But that's not all. I saw an email too.'

'An email?' I ask, before looking at Bev in confusion, but she doesn't seem to know what he is referring to either.

'I had I.T. send me every historic email in this company and went through those belonging to anyone I thought might have had a vendetta against my father. That's how I saw the email Natasha sent to him before his death. The one in which she told him he would pay for what he had done, not only to her but to Liz and Bev too.'

Natasha sent an email like that? It must have been after that night when she turned up at my place in tears. She would have still had access to her company email account then on her work mobile because she hadn't been paid off by Edwin yet. If so, no wonder Phillip has been on to us.

'I don't know what Natasha said in her email, but-'

'She said enough,' Phillip says, cutting off my sentence. 'But don't worry, only I have read it. I.T. don't go through everyone's emails individually unless they are requested to do so. But I have been through them and once I saw that message, I knew the pair of you were worth looking into. Then I read a message from you, Bev, that said you hope you get away with it and that nobody ever finds the body. You know the one, Liz, because you would have read it. It was sent to your phone, after all.'

Phillip has hard evidence on us now, which is why I don't even bother trying to deny anything. Instead, I just try to make what we did seem acceptable.

'We're sorry, but we can explain! Your father did some terrible things to all of us! We were just trying to protect ourselves from him; you have to believe us!'

I'm wondering if my pleas are going to fall on deaf ears, but Phillip raises a hand to signal for me to be quiet and once I am, he doesn't look like a man who is desperate to call the police.

'Relax, I'm not angry at you. I'm actually quite impressed.'

What? Did he really just say that?

'You think you were the only ones who knew what my father was like?' Phillip says as he stares into the bottom of his whiskey glass. 'You weren't the only ones he mistreated. You just worked for him. Try being raised by him.'

Bev and I share another confused glance before Phillip goes on.

'I hated that man,' he says quietly. 'He thought I was proud of him, but how could I be? Not after what I'd seen him do in private. He liked to present himself as this brilliant man, but he was so flawed. He cheated on my mother multiple times. He was vicious to anybody who didn't agree with him. He told me numerous times that I was nothing like him, which, for me, was a compliment, but I know he meant it in a disparaging way. But that's not even the worst of it.'

'You're right about that,' I say as I shake my head. 'He was a bad man, and he deserved what happened to him.'

'Which was?'

Phillip's question hangs in the air, and the office is deathly silent as I ponder whether or not I should confess what we did to him. Bev looks unsure, but Phillip seems to be on our side here. But is he really?

'I'll only tell you if you can promise that this conversation never leaves this room,' I say to the man on the other side of the desk. 'This stays between us. Forever.'

Phillip agrees, but Bev still looks nervous, and she suggests we just leave it as it is.

'We all hated him, and now he's gone,' Bev says. 'Can this be the end?'

'No, I still need to know what happened,' Phillip tells us. 'For closure. Do you understand?'

I do because, in his position, I wouldn't be able to rest until I knew what had happened to my father, even if I hated him just as much. So that's why I tell him everything. Well, almost everything. I talk about the plan Bev and I made with Natasha, all the way up to the point where Edwin was tied up at her home, and I used the knife to take his life. I then talk about how we moved his body and hid it in a place where it remains unfound until this day. By the time I've finished talking, Phillip looks stunned, but most importantly, he does not look like he is going to tell anybody what I just said.

'Thank you,' is all he says after I have finished talking. 'Thank you for getting rid of that man, and thank you for telling me so I can move on.'

Is that it? As easy as that? It seems so because Phillip is still not reaching for his phone to call the police.

'I'm sorry for what my father did to you and your friends,' Phillip says then. 'You didn't deserve any of this, and I'm sorry your lives have been affected by him just like mine has.'

From walking into this office feeling both hatred and fearful respect for this man, I am now simply feeling sorry for him because he just looks broken, like any son would do after being raised by someone undeserving of having a child of their own.

'What happens now?' Bev asks, and that focuses all our minds back onto the present.

'Now we all get on with our lives,' Phillip replies. 'You can leave now.'

That's it? The meeting's over? After everything we just talked about?

'You're not going to go to the police?' I ask Phillip, still nervous, but he shakes his head.

'No, I'm not. I've got a company to run, and you have your own lives to get on with. My father is missing, and I guess he always will be. Let's just leave it at that. What do you say?'

I say that sounds good to me, before suggesting to Bev that we leave as quickly as we can, and as we head for the door, it feels like this is finally over. By the time we walk out of the office and get back into Bev's car, I see no police officers coming to arrest us, nor do I see Jack Ferdinand spying on our next move, so it really must be finished.

Finally, after all this time, the spectre of Edwin van Dekker is no longer hanging over me.

Does Bev feel the same? Something tells me she's still not so sure.

But for now, we are free, and I intend to enjoy that freedom. That's why I suggest we go for a strong drink while we go over what just happened tonight. Bev agrees, and we set off on our way to the nearest bar, both of us looking forward to a cold glass of white wine on this warm, stressful night.

Little did I know it was going to be the last glass of wine I savoured for a very long time.

34

PRESENT DAY

As I hoped it would be, the glass of wine was refreshing and helped soothe the last of the nerves I had been carrying with me ever since we left Phillip's office earlier tonight. But I decided not to order a second drink, preferring to keep a clear head because the way I saw it, tomorrow was the first day of the rest of my life. Bev agreed with that sentiment, and as she drove me home from the bar, the pair of us chatted about what we hoped our future might look like now that our eventful past was firmly behind us.

Bev suggested a holiday was in order, and I couldn't argue with her there, which is how the two of us made tentative plans to book a week away somewhere warm and sunny very soon, all-inclusive ideally, but we'd just see what the best deal was that we could get nearer the time. But there was also time for us both to discuss future plans that weren't quite so simple as booking a trip abroad. Perhaps it was the adrenaline from the evening, or maybe just that the wine had affected me more than usual, but I found myself telling Bev about something I hoped for in the future that was much more substantial than sitting on a sunlounger by a pool, reading a good book.

I told her that I wished to meet a man and start a family.

Far from being surprised by my admission, Bev told me she wanted the same thing, and we shared a poignant moment in the car as we both realised that as we approached forty, each of us had almost been too embarrassed to admit to each other what it was we most wanted in life. It's stupid, but it seems it took the pair of us almost going away to prison for the rest of our lives to be honest with not just each other but ourselves too.

All the stress of the last few months culminating with tonight's daunting trip to see Phillip and hearing him tell us he knew we killed his father seems to have been the catalyst for me to take stock of my life and now I have, I can clearly see what is important to me. I've spent so long working on my career and my friendships, but now I can see that unless I have a family, I'll feel unfulfilled. There is still time - Bev and I both agreed on that - though not enough to delay things much longer. If we both want to find a man, get married, and have at least one baby, then we should do something about it sooner rather than later. That's why, as Bev steers us onto my street, we have both vowed to get serious about online dating and encourage each other to put ourselves out there and see what might happen for us.

At least that was the innocent plan.

Unfortunately, as I arrived home, it was the criminal plan that preceded it that reared its ugly head again.

'What's going on? Are they at your house?' Bev asks me as she hits the brakes whilst staring at the numerous police cars parked on the street ahead of us, and sadly for me, it does seem like they are all parked outside my property. Not only that but I can see officers walking across my lawn, and one of them appears to be going around the back of the house, making it painfully obvious they are looking for the owner.

What should I do?

The tap on the glass window beside my head causes Bev and I to both jump, and when we see who it is, nausea almost overcomes me. It's a police officer, and now there's another one on Bev's side of the car. They are both signalling for us to exit the vehicle, and I don't see that we have any other choice but to comply. Bev isn't so stupid as to think we could try and outrun them, so she turns the engine off, and as we open our doors, we are quickly pulled out and pressed up against the body of the vehicle. As Bev and I make eye contact, our wrists are wrapped in cold stainless steel, and once the handcuffs are on, we are told exactly what this is about.

'I'm arresting you on suspicion of murder. You don't have to say anything, but it may harm your defence if you don't say something that you later rely on in court.'

No, this can't be happening.

"Murder." They know what we did. They know about Edwin.

My worst nightmare has been realised.

But how?

Before there is any time to think, the pair of us are marched to separate police cars, where we are bundled onto the back seat, and the door is slammed in our faces.

'Hey! What's going on?' I cry, but the driver ignores me as he sets off, and as we move down the street, I see all my neighbours looking on from their doorsteps, utterly aghast at what is occurring. But if they're shocked, then they should try swapping places with me because I'm totally baffled as to what is happening.

However, I retain the sense of mind to refrain from saying anything that might make things worse for me, opting to stay silent until I have had a chance to speak to a lawyer, one of which I most certainly need now. How does a person even go about getting a lawyer? I only know what I do from crime dramas on TV. I think I'm entitled to a phone call. Is that right, or am I confusing the British justice system with the American one? Damn it, I watch so many US legal dramas that I can't remember what applies to me here in England and what doesn't. But that's the least of my worries because if the police seem sure about me being guilty of murder, maybe there isn't anything I can do to save myself anyway. They might have me bang to rights, and if so, all the hopes and dreams I just shared with Bev will be going up in smoke almost as quickly as I voiced them just a few minutes ago.

As the police car moves on through traffic, edging its way ever nearer to the station, I think about how my best friend must be feeling sitting in the back of her own vehicle and experiencing all the same emotions as me. Is she more afraid or angry than I am? I can only speak for myself, and currently, the shock I feel at my arrest has started to wear off a little, and I am starting to feel an anger burning inside me. It's an anger that is directed at Phillip because it's now painfully obvious what must have happened.

He betrayed us. He lied. He told us our secret was safe, but he must have shared it with the police as soon as we left his office. How else would they know, and why else would they be so quick as to be waiting at my house when I got home?

I'm stupid. I never should have trusted that man. I should have known he would be just like his father. Manipulative. Deceitful. Scheming. He's well and truly played us, and now we seem to be screwed. But I haven't had a detective tell me exactly what they know yet, so until then, I'll try and stay calm whilst praying that there isn't enough evidence to get a conviction, and somehow, Bev and I can still walk free to go on and do all the things we just talked about.

At least that's what I thought until I did end up in an interrogation room sitting opposite a detective, with a lawyer by my side and a tape recorder on the table between us. That was when the detective told me what he had, or rather, he played me what he had.

It was a record of the conversation I had earlier that night with Phillip. He must have secretly recorded the whole thing and because he did, he has captured my confession, the part where I admit to hatching a plan to kill Edwin and then carrying it out to its grim conclusion.

'What do you have to say to that?' the detective asks me after he presses pause on the recording, the most damning parts of it already aired and leaving little room for dispute.

Perhaps unwisely, I glance at my lawyer, the one who was provided for me after I admitted to not having a clue how to get one myself, and that seems to be all the detective needs to see before he shakes his head and considers this case closed.

'That was you in the recording? You know, if you admit to this, it will be a lot easier for you,' he says, though by the sounds of that recording, I've already admitted to plenty. That's why I stay quiet, and the silence is only broken when my lawyer requests a private conversation with me.

The detective grants the wish, probably because he doesn't think it will make much difference in the long run, so he stands up to leave and as he goes, I envy him for the fact that he is free to just stand up and walk out of this room. I won't be going anywhere for a while, but once the detective has gone, I ask the lawyer if there is any possibility I can get out of this mess.

'You admitted to murder, and it was caught on tape,' I'm told.

'But I didn't know I was being recorded. That's a crime in itself, right?'

'Well, yes, but not quite as serious as murder.'

'But is it admissible evidence if I didn't know the conversation was being recorded? I read somewhere that it can't be used in court.'

'You mean you saw it on a TV show once? I can try and discredit the recording, but it's going to be tough. The fact is the police have been trying to solve Edwin van Dekker's disappearance for some time, and now you have just given them a strong indication of what happened.'

It really does seem like I'm screwed and not only me but Bev as well because she will be in another room talking to her own lawyer right now. What if she is advised to just admit to everything for a lesser sentence, further condemning us both in the process and leaving my lawyer with nothing to work with to get me out of here? It's frightening enough being in here, but it's even scarier when I feel like I'm not in control of my destiny while Bev has the chance to admit to everything for me elsewhere.

But then I tell myself that I did have a Plan B, just in case Phillip turned out to backstab us, and it's a Plan B that Bev was privy to. She knows what I said in that room with Phillip earlier, but more importantly, she knows what I didn't say.

I told Phillip everything, but one very crucial piece of the story was false. Instead of telling him that his father's body was at the bottom of the canal, I told him that he was buried in the woods. I did that because one, Phillip would never know I had lied about that and two, it was insurance just in case he turned out to be untrustworthy. Now that he has, I wonder if my lie about the location of the body is going to help me because if the police are looking for Edwin's corpse in the wrong place, they'll never find it.

'There's no body? If there's no body, there's no case, right?' I suggest, and my lawyer thinks about that for a moment.

'The confession is still problematic, but you are right that the lack of a body will make it more difficult for the police. Unfortunately, you told Phillip where the body was, and the police are searching in the woods as we speak.'

'Let them search,' I say, sitting back in my chair and folding my arms. 'They won't find anything because Edwin is not there. Now, all I need you to do is tell the detective that I was lying in that tape recording, or that I made the confession under duress, whatever you have to say. Just discredit it and get me out of here. You think you can do that?'

My lawyer is just about to answer me when the door opens again, and the detective walks in, worryingly, with a big smile on his face. What's he so happy about? I find out after he has taken a seat and still smiling, enlightens me on what just happened while he was out of the room.

'We've found Edwin's body,' he says, looking very pleased with himself.

'What? It's not possible. How? I didn't do anything. Where? What are you talking about?'

I'm not making much sense, but it doesn't matter because the detective seems clear enough on this subject for the both of us.

'We've just pulled him from the canal,' he tells me. 'So, now that we have the body and the confession, how about we start this conversation again? And this time, Liz, do try and tell the truth, okay?'

35

PRESENT DAY

How does it feel to be backstabbed by your best friend? I'll tell you when the shock has worn off. For now, all I know is that I am in a daze as I am led to a police cell after being formally charged with the murder of Edwin van Dekker.

The discovery of his body in the canal has been crucial to these charges being laid against me because now there is a body, there can be a full investigation into the cause of death and when there is, the stab wounds that I inflicted are not going to make for good reading in a coroner's report. Despite lying to Phillip and saying his father's body was buried in the woods, it seems somebody else has told the truth, and they have done so simply to save their own skin.

Bev.

She has broken our bond. She has told the police everything, despite the pair of us making a pact to stick together in secrecy. Worst of all, she has done it so that I will take the fall for our crimes while she gets a much lesser sentence.

Having my lawyer explain to me exactly what my so-called best friend had said to the police was traumatising, not least because I couldn't believe what I was hearing. But it was true, and I'll have plenty of time to think about it further once I am in my cell and the door is locked behind me.

Reaching said cell, I notice how small it is, but at least it doesn't appear that I'll be sharing it with anybody, for the time being at least. However, being alone is not necessarily the best thing for a woman in my position, and as the door is locked, I feel cut adrift, disconnected from the outside world and everybody I know.

I guess that's the idea of prison.

I hate the fact that I've ended up in here, but worse than this is how I ended up here. Bev sealed my fate, and she did so by telling the police everything before they had a chance to throw her into a cell alongside me.

From what I've heard, Bev was being questioned by a detective, just like I was. During that questioning, the recording of our conversation with Phillip was played, the one in which it sounds like we - but mostly me - were confessing to the murder of Edwin. I can understand how that would have been terrifying for her because it was scary for me too, but whilst I was planning on making up excuses for what I had said and ensuring the location of the body remained a secret, Bev decided to do something else.

Panicked at the thought of several long years behind bars, she fabricated a story that the police now believe, and they believe it because it has resulted in them finding Edwin's body in the canal.

Bev has told them that killing Edwin was all my idea and that I coerced both her and Natasha into helping commit the crime. Apparently, I was the mastermind behind the whole thing, from luring Edwin into our clutches to stabbing him myself and then deciding where his body should be dumped. Of course, I played a big part in all of that, from helping form the plan to stabbing Edwin and helping move his body, but I was just a part of it. All three of us were happy to go along with it at the time, although that's not at all how Bev has told it. According to her, I preyed on my friends' vulnerabilities and forced them to partake in a heinous crime before making them stay quiet about it with threats and intimidation.

It's laughable, but Bev has concocted a story that seems plausible, and that's my problem. She even went as far as to say that the reason Natasha killed herself was because of how guilty she felt after I had forced her to help with Edwin's murder. That's disgraceful because it's using the death of our friend for her own benefit, but Bev said it anyway. No mention of Edwin hurting women or trying to frame me for financial crimes. No, Bev chose to omit all that and just said the whole reason for me wanting Edwin dead was because I held a grudge against him after he had terminated my employment due to me stealing money from his company.

The lies would be laughable if they weren't so damaging, but as it is, I'm the one in a police cell struggling to figure out a way to get out of this. Of course, the police aren't so stupid as to simply believe every word that comes out of Bev's mouth because she wouldn't be the first person to tell lies to get herself out of trouble. But Bev has even had a plan for that because rather than try and convince the police that she is entirely guilt-free in all of this, she actually admitted that what she did was wrong and she deserved some punishment for her part in covering up Edwin's death. However, she had a convenient way of negotiating that punishment to make sure it wasn't as harsh as it could be.

She offered to give up the real location of Edwin's body in exchange for some leniency.

That offer, along with Bev also offering to tell the full 'truth' about the motives behind 'my plan' to kill Edwin, was obviously appealing to the police because before Bev suggested it, they were potentially looking at having to take us both to trial, and it might have been a trial they lost. But the second Bev told them about the body in the canal, two big things happened. One, the police had concrete evidence that a serious crime had occurred and two, they had caught me in a lie, making Bev look like the only honest one out of the pair of us.

My voice on the recording clearly states that the body was in the woods, so now the police have found it in the canal, who are they more likely to believe in future? Bev, the woman who has given them something factual, or me, the woman who is on tape telling a lie?

My lawyer didn't have to say anything more once he had finished telling me what was going on because the look on his face said it all.

I'm screwed.

Sure, I can try and fight it, and I definitely will because I can't let Bev get away with this. If she's willing to do such a thing to me, then our friendship is over, and now I have to defend myself against her as desperately as if I am fighting for my life, because maybe I am. Who knows how long my sentence might be, and I might never make it out alive. If I'm going down, and it sure looks like I am, then I will drag Bev down with me. She can't weasel out of this by saying I pressured her into killing Edwin. How ridiculous is that? She's a grown woman, and what grown woman gets coerced into murder? She could have just said no and walked away, but she didn't. She stood right beside me as I stabbed Edwin, and then she helped carry his body to the car. She was fully on my side once, and even though she is not anymore, she can't change the past any more than I can.

I'm not sure how long I will have to stay in custody and in limbo as to what my future has in store for me. I guess that depends on what I say to the police when I speak to them again. My lawyer thinks I should just admit my part in all of this, and that way, I'll get some leniency myself. But while there's bound to be DNA evidence of me on Edwin's body, be it hairs, sweat, or something else, and while I am on tape confessing to murder, I am not willing to let people think I forced others into doing such a thing with me.

I can't bear the thought of Natasha's poor family thinking that the only reason she is dead is because I put unbearable pressure on her to stay quiet, and she killed herself over the guilt of what I made her do. That is nonsense, and I don't deserve to be tarred with such a brush. I also cannot bear the thought of having to serve multiple more years than Bev, the woman who has betrayed me. If I get ten years for this, then so be it, but surely, Bev has to get the same. Anything else would be an injustice, especially after she has proven to be a bigger liar than me.

But our fates remain to be seen.

The police, or perhaps a judge and jury, will decide what happens to us.

Until then, all I can do is stare at the walls of my cell and pray that I won't spend the entirety of my forties with the same view.

But is that my fate?

36

FIFTEEN YEARS LATER

'How does it feel to be a free woman again?'

The question from my taxi driver might be well-intentioned, but to me, it's just another reminder of how much time I have lost in police custody. That's why I want to tell the driver to mind his own business and just get me to where I have asked him to take me. However, something makes me refrain from being that abrupt, and instead, I opt for a little conversation to help pass the time on this journey.

'It feels good,' I say, understating that somewhat because it doesn't just feel good to be free again. It feels fantastic. How can it not? I've spent the last fifteen years behind bars, staring at the same walls, eating the same meals, and being surrounded by the same prison wardens wearing those same uniforms and flashing those same keys. I've spent countless nights wishing to be out of that environment and now I am, so I have nothing to complain about, right?

Wrong.

I have a lot to complain about, and after opting to be chatty with my taxi driver as he steers us away from my home for so many long years, I should probably go into a little more detail about my life inside, especially when he asks me for more information.

'Is it like what we see on TV, or is it different?' my nosy driver asks as he turns a corner and further increases the distance between me and that prison.

'Oh, it's very different.'

'I read somewhere that prisoners have televisions in their cells and PlayStations and Xboxes. Is that true?'

'We have TVs, but it's just basic channels.'

'No Sky Cinema then?'

'Not quite.'

My driver seems amused by that before going on to ask me about the dangers of prison life.

'Does it get violent in there? I imagine you had to watch your back.'

'Yeah, it can be dangerous. I just mostly kept to myself though. Nobody really picked on anybody unless they were asking for it.'

'Fair enough. I get that you should be punished for whatever crime you committed, but I don't think you should be living in fear in there.'

'No, I wasn't living in fear,' I confirm. 'At least not after the first few months once I'd got used to it. But I was living in boredom. The days are long in there.'

'It's not supposed to be a holiday camp,' my driver quite rightly reminds me.

'That's true, and it's certainly no holiday. But it's over now.'

'What did you go in for, if you don't mind me asking?'

This driver certainly is prying into my business, but then again, it's probably not every day he gets to pick up a passenger who has just been released from the town's prison, so he probably doesn't want to miss this opportunity to ask me questions he must have had for a while. I'm sure he's memorising all the information I give him so he can relay it to his mates in the pub this weekend, no doubt thrilled because his fairly mundane job has suddenly become exciting, at least until this particular journey ends, and he returns to ferrying less-interesting passengers around. If that's the case, he's really going to be interested in my next answer.

'Murder,' I say simply, in response to his last question.

I notice the driver's eyes on me in his rear-view mirror and wonder if I've just made him feel uncomfortable. Probably, because I expect it's difficult to relax when you find out you're in the presence of a killer. However, if he is afraid, he's doing a good job of controlling his emotions because his driving is still steady, and he hasn't parked up and told me to get out of his vehicle yet.

'Oh, okay,' he says a little awkwardly.

'Do you want to know what happened?' I ask then, almost enjoying this conversation now because I've just realised that now I'm free, with my backstory, I'm always going to be the most interesting person at any dinner party I go to in the future.

'It's okay. You don't have to tell me if you don't want to,' the suddenly shy driver says, but it's a bit late for that because he was the one who pried, so now he can be the one to hear my story.

'I killed my old boss,' I say nonchalantly. 'I stabbed him several times in the stomach, and then I put his body in the canal. You might remember hearing about it in the news. He was called Edwin van Dekker.'

I can see that my driver remembers it because he has gone pale and is nervously scratching at the stubble on his chin with one hand while the other grips his steering wheel tightly.

'So, anyway, I got caught, and I've been away for a very long time. But do you know what? I deserve it. I killed a man. I can hardly have expected to get away with that, could I? What kind of world would it be if people got away with murder? No, I accept my punishment. I did the crime, so I had to do the time.'

That might all sound very understanding, but as always with me, it's only half the story, and I'm not willing to share the other half with this driver for fear that he might go straight back to the prison after dropping me off and tell them what he just heard. That would be the part where rather than decide to be a reformed character and try to get my life back on track, I am choosing, instead, to get revenge on the two people who I believe wronged me. That would be Phillip van Dekker for recording our private conversation in his office and then running to the police with it, after telling me he wouldn't say a word. It would also be Bev, my ex best-friend, who, after betraying my trust and lying about me to make my part in Edwin's death bigger and hers smaller, only served two years for her part in the crime.

Two years, while I got fifteen. Does that seem fair? Never mind that she made me look worse in front of the police, saying that I was the ringleader of the pre-meditated murder plot, which greatly added time on to my sentence, but by lying and seeming to be cooperative, she greatly reduced her own punishment.

My lawyers told me that the police were actually grateful for Bev because she helped them solve a crime that was going unsolved, even if she had been a part of it. I became the fall guy, and that gave Bev the opportunity to be out of prison not long after her fortieth birthday, while I am beyond my fiftieth now that I'm released. That extra time she bought herself allowed her to get married and have a child, something I dreamt of for myself once upon a time, but something she robbed me of when she decided to spill all my secrets to the police and leave me without any way of talking myself out of it.

Bev and Phillip screwed me, but unbeknownst to them, this taxi driver, and the prison officials who believe I am safe to let back out into society on the grounds of good behaviour, I am planning on getting my own back.

Revenge will be sweet.

Even sweeter than breathing fresh air as a free woman.

Having started off this journey incredibly chatty, my driver has not been much of a conversationalist ever since he found out he had a murderer sitting on his back seat, but he's forced to speak again when we reach my desired destination.

'Where would you like me to park? Anywhere around here okay?' he asks me as he taps the brake pedal and slows us down.

'Anywhere around here will be fine,' I say breezily before reaching into my purse for the necessary payment. As far as saving money goes, prison works wonders because I haven't touched the money in this purse since the night of my arrest. All my belongings, from this purse to the clothes I am wearing now, were stored away until my release, meaning I am now spending money that I originally withdrew from a cash machine several years ago.

It feels strange to do something as simple as pay a taxi fare after spending so long living under strict rules in a harsh environment, and it is satisfying when the driver thanks me and wishes me a good day. I'm back to being a functioning member of society again, someone who can contribute rather than be a burden, although with what I have planned, I'm not going to be contributing wholly positive things to society.

Pretty soon, I will be a burden on the police force again.

That's because by the time I'm finished, there will be another murder for them to investigate.

It all starts right here, and as the taxi drives away, I look up at the place where he has just dropped me off. It's Van Dekker Logistics, and wouldn't you know it, there is Phillip's car parked beside the front door.

Perfect.

He's exactly where I thought he would be.

Unlucky for him.

37

Marching into the familiar office, I breeze straight past the reception desk because it's currently unmanned. I expect almost all the desks upstairs are the same because it's after five o'clock now, and the only person who ever stays late here is the boss.

I'm sure I'll find him upstairs in his office, and I'm very much looking forward to surprising him as I ascend in the elevator. Even though I've not been here for many years, the place still looks exactly the same as it did before my incarceration, especially the kitchen, which is the first place I visit after leaving the elevator.

Out of sight of Phillip's office, I roam freely in the quarters reserved for staff to enjoy their lunch and make a cup of tea, but I'm not in here for refreshments. I'm in here to take out the sharp knife in the top drawer, and once I have it, I carry on my way to see the boss.

With the knife held down by my side, I'm not making any attempt to hide it, but I'm not walking in with it raised either because I want the man I'm going to see to be nervous, but not panicked, when I walk in. I need to look like I might do something dangerous but that I've still not quite convinced myself of doing it yet, which will give my target the hope he can talk me out of it.

Now, here I am, standing in front of the closed door, behind which is the man who helped send me to prison.

I hope he's happy to see me.

Entering confidently, I find Phillip hunched over his laptop, but he quickly rises to his full height when he sees me arriving, and his eyes go even wider when he spots the knife by my side.

'Liz!' he cries, about as shocked as I had expected him to be.

'Phillip. Nice to see you again. It's been a while. Fifteen years, in fact.'

'What are you doing here? I thought-'

'You thought I was still in prison? Nope. I got out today. I'm a free woman. Free to do anything I want, and what I wanted to do most of all is come and see you.'

Phillip's eyes flit from my face to the weapon I hold, and I take pleasure in his grave uncertainty for a few seconds.

'What do you want?' he asks me nervously, and I make sure to lift the knife at that precise moment for dramatic timing.

'I just want you to do something for me. Just one thing. If you do it, I'll leave you alone.'

'What is it?'

'I want you to make a phone call.'

'What?'

'A phone call. This is an office, is it not? I've been away for a long time, but offices still have phones, right?'

Phillip nods his head, whilst not appreciating my jokey question, but I didn't expect him to.

'Good. Then sit down at your desk and pick up your phone.'

'Who am I calling?'

'Our old friend, Bev.'

Phillip is surprised again, but he better get used to it.

'Come on, pick up the phone. I'll tell you the number to dial.'

'What are you doing?'

'You'll see. Now come on, pick up the phone.'

Phillip reluctantly does as I say before staring at me uselessly with the receiver in his hand.

'Now, when Bev answers, you're going to tell her that you need to see her and that she has to come here as quickly as she can.'

'Why?'

'Because that's what I'm telling you to say, and I'm the one with the knife, okay?' I state in a very matter-of-fact manner.

'But what if she says no?'

'She won't. Not if you're persuasive, and I know you can be, so it shouldn't be a problem. Just tell her that something has happened, something to do with me, and that you're worried the pair of you could go to prison unless you make a plan. But whatever you do, do not tell her that I'm here. Like you, she'll still think I'm behind bars.'

'But why would she come and see me? She hates me as much as you do.'

'Oh no, not quite. Nobody hates you as much as I do.'

Phillip looks like he regrets testing me on that point and then starts pleading for forgiveness.

'I'm sorry about what happened.'

'You mean for recording our private conversation and giving it to the police? Yeah, I thought you might be sorry now that I'm standing in your office with a knife, and there's no one else around to help you.'

'I am sorry! I shouldn't have done it. I meant what I said about my father. I knew he was a bad man, and I am glad he's dead. I'm glad you killed him.'

'So glad that you just couldn't wait to report his killer to the police?'

'He's still my father. I thought I had to get justice.'

'Justice is fine, but what happened in the end was not justice. Bev screwed me over. That's why I want you to get her to come here now.'

'What are you going to do to her when she arrives?' Phillip asks me, even though it might seem obvious, considering I am still brandishing a blade.

'That's between me and her,' I say. 'All I need you to do is get her here. If you can do that without giving away the fact that I'm out of prison, then everything will be okay for you, I promise.'

Phillip has no choice but to trust me, and once he has stopped with the questions, I tell him the number to dial. Once he has, he puts the receiver to his ear, his hand shaking as he holds it, and I can see how anxious he is, so I opt to give him one last pep talk before his big task.

'Just stay calm. Say exactly what I just told you to and nothing more. Then this will all be over.'

Phillip nods his head to show that he understands, and then the call connects.

'Bev? It's me, Phillip van Dekker. I need to see you immediately at my office.'

I can't hear the other end of the line, but I suspect Bev is shocked to receive a call from this man and is already thinking about hanging up. That's why I step forward and whisper to Phillip that he is to keep talking.

Maybe it's the urgency of my whispering, or maybe it's the fact I have just got a little closer to him with the knife, but he does what I say and speaks again before Bev can end the call.

'It's about what happened with my father and Liz. The police have started asking a few more questions, and I think Liz must be talking to them in prison. I don't know what she's saying, but if both of us want to avoid any investigation again, then we need to get our stories straight, just in case. Do you understand?'

I'm impressed by Phillip's ability to work under pressure, and his improvisational skills seem to be doing the trick because Bev hasn't hung up yet. Things get even more promising when I hear Phillip nod to me whilst telling Bev that he will see her soon.

It sounds like she is on her way, and after he has hung up, Phillip confirms that is the case.

'Well done,' I tell him, aware that it's good to offer praise when it's deserved.

'What do you want me to do now?' he asks me as he stands up. 'Bev's on her way. Can I leave? I don't want to be part of whatever you are going to do to her.'

'I understand, and yes, you can leave now,' I say, standing aside so the path to the doorway is clear. 'Just do me a favour and don't call the police as soon as you get out of here. Go home, make dinner, and forget this little conversation ever happened. Do you think you can do that?'

'Yes,' Phillip replies, though I know far better than to believe anything that comes out of this man's mouth anymore.

But I'm still standing aside and allowing him to pass, so he takes his chance and heads for the door. Unfortunately for him, he still has to walk past me and the knife, and no sooner is he within striking distance then I make my move.

Plunging the knife into his stomach, I repeat the motion several more times until he has collapsed onto the carpet, his white shirt soaked in blood and his eyes looking up at me with abject terror.

'Oh, sorry. Did I not do what I said I was going to do?' I say coldly. 'Silly me. Sorry about that. It's no fun to be lied to, is it?'

I think Phillip gets the message before his eyes close, or at least I hope he did, as his breathing stops and his body is still.

He's gone, but soon, Bev will be here.

That means I still have a lot of work to do.

EPILOGUE

Having spent so long inside a prison, it might be easy to assume a prison would be the last place I'd ever want to see the inside of again. But I'm returning to the scene of my lengthy ordeal, although this time, I'm not here because I have a long sentence to serve.

I'm here because someone else has one.

Smiling at the prison warden as he lets me, and the other people whom I am waiting with, know that visiting hours are about to begin, a door is unlocked, and we all filter through it before entering a large room where we have to spot the person we have come here to see. Fortunately, that's not too difficult, and I easily lay my eyes on the person I am here for.

She's the one who looks like she doesn't really belong in here, but that's just how I probably looked when I was an inmate. She's the one who looks afraid, exhausted, and frustrated all at the same time - again, exactly how I was when I was here. She's the one who is now looking at me as I approach the table she sits at, and when I reach her, she's the one who doesn't seem to know what to say.

That's why I speak first.

'Hello, Bev.'

The prisoner doesn't react in any way to my greeting, so I take the opportunity to sit down opposite her before speaking again.

'How are you finding it in here? It's tough, right?'

'What do you want?'

Bev's first words are straight to the point.

'What do I want?' I muse, sitting back in my seat. 'Nothing. I've already got everything I want. I'm free, and justice has been done.'

'Justice? How can you say that? You framed me.'

Bev is showing remarkable restraint to keep her voice low as she speaks. If I was in her position, I'd be shouting and screaming, and I might even have reached across this table and had a go at attacking my visitor by now.

'I don't know what you are talking about,' I reply, as a sly smile curls up my lips. In reality, I know exactly what she is talking about, but I'm far too experienced now to make the same mistake I have made before. For all I know, Bev might be secretly recording this conversation because she sees it as her potential ticket out of here. All she has to do is get it on tape that I'm the one who actually killed Phillip and not her, and then we would be sitting in opposite seats. But I'm not going to make it that easy for her, especially after being burned before by Phillip and his secret recording of our private conversation. That's why I'm not going to admit to being guilty of anything here, which will only serve to frustrate Bev even more.

Perfect.

'I know what you did and how you did it,' Bev says to me, clearly taking this opportunity to tell me that I'm not quite as clever as I think I am. But she'll have a hard job making me think that because from where I'm sitting, my plan worked to perfection.

That would be the plan in which I killed Phillip and fled the scene of the crime, but having had him call Bev before his death, she came to see him at his office and discovered his bloodied corpse lying on the floor beside his desk. As I expected she would do, Bev had run from the scene as quickly as she could for fear of being associated with what was clearly a murder, but the problem with taking that course of action was that she was caught on camera running through the office car park before speeding away in her vehicle. It was the camera situated by the front gate that captured her going in and out of the office on the night Phillip van Dekker was so brutally killed, so once the police checked the CCTV footage, it was pretty obvious who they were going to go and see first as part of their investigation.

But obviously, Bev was not the only person who had been at the office that night. I had been there too, so why wasn't I captured on camera going in and out of the office as well? It might have had something to do with the fact that I had made sure the footage showing my presence there that evening had been deleted long before any police officer could check it.

To have such a thing done required me to rekindle my brief romance with Barry, the security officer at Van Dekker Logistics. It's a lot easier to get somebody to do you a big favour if you give them something they want first, and I certainly gave Barry what he wanted. In exchange, he made sure the footage of me going to visit Phillip in his office just before his death was never seen by anybody else. I'll most likely have to keep 'visiting' Barry for many years to come, at least until he starts to find me unattractive, but so what? I can do that. It's not as if there is a multitude of other men interested in me these days, anyway.

Still, even with the CCTV recording of Bev fleeing from the office where Phillip lay dead, there was a chance a lawyer could get her out of it. That was why I made sure to take the murder weapon and plant it in her back garden while she was busy at the office. I left Phillip before Bev could get to him, and so, while she was driving towards him, I was going in the opposite direction, to her house, and that's where I left the knife, hidden inside a box and buried in a shallow hole at the bottom of her garden, making it look like she had tried to hide it quickly after the attack. Of course, I knew a defence lawyer would try to throw doubt on her guilt by asking why a killer would bury the murder weapon in their own garden, but the discovery of the bloodied knife on her premises, along with the surveillance footage putting her at the scene, was more than enough to convince a jury that Bev was Phillip's killer. It also looked like pre-meditated murder, too, so that is why Bev was sentenced to fifteen years behind bars, the same as what I ended up getting for Edwin's death, which, of course, made me smile even more.

'Do you regret it?' I ask Bev, still choosing my words carefully but also needing to broach this subject so the person I am talking to is in no doubt as to why I did what I did.

'Regret what?'

'Lying to the police about Edwin and telling them that his murder was all my idea and not yours too, not to mention giving them the real location of his body in exchange for leniency,' I say calmly. 'You do remember doing that, right? It's the reason why I went to prison for fifteen years while you only got two. It's also the reason you were able to get married and have a child, whereas I lost that chance thanks to your 'confession'.'

I use my fingers to highlight the last word of that sentence before shaking my head at this woman who used to be so dear to me. As she hasn't answered my last question, I fill the silence for the both of us.

'Do you think I wanted this to happen? For one of us to be in a place like this?' I ask, looking around at the concrete walls, the watching wardens, and the other prisoners who all carry the same abject look of despair on their faces. 'We should have both been free to live our lives and make the most of still having them despite what we had been through. But I guess it wasn't meant to be.'

Bev is still quiet, so I'm thinking it might be time for me to conclude this little visit and forget all about this chapter of my life. But just before I can get up and walk away, concluding my revenge without further need for anything else in the future, Bev leans forward and has something she would like to ask me.

'Do you think I'll let you get away with this?' she wants to know, heavily hinting that she will take revenge on me the first chance she gets. But if she's expecting me to look nervous about that, she would be wrong.

'I wouldn't expect you to forget about this and leave me alone, no,' I reply calmly. 'In fact, I'd almost be disappointed if you did.'

With that, I wink at Bev before getting up from my seat and walking away from her, not bothering to look back over my shoulder as I go because there'll be plenty of time for that later. I know I'll have to stay on my guard for the rest of my life because Bev might try and have her revenge on me. She could try and get somebody on the outside to hurt me, or maybe she'll figure her own way out of prison and come for me herself. They are all possibilities that I will have to be on my guard against.

A lifetime of worry and fear, just waiting for one little thing to go wrong! Isn't that going to be hell? Am I actually as free as I look, or am I merely trapped in a not-too-dissimilar way to the one in which Bev already is?

No, I'll be fine. If not fine, I'll at least manage to keep going and do my best to have a normal life. After all, isn't that what everyone is doing? Carrying on until something inevitably goes wrong? Some people look over their shoulders because of money issues, or health issues, or, like me, because a person they wronged might one day come back to have their vengeance. But isn't it all the same? Time is ticking; enjoy it while we can.

Goodbye, Bev, I think as I leave the prison. *Maybe I'll see you again one day, or maybe I won't.*

Either way, there are no real winners here, just like there are no real winners in life, only people who think they are ahead.

Until suddenly, they aren't anymore.

There is one more person who probably thinks they got out ahead in all of this. It's the woman who helped both Edwin and Phillip get away with so much for so long, the woman who dealt out NDA's as easily as they dealt out crimes.

Amy, the personal assistant to those two horrible men, probably thinks she's been lucky to have come out of this unscathed. The last I checked, she was working at another large company across town, presumably as the PA to some other tyrannic boss. She might even have forgotten about the past and the part she played in it. But I haven't. That's why I will make sure to pay her a visit one day. Not quite yet, because I need enough time to pass so as not to arouse suspicion. I can't go getting revenge on everybody so soon after my release, can I?

But I will get Amy, make no mistake about it.

Only then will I be able to go to Natasha's grave and truly tell my dearly departed friend that this is finally over.

THE END

Thank you for reading

If you would like to receive a FREE copy of my psychological thriller 'Just One Second', then you can find the link to the book at my website www.danielhurstbooks.com

Thank you for reading *The Colleagues.*

If you have enjoyed this psychological thriller, then you'll be pleased to know that I have several more stories in this genre, and you can find a list of my titles on the next page. These include ***The Doctor's Wife***, which became the #1 selling book in the UK Kindle Store in February 2023, and has now become a four-book series, continuing with ***The Doctor's Widow, The Doctor's Mistress*** and ***The Doctor's Child***.

Other popular titles include ***The Couple's Revenge,*** about two parents trying to save their child from a threat at school, and ***My Daughter's Boyfriend,*** about a mother who follows her daughter to America to meet her new boyfriend, only to discover a terrible danger awaiting them both…

ALSO BY DANIEL HURST

THE DOCTOR'S WIFE
THE DOCTOR'S WIDOW
THE DOCTOR'S MISTRESS
THE DOCTOR'S CHILD
MY DAUGHTER'S BOYFRIEND
MY DAUGHTER'S HUSBAND
THE COUPLE'S REVENGE
TIL DEATH DO US PART
THE PASSENGER
WE USED TO LIVE HERE
THE COUPLE AT TABLE SIX
THE INTRUDER
WHAT MY FAMILY SAW
THE HOLIDAY HOME
HER HUSBAND'S MISTAKE
THE BRIDE TO BE
HER LAST HOUR
THE PERFECT ESCAPE
RUN AWAY WITH ME
THE RIVALS
WE TELL NO ONE
THE WOMAN AT THE DOOR
HE WAS A LIAR
THE BROKEN VOWS
THE WRONG WOMAN
NO TIME TO BE ALONE
THE TUTOR
THE NEIGHBOURS
THE BREAK

THE ROLE MODEL
THE BOYFRIEND
THE PROMOTION
THE NEW FRIENDS
THE ACCIDENT

(All books available now on Amazon and Kindle Unlimited – read on to learn a little more about selected titles...)

THE DOCTOR'S WIFE

The UK Kindle Store #1 Bestseller!

He thinks his secret is safe. But she knows the truth…

My husband is a doctor. He's smart and charming and everybody trusts him. **Except me.**

On the surface, it looks like I have it all – the perfect marriage, the perfect husband, the perfect life. But it's far from the truth. **Doctor Drew Devlin** is not the respectable figure he makes out to be. The reason we moved to this beautiful, old property with a gorgeous view of the sea was because we needed to put our past behind us. It should've been a fresh start for us both.

Except I've discovered my husband has been lying to me again. He's using the power he has in his job to mess with people's lives, and to get exactly what he wants – no matter who it hurts. But he's underestimated me. I've had plenty of time, in this big, isolated house, to think about all of his mistakes. *And my husband has no idea what's about to happen next…*

If you enjoy this, the series continues with The Doctor's Widow!

THE COUPLE'S REVENGE

How far would you go to protect your child?

I knew something was wrong. It's a mother's instinct. I could tell when my son started hiding things from me. He used to walk to school with a mischievous grin on his beautiful face. Now he avoids eye contact and keeps his head down.

Since I discovered he's being bullied by a classmate, I've spent every day worrying, my stomach churning with anxiety from the moment he leaves the house to the second he walks back through the door. Everyone keeps telling me I'm overreacting, but I won't risk my child's safety. My husband and I try to talk to the other boy's parents, but it only makes things worse…

Then our precious child is hurt. Enough is enough. It has to stop. Even if that means taking matters into our own hands. Because we know the truth about the family targeting our son – it's not the first time they've done this.

So the question is, exactly how far will we go to get revenge?

TIL DEATH DO US PART

What if your husband was your worst enemy?

Megan thinks that she has the perfect husband and the perfect life. Craig works all day so that she doesn't have to, leaving her free to relax in their beautiful and secluded country home. But when she starts to long for friends and purpose again, Megan applies for a job in London, much to her husband's disappointment. She thinks he is upset because she is unhappy. But she has no idea.

When Megan secretly attends an interview and meets a recruiter for a drink, Craig decides it is time to act. Locking her away in their home, Megan realises that her husband never had her best interests at heart. Worse, they didn't meet by accident. Craig has been planning it all from the start.

As Megan is kept shut away from the world with only somebody else's diary for company, she starts to uncover the lies, the secrets, and the fact that she isn't actually Craig's first wife after all...

THE PASSENGER

She takes the same train every day. But this is a journey she will never forget…

Amanda is a hard-working single mum, focused on her job and her daughter, Louise. But it's also time she did something for herself, and after saving for years, she is now close to quitting her dreary 9-5 and following her dream.

But then, on her usual commute home from London to Brighton, she meets a charming stranger – a man who seems to know everything about her. Then he delivers an ultimatum. She needs to give him the code to her safe where she keeps her savings before they reach Brighton – or she will never see Louise again.

Amanda is horrified, but while she knows the threat is real, she can't give him the code. That's because the safe contains something other than her money. It holds a secret. *A secret so terrible it will destroy both her's and her daughter's life if it ever gets out…*

THE NEIGHBOURS

It seemed like the perfect house on the perfect street. *Until they met the neighbours...*

Happily married couple, Katie and Sean, have plenty to look forward to as they move into their new home and plan for the future. But then they meet two of their new neighbours, and everything on their quiet street suddenly doesn't seem as desirable as it did before.

Having been warned about the other neighbours and their adulterous and criminal ways, Katie and Sean realise that they are going to have to be on their guard if they want to make their time here a happy one.

But some of the other neighbours seem so nice, and that's why they choose to ignore the warning and get friendly with the rest of the people on the street. *And that is why their marriage will never be the same again...*

THE TUTOR

What if you invited danger into your home?

Amy is a loving wife and mother to her husband, Nick, and her two children, Michael and Bella. It's that dedication to her family that causes her to seek help for her teenage son when it becomes apparent that he is going to fail his end of school exams.

Enlisting the help of a professional tutor, Amy is certain that she is doing the best thing for her son and, indeed, her family. But when she discovers that there is more to this tutor than meets the eye, it is already too late.

With the rest of her family enamoured by the tutor, Amy is the only one who can see that there is something not quite right about her. But as the tutor becomes more involved in Amy's family, it's not just the present that is threatened. Secrets from the past are exposed too, and by the time everything is out in the open, Amy isn't just worried about her son and his exams anymore. She is worried for the survival of her entire family.

HE WAS A LIAR

What if you never really knew the man you loved?

Sarah is in a loving relationship with Paul, a seemingly perfect man who she is hoping to marry and start a family with one day, until his sudden death sends her into a world of pain.

Trying to come to terms with her loss, Sarah finds comfort in going through some of Paul's old things, including his laptop and his emails. But after finding something troubling, Sarah begins to learn things about Paul that she never knew before, and it turns out he wasn't as perfect as she thought. But as she unravels more about his secretive past, she ends up not only learning things that break her heart, but things that the police will be interested to know too.

Sarah can't believe what she has discovered. But it's only when she keeps digging that she realises it's not just her late boyfriend's secrets that are contained on the laptop. Other people's secrets are too, and they aren't dead, which means they will do anything to protect them.

RUN AWAY WITH ME

What if your partner was wanted by the police?

Laura is feeling content with her life. She is married, she has a good home, and she is due to give birth to her first child any day now. But her perfect world is shattered when her husband comes home flustered and afraid. He's made a terrible mistake. He's done a bad thing. *And now the police are going to be looking for him.*

There's only one way out of this. He wants to run. *But he won't go without his wife...*

Laura knows it is wrong. She knows they should stay and face the music. But she doesn't want to lose her man. She can't raise this baby alone. *So she agrees to go with him.* But life on the run is stressful and unpredictable, and as time goes by, Laura worries she has made a terrible mistake. They should never have ran. But it's too late for that now. Her life is ruined. The only question is: *how will it end?*

THE ROLE MODEL

She raised her. Now she must help her…

Heather is a single mum who has always done what's best for her daughter, Chloe. From childhood up to the age of seventeen, Chloe has been no trouble. That is until one night when she calls her mother with some shocking news. There's been an accident. *And now there's a dead body…*

As always, Heather puts her daughter's safety before all else, but this might be one time when she goes too far. Instead of calling the emergency services, Heather hides the body, saving her daughter from police interviews and public outcry.

But as she well knows, everything she does has an impact on her child's behaviour, and as time goes on and the pair struggle to keep their sordid secret hidden, Heather begins to think that she hasn't been such a good mum after all. *In fact, she might have been the worst role model ever…*

THE BROKEN VOWS

He broke his word to her. Now she wants revenge…

Alison is happily married to Graham, or at least she is until she finds out that he has been cheating on her. Graham has broken the vows he made on his wedding day. How could he do it? It takes Alison a while to figure it out, but at least she has time on her side. *Only that is where she is wrong.*

A devastating diagnosis means the clock is ticking down on her life now, and if she wants revenge on her cheating partner, then she is going to have to act fast. Alison does just that, implementing a dangerous and deadly plan, and it's one that will have far reaching consequences for several people, including her clueless husband.

WE USED TO LIVE HERE

How much do you know about your house?

When the Burgess family move into their 'forever' home, it seems like they are set for many happy years together at their new address. Steph and Grant, along with their two children, Charlie and Amelia, settle into their new surroundings quickly. But then they receive a visit from a couple who claim to have lived in their house before and wish to have a look around for old times' sake. They seem pleasant and plausible, so Steph invites them in. And that's when things start to change…

It's not long after the peculiar visit when the homeowners start to find evidence of the past all around their new home as they redecorate. But it's the discovery of a hidden wall containing several troubling messages that really sends Steph into a spin, and after digging deeper into the history of the house a little more, she learns it is connected to a shocking crime from the past. *A crime that still remains unsolved...*

Every house has secrets. But some don't stay buried forever…

THE 20 MINUTES SERIES

What readers are saying:

"If you like people-watching, then you will love these books!"

"The psychological insight was fascinating, the stories were absorbing and the characters were 3D. I absolutely loved it."

"The books in this series are an incredibly easy read, you become invested in the lives of the characters so easily, and I am eager to know more and more. Roll on the next book."

THE 20 MINUTES SERIES (in order)

20 MINUTES ON THE TUBE
20 MINUTES LATER
20 MINUTES IN THE PARK
20 MINUTES ON HOLIDAY
20 MINUTES BY THE THAMES
20 MINUTES AT HALLOWEEN
20 MINUTES AROUND THE BONFIRE
20 MINUTES BEFORE CHRISTMAS
20 MINUTES OF VALENTINE'S DAY
20 MINUTES TO CHANGE A LIFE
20 MINUTES IN LAS VEGAS
20 MINUTES IN THE DESERT

20 MINUTES ON THE ROAD
20 MINUTES BEFORE THE WEDDING
20 MINUTES IN COURT
20 MINUTES BEHIND BARS
20 MINUTES TO MIDNIGHT
20 MINUTES BEFORE TAKE OFF
20 MINUTES IN THE AIR
20 MINUTES UNTIL IT'S OVER

About The Author

Daniel Hurst lives in the Northwest of England with his wife, Harriet, and daughter, Penny, and if that doesn't make him lucky enough, he considers himself extremely fortunate to be able to write stories every day for his readers.

You can visit him at his online home www.danielhurstbooks.com

You can connect with Daniel on Facebook at www.facebook.com/danielhurstbooks or on Instagram at www.instagram.com/danielhurstbooks

He is always happy to receive emails from readers at daniel@danielhurstbooks.com and replies to every single one.

Thank you for reading.

Daniel

THE COLLEAGUES by Daniel Hurst published by Daniel Hurst Books Limited, The Coach House, 31 View Road, Rainhill, Merseyside, L35 0LF

Front Cover Design by 100Covers

Printed in Great Britain
by Amazon

39239272R00179